ACCLAIM FOR ALEX RIDER:

"Explosive, thrilling, action-packed – meet Alex Rider."
Guardian

"Horowitz is pure class, stylish but action-packed ... being James Bond in miniature is way cooler than being a wizard."
Daily Mirror

"Horowitz will grip you with suspense, daring and cheek – and that's just the first page! ... Prepare for action scenes as fast as a movie."
The Times

"Anthony Horowitz is the lion of children's literature."
Michael Morpurgo

"Fast and furious."
Telegraph

"The perfect hero ... genuine 21st century stuff."
Daily Telegraph

"Brings new meaning to the phrase 'action-packed'."
Sunday Times

"Every bored schoolboy's fantasy, only a thousand times funnier, slicker and more exciting ... genius."
Independent on Sunday

"Perfect escapism for all teenage boys."
The Times

"Addictive, pacey novels."
Financial Times

"Adults as well as kids will be hooked on the adventures of Alex Rider ... Harry Potter with attitude."
Daily Express

Titles by Anthony Horowitz

The Alex Rider series:
Stormbreaker
Point Blanc
Skeleton Key
Eagle Strike
Scorpia
Ark Angel
Snakehead
Crocodile Tears
Scorpia Rising
Russian Roulette
Never Say Die
Secret Weapon

The Power of Five (Book One): *Raven's Gate*
The Power of Five (Book Two): *Evil Star*
The Power of Five (Book Three): *Nightrise*
The Power of Five (Book Four): *Necropolis*
The Power of Five (Book Five): *Oblivion*

The Devil and His Boy
Granny
Groosham Grange
Return to Groosham Grange
The Switch
Scared to Death

The Diamond Brothers books:
The Falcon's Malteser
Public Enemy Number Two
South by South East
The French Confection
The Greek Who Stole Christmas
The Blurred Man
I Know What You Did Last Wednesday

ALEX RIDER

SECRET WEAPON

ANTHONY HOROWITZ

Marino Branch
Brainse Marino
Tel: 8336297

WALKER BOOKS

For JF and S

This is a work of fiction. Names, characters, places and incidents
are either the product of the author's imagination or, if real, used
fictitiously. All statements, activities, stunts, descriptions, information
and material of any other kind contained herein are included for
entertainment purposes only and should not be relied on for
accuracy or replicated as they may result in injury.

First published 2019 by Walker Books Ltd
87 Vauxhall Walk, London SE11 5HJ

2 4 6 8 10 9 7 5 3 1

This collection © 2019 Stormbreaker Productions Ltd
Individual stories © 2003, 2009, 2010, 2012, 2019 Stormbreaker Productions Ltd
Cover illustration © 2019 Walker Books Ltd
Trademarks Alex Rider™; Boy with Torch Logo™
© 2019 Stormbreaker Productions Ltd

The right of Anthony Horowitz to be identified as author
of this work has been asserted by him in accordance with
the Copyright, Designs and Patents Act 1988

This book has been typeset in Officina Sans

Printed and bound by CPI Group (UK) Ltd, Croydon CR0 4YY

All rights reserved. No part of this book may be reproduced,
transmitted or stored in an information retrieval system in
any form or by any means, graphic, electronic or mechanical,
including photocopying, taping and recording, without
prior written permission from the publisher.

British Library Cataloguing in Publication Data:
a catalogue record for this book is available from the British Library

ISBN 978-1-4063-4017-4
ISBN 978-1-4063-8746-9

www.walker.co.uk

MIX
Paper from
responsible sources
FSC
www.fsc.org
FSC® C020471

CONTENTS

INTRODUCTION

In 2015, after *Russian Roulette* was published, I thought I would never write another Alex Rider adventure. Ten novels taking Alex to the UK, France, Italy, America, Russia – even outer space! – seemed quite enough.

But then I got a call from my publisher asking me if I would revisit the short stories I had written over the years. Some had appeared in newspapers, others as "extras" in previous editions of the books. The idea was that, if I polished them up a bit, we might bring them together in one collection. This is the book that emerged but, in the end, I wrote three brand new stories, appearing in print here for the first time.

What happened was rather strange. After I'd been reintroduced to Alex and started working on the stories, I found I couldn't stop. All sorts of ideas tumbled into my head. A mission to Afghanistan. A glimpse into Smithers's private life with a twist at the end. The return of an old enemy.

A nightmare hospital that most certainly isn't what it seems. As I began writing, I found myself creating action sequences that simply made me smile. Look at the way Alex escapes from Falcon's Edge or, for that matter, from Bellhanger Abbey. I can't tell you how much fun I had dreaming these up.

But that's the joy of the short story. A novel can take me seven or eight months to write. The plots have to be quite complicated. There are dozens of characters I have to create. A short story, on the other hand, allows me to dive straight into the action, to think up a situation and then to enjoy it. In a way, it's the same for Alex. Because all these adventures take place over a matter of days (or even hours) he doesn't have time to hang around. He just has to get to grips with whatever I throw at him and deal with it. I like that fast pace, the sense of immediacy.

There is something else I want to mention. Since *Russian Roulette* came out there has been another Alex Rider novel, *Never Say Die*, published in 2017 and there's going to be a thirteenth, *Nightshade*, coming out soon. These two books would never have happened if it hadn't been for this collection. Sitting down and writing about Alex again, I realized how much I'd missed him and, although I'd suspected otherwise, I still had plenty of ideas for escapes, fights, gadgets and all the rest of it. In other words, it was this book that persuaded me to write the others. That's another reason why I'm glad I wrote it.

There's never been a better time for Alex Rider. By the time you read this, they'll have started shooting an eight-part TV series based on *Point Blanc* and of course the hope is that the other books will follow. We'll soon be celebrating Alex's twentieth anniversary. And for what it's worth, I think this could be my fiftieth published book.

Lots of reasons to celebrate. I hope you enjoy the read.

Anthony Horowitz
April 2019

ALEX IN AFGHANISTAN

FALCON'S EDGE

There were five men sitting around the fire, huddled together in the Herat mountains in the north-west corner of Afghanistan. Although it was May and the plains were dotted with spring flowers, up here, five thousand feet above sea level, the winds still came rushing round the corners in icy blasts and the temperature tumbled towards zero once the sun had set. The men had erected a tent, made from woven goat-hair and tied down with long ropes nailed into the hard ground. They had rested here for three hours and now squatted down with their backs to it, waiting for their meal to cook. The horses that had brought them here were tethered near by.

Five men and a boy.

Alex Rider came out of the tent and took his place on the rough piece of carpet that had been set down for him. He examined the food that was bubbling away in the metal cauldron in the middle of the fire. It was some sort of lamb stew and he had to admit that it smelled delicious. The men had barely spoken to him since they had picked him up at the rendezvous point, a day's ride away on the other side of the Afghanistan border. He knew that they were Kochis – Afghan nomads – and that they were loyal only to themselves. They would have been paid to bring him this far ... gold, weapons, food, or all three. He wasn't sure if he trusted them. Certainly, from the moment they had set eyes on him, they hadn't trusted him.

They had not been told why it was necessary to escort a fourteen-year-old English boy into a landscape that really could be described as the middle of nowhere. They knew only that he was important. He had been brought to them in a Lynx Mk9A, the British Army primary battlefield utility helicopter said to be the fastest in the world. It had landed on the outskirts of the town of Yazdan, in Iran, and that had told them something at once. It could not have been there without the permission of the Iranians. The British and the Iranian government working together! This was serious.

The food was ready. The leader of the Kochis, a man Alex knew only as Rafiq, unwrapped a piece of cloth and laid out several pieces of flatbread, which they would use as plates. There were no knives or forks. He scooped out some of the meat and vegetables and handed it to Alex.

"*Mamnoon*," Alex said. It was the Farsi word for "thank you".

The other men served themselves and they all began to eat. The moon had come out, giving them enough light to see what they were doing and the sky was also crowded with hundreds of stars, shimmering over the mountains with a silver glow. Holding the flatbread in both hands, Alex tore into it with his teeth. The lamb was cooked in yoghurt, lotus roots, chickpeas and garlic. After the long journey he would have eaten anything, but it was even better than he'd expected. As he ate, he glanced at his companions. They all looked very similar with skin beaten dark by the sun and the wind, tangled black hair, hooded eyes. They were dressed in loose-fitting clothes, neutral colours, with either turbans or the soft, round-topped berets that were known as *pakols*. Rafiq had a velvet waistcoat, which might have been green and gold when his grandfather wore it, but was now threadbare and faded. It was impossible to tell their age. They could have been twenty. They could have been fifty. They hardly seemed to belong in the modern world.

And what did they think of him, he wondered. He had seen their astonishment when he had climbed out of the helicopter, and as they travelled together towards the mountains they had kept glancing at him as if they still couldn't believe he was there. He couldn't have looked more different to them. He was half their size, fair-haired, European. He was wearing a black combat suit with hiking boots and a backpack. It was unfortunate that horse-riding was one of the few outdoor activities that he had never fully mastered. They had given him a sleek, Egyptian black colt with a white blaze on its chest but he was barely able to control it, bouncing along helplessly.

He was very glad to dismount for a rest. The lower parts of his body felt like they'd been mangled.

"English boy!" It was Faisal, the second in command who had spoken. Alex didn't like him. He had an ugly, crooked smile and a cataract had turned one of his eyes a milky white.

Alex looked up.

"You living in London?"

Alex nodded. He didn't want to pass on any information, but there was no point denying it.

"Big Ben! The Queen! Chelsea football!" Faisal roared with laughter as if he had said something hilarious.

Rafiq muttered something in Farsi but Faisal snapped back angrily, then turned to Alex once again. "Why you come here?" he demanded.

Alex shrugged. "There's no school at the moment," he said. "And I didn't know what else to do."

Faisal had only half understood and frowned. "You go to Falcon's Edge," he said.

A gust of wind tugged at the flames and Faisal's face seemed to become distorted. The other men were waiting to hear what Alex said. Even Rafiq was gazing at him intently. Once again, Alex didn't want to reply. But they knew anyway. They had been paid to take him there. "Yes," he said, simply.

"Why?"

Alex ignored him. But then another of the men spoke. His name was Usman. As well as a rifle strapped across his shoulders, he had an ornate dagger with a curved blade hanging from his waist. "You no go there, English boy," he said. "You enter Falcon's Edge, you no come out." The others nodded in agreement.

"Nice lamb," Alex said, holding up his food. "What's for pudding?"

Falcon's Edge. Alex had never heard the name until a few days before. Suddenly he was three thousand miles away, back home in Chelsea, relaxing in the comfort of his bedroom. The sun was shining. It was going to be a warm day. Alex had schoolwork to do – but no school. A large part of Brookland had burned down and all the students had been sent home while the police investigated what had happened. Alex could have told them, of course. He had been there when the fire began. He was lucky he hadn't died in the flames.

The doorbell rang.

Alex waited for Jack Starbright to answer it, then remembered that she had gone out shopping. He swung himself off the bed and padded downstairs with no shoes on. This was the house

17

that his uncle had bought. All his life, while Alex was growing up, Ian Rider had pretended to be a banker, but it was only after his death that Alex had discovered the truth. He was a spy, working for the Special Operations Division of MI6. As Alex had unravelled all the lies, there had been a part of him that had wanted to sell the house, to move out of London, to start living a life that was actually real. In fact, the exact opposite had happened. MI6 had come for Alex, sucking him into their world, sending him on two missions – first to Cornwall and then to a private academy in the French Alps. He had been lucky to escape from Point Blanc. He had even been invited to his own funeral.

He reached the front door and opened it. Who had he been expecting? The postman? Of course it wasn't as easy as that. Mrs Jones, the Deputy Chief Executive and number two to Alan Blunt, was standing there, wearing a light raincoat, with her hands in her pockets. Alex recognized the man who was with her, dressed as he always was in a cheap suit and what looked like an old school tie. This was John Crawley. "Crawley from Personnel..." That was how he had described himself after Ian's death.

"Can we come in, Alex?" Mrs Jones asked.

"Maybe you should wait for Jack to get back," Alex said.

"Actually, we waited until she'd left."

Alex didn't remember inviting them in but

somehow the two agents made their way past him and entered the house. Alex led them into the kitchen. He didn't offer them coffee.

"You're not at school," Mrs Jones began.

"You know very well that the school burned down," Alex said.

"Yes. That was very unfortunate. We should have realized that one of Dr Grief's clones was still on the loose."

Alex had been chased around the building by a boy who was an exact replica of himself. It was like being attacked by his own reflection. He remembered the last moment, seeing the boy falling through a crater in the roof, disappearing into the smoke and flames. "What happened to him?" he asked.

"We're looking after him," Mrs Jones said. Alex didn't even want to think what that might mean. "How are you?"

"I'm still alive. No thanks to you."

Mrs Jones smiled thinly. She took out a packet of mints and, without offering one to Alex, slipped one into her mouth. She always sucked peppermints when she was about to deliver bad news. Behind her, Crawley was perched on a kitchen chair with his hands on his knees. He somehow reminded Alex of a ventriloquist's dummy. "We need your help again," Mrs Jones said.

"I'm afraid I'm not interested," Alex said. "I've got maths homework."

"I know..."

"And science homework, history homework, geography homework, French homework. I'm still trying to catch up from last term."

"Mr Blunt asked me to pay you a visit. Something's come up, and from what we understand, Brookland won't be open for at least another week. That gives you plenty of time to do what we have in mind and to be back without anyone noticing."

"You'd have thought most young people would jump at a chance to visit Afghanistan," Crawley said, speaking for the first time.

"Afghani—?" Alex's head swam. "No!" he exclaimed. "Forget it! You've got to be joking! Why do you keep asking me? Why can't you leave me alone?"

"Because you're very good, Alex," Mrs Jones replied. "Ian Rider trained you for this. All your life you were prepared for it and you've already proved yourself twice. That business with Dr Grief really was spectacular."

"You forced me into all that," Alex reminded her. "Why should I be interested now?"

"I'll explain." Mrs Jones turned to Crawley. "John, would you mind making us some coffee?"

"Certainly, Mrs Jones." Crawley swung himself off the stool and busied himself in the kitchen.

Alex watched him in disbelief. "Do you know where the milk is?" he asked.

"Oh yes." Crawley smiled. "I know everything."

Mrs Jones looked back at Alex and began to explain. "I'm sure I don't need to tell you, Alex, that terrorism is now the greatest threat to world peace. You'll have read about horrible incidents in New York, in London and in Paris. The whole of the Middle East is a cauldron and for the security services, it's a situation that's almost impossible to control ... especially when you have so many tiny groups that are ready to strike at any time with no overall plan.

"Imagine how much worse it would become if those groups were able to get their hands on the most advanced weapons, by which I mean nuclear or bio-chemical technology. That's our biggest nightmare. A terrorist with a nuclear bomb – and intelligence services all over the world have been working together to make sure it never happens."

"Caffeinated or decaffeinated?" Crawley asked. He had filled the kettle and flicked it on.

"I don't really mind, thank you." Mrs Jones hadn't taken her eyes off Alex. "It could be about to happen," she went on. "And all because of a man called Darcus Drake."

"Who is he?" Alex had to ask.

"He's a very interesting person. For many years, he was a photographer, working for the international press. He lived in London. He was wealthy. He won a great many awards. Darcus travelled the world, taking photographs of war zones. That was speciality. When bombs went off, when children re hurt, when the hospitals began to fill up, somehow he'd be there. He didn't care about his own safety. He made it his mission to show people what was happening in places like Syria, Yemen, Iraq, Sudan and Ethiopia. The strange thing is, Alex, there was something almost beautiful about the images he took. He had a knack of capturing horror in a way that made you want to look."

"He sounds like a good guy," Alex said.

"He was. There's no doubt about that. But somewhere along the way, he changed. I suppose it's impossible to keep witnessing so much pain and suffering and just to click away with your camera as if it's got nothing to do with you. Darcus Drake came to believe that the West was responsible for everything that he was seeing. He became more and more interested in terrorism until the inevitable happened and he became a terrorist himself.

"The thing is, he had travelled all over the Middle East. He had made hundreds of contacts. He knew journalists, intelligence officers, field agents, local tribesmen ... he'd even met some of the terrorist groups. He spoke four languages, including Arabic and Farsi. There's no question that he had a brilliant mind. I don't know exactly what happened. I don't know if there was a light-bulb moment. But suddenly, he realized he was in a perfect position to take control, to form his own terrorist group, fighting against the West. And that is what he did."

"What's all this got to do with me?" Alex asked.

"I'm coming to that, Alex. For the last two years, Darcus Drake dropped out of sight, but he recently emerged again in Afghanistan. We've received intelligence that he's holed up in the Herat mountains, quite close to the border with Iran. He's occupying an ancient citadel that was actually built around 300 BC by Alexander the Great. It's been rebuilt many times since then. In the nineteenth century, British soldiers fighting in Afghanistan gave it a name: Falcon's Edge. That's how it's been known ever since.

"It's a fantastic place. It looks out over an empty plain with Iran just to the west. The entrance to the citadel is very high up. There's a wide, stone platform open to the elements with a three hundred metre drop. During the First Anglo-Afghan War, the local tribesmen used to tie up their prisoners and throw them to their deaths. Only one track winds up through the mountains to this entrance and it's heavily guarded. It would be impossible to approach without being seen. And there's more to Falcon's Edge than meets the eye. It's perched on the edge of the mountain, but more recently it's been extended ... into the mountain itself. There's a network of tunnels and chambers. It has electricity and advanced telecommunications. But there's worse. According to our latest reports, the citadel is hiding a terrible secret."

"Here you are!" Crawley brought a tray over to

the counter. He had set out three cups and a small jug of milk. He glanced at Alex reproachfully. "You don't have any biscuits."

"I try not to eat them," Alex growled. He was annoyed. He had allowed himself to be drawn into this story. Despite himself, he wanted to know more. "What secret?" he asked.

"For the answer to that, you have to go back to nineteen seventy-nine," Mrs Jones replied. "That was when the Soviets occupied Afghanistan at the start of what turned out to be a disastrous nine-year war. While they were there, for their own reasons, they decided to build something called a calutron. I don't suppose you know what that is."

"It's a giant particle accelerator," Alex said. "It produces uranium-235, which you can use to make a bomb. We did it last term in science." He sighed. "I was actually there for that lesson..."

"Well ... yes." Mrs Jones blinked. "A calutron is used to produce small quantities of pure uranium. For what it's worth, it needs a huge amount of electrical power to run it and an equally huge cooling system to stop it blowing up." Crawley handed her a cup of coffee and she took it. "We've learned that there's a Soviet-built calutron inside Falcon's Edge and Darcus Drake is trying to get it working. He's planning to produce uranium and basically what he's going to do is to open a nuclear supermarket. He's offering to arm every terrorist group in the Middle East with nuclear weapons."

She paused. Was it Alex's imagination or had it suddenly got very quiet outside?

"Think about it Alex," Crawley muttered. "A nuclear explosion in London or Paris..."

"Go on," Alex said.

"To begin with, we didn't believe it," Mrs Jones said. "A plant that size would have to show up. We've had planes over the country looking for heat signatures. Satellite photography. Nothing. But then, two weeks ago, we were contacted by a Russian scientist who had worked on the project. He confirmed that the calutron is there, buried deep in the mountain, invisible to the world outside. And very soon it's going to start production."

"So why don't you bomb it?" Alex asked.

"Because it's too well protected. The walls of the citadel are far too thick and the mountains make it almost impossible for an air-to-ground missile to get a proper sighting on the target. Anyway, these days you can't fly bombing missions without evidence that you can show the world first. Photographic evidence. That's what we need now. Someone has to get into the mountain and prove that the calutron is really there. Then we can go to the United Nations and persuade them to take action."

There were many questions Alex could have asked, but in the end, he knew it boiled down to two words. "Why me?"

"We've managed to look at some blueprints and

as far as we can see, there's only one way into Falcon's Edge. As I've explained, the front entrance is impossible. But if you were to climb through the mountains and go in the back way, there is a possibility. The Soviets built a network of pipes and ventilation shafts and there's an access panel that could be opened. It's the one weak link in their security and the reason it's been overlooked is simple. Some of the pipework is very narrow. Too narrow for a man..."

But not too narrow for a boy...

Alex found himself staring into the flames of the bonfire, the cool breeze tugging at his hair as he remembered the conversation with Mrs Jones. The man called Usman had brewed mint tea. He handed Alex a tiny bowl that burned his fingers. He raised it to his lips and sipped. The tea was hot and sweet. The other men had lit cigarettes. They were talking among themselves in low voices, ignoring him now. How had he allowed MI6 to talk him into this? It seemed to Alex that everything had happened in a whirl. He had been driven to the seventeen-storey building near Liverpool Street Station which pretended to be a bank and where Special Operations was based. There had been further briefings. He had been provided with all the equipment he would need. And then, finally, a Royal Navy Jetstream T3 aircraft had flown him halfway across the world. He had transferred to the Lynx Mk9A helicopter in Cyprus and then – after refuelling on an aircraft carrier in the south Mediterranean – he had been dropped on the edge of a dusty town in Iran. And now he was here.

Why him? There was no answer to that question and, anyway, it was already far too late to ask.

IN THE PIPELINE

The Kochis knew what they were looking for, but even so, Alex was amazed that they had been able to find it without satnav or highly detailed maps. The entrance to the pipework was a round hole set in a block of concrete, covered with thick steel wire. The whole thing was built into the side of a hill and half covered by rubble and wild grass. Even in broad daylight they could have walked past without seeing it, but they had come here in the middle of the night and they hadn't even hesitated. The man called Usman had cried out and beckoned them over. They set to work at once.

They had brought with them an oxyacetylene torch and gas cylinder, strapped to one of the horses, and now they used the equipment to burn through the wire. Alex watched the heavy strands as they glowed red and then peeled away. Part of him was afraid that the brilliant light of the cutter would alert someone that they were there but, as with the bonfire, the tribesmen showed no concern. They were surrounded by the great bulk of the mountains with nobody in sight. Falcon's Edge itself was half a mile away and below them, tucked away in its own rock face. A passing satellite might notice the sudden glare but by the time it had communicated the information to whichever intelligence agency controlled it, they would have long gone. It was probably safe enough.

Alex found himself staring into the black, round hole that could have been the barrel of a gun pointing straight at his head. He could just make out the curve of the pipe as it burrowed into the hillside and the thought of crawling into it filled him with horror. Mrs Jones had been right about one thing. Alex was slim and small for his age, but even so, his shoulders would barely pass through and certainly no adult would be able to follow. He realized that once he began, it would be impossible to turn round. If the plans that he had been shown were wrong, if he came to a dead end, he would be trapped. Effectively, he was being asked to bury himself alive.

"Tomorrow." Rafiq, the leader of the group who had brought him here, hadn't dismounted from his horse. Glancing down at Alex, his face was full of doubt. "We meet ... the Shuja cemetery."

"Midday," Alex said. Mrs Jones had described the operation while he was in London. Getting out of Falcon's Edge was going to be easier than getting in. If all went well, in less than twelve hours' time, Alex's work would be done and he would be escorted back across the border into Iran. If not ... Alex didn't like to think about the possibility of failure – and why should he? There were only about a hundred things that could go wrong.

Rafiq nodded. He took one look at the mad English boy who seemed determined to kill himself, then wheeled his horse round and rode away. The others followed him. Faisal, the man who was blind in one eye, twisted in his saddle and spat at the ground. It was as if that summed up everything he had to say about the adventure. He rode off, leading Alex's horse behind him.

Alex was alone. Suddenly he felt very lonely, lost in the mountains. The wind was still gusting over his shoulders. He ran a hand through his hair, clearing it out of his eyes. Well, there was no point standing here having second thoughts. Right now, there was only one way back home.

He gathered his things together. Nothing that he was wearing was quite what it seemed. Derek Smithers, the ever cheerful, overweight technical specialist at MI6, had supplied Alex with all the gadgets he had needed on his last two missions and he had equipped him for this one too. First, Alex checked the belt that he was wearing. It was divided into various pockets, each one containing different items – weapons, medical supplies, maps, food, water – that he might need. The belt also had what looked like four suction caps, surrounding his body like points on a compass. Alex would need these later.

He had taken off the backpack. It would be impossible to fit into the pipe while he was wearing it. Inside the backpack were two batteries and a miniature computer that controlled all the equipment hidden in Alex's combat suit. This extended to his hiking boots, which looked ordinary when seen from above, but in fact had two small, glass plates concealed in the instep, in front of each heel. Finally, Alex slipped on a charcoal-grey helmet, made out of some sort of impacted plastic. It wasn't just there to protect his head. It housed a miniature digital camera, barely larger than a matchbox, which would record his journey through an opening 1.5 millimetres wide. Alex had been given a professional camera to photograph the calutron when he found it but the digicam would act as back-up. The helmet was also fitted with a Petzl Ultra Vario Headtorch, powered by a built-in lithium-ion battery – the lightweight, state-of-the-art torch favoured by potholers.

He flicked it on and the beam shot out ahead of him. Alex directed it into the yawning mouth that waited to devour him. "The first part's the worst part," he muttered to himself. It was something Ian Rider had often said ... helping him with his homework or teaching him to climb mountains. It was a joke between them because they both knew that the first part never was. It just got worse as it went along. Alex lowered himself onto his knees. He grabbed the backpack in both hands and, pushing it ahead of him, plunged in.

The wind was cut off as if by a giant blade. The stars disappeared. He was completely surrounded by the smooth, metal surface of the pipe. He could feel it pressing down on his shoulders, rubbing against his arms and legs. It seemed to go on for ever. Looking ahead of him, he saw the light from his helmet slicing through the darkness, illuminating ... nothing. There was just the pipe, a perfect circle glinting in the light, and him, the insect who had been foolish enough to crawl into it. He would have to worm his way along, pushing the backpack ahead of him. And suppose the diagrams that Mrs Jones had shown him were wrong? Suppose the pipe narrowed? Alex put these thoughts to one side. There was no point wasting energy on problems until they became real.

He crawled forward, following the beam. It would be impossible to tell how far he had travelled, when every section of the pipeline looked the same. Nor did he waste time checking his watch. He only knew that the further he went, the more his elbows and knees, unused to bearing his weight, began to hurt. He also had to fight to stop himself panicking. His brain was screaming at him to stand up, to turn round, to go back. But that was out of the question, he reminded himself. He had a job to do. He just had to focus on that. What would he do if the light went out? No. The lithium-ion battery would last eleven hours and, in case of an emergency, he had a spare in his belt. *Stop worrying about nothing.* Alex knew perfectly well that the real danger was still to come.

A whole hour passed. At least, it felt like an hour. The pipe seemed to be getting narrower. Alex was sure he could feel it closing in on him. Was he imagining it or was it getting harder to breathe? He must be about a quarter of a mile into the mountain now and he could only imagine thousands of tonnes of soil and rock bearing down on him from above. He stopped and forced himself to relax. A trickle of sweat slid down his face, finding its way through the crack between his helmet and the side of his head. It had been cold outside but as he penetrated further into the ventilation system he began to feel warm air being blasted up from somewhere far below. The deeper he went, the closer it seemed to get and he was also aware of a strange smell. It was mechanical, a mixture of oil and metal.

He came to a T-junction. He had arrived before he knew it, almost hypnotized by the single beam of light. The second pipe, running left and right, was twice the size of the one he was in and he hauled himself into it, feeling like toothpaste coming out of a tube. It was still pitch-dark but at least he no longer had the feeling of being trapped.

"You'll be starting in one of the auxiliary outlets.

It feeds into the main air shaft – and all I can say is that I'm glad they didn't send me. I'm not sure I'd have got very far!"

It was Smithers speaking, his hands resting on his enormous stomach. Suddenly Alex was back at MI6, studying the charts and diagrams that were spread out in front of him. Mrs Jones was in the room and there was another, thin-faced man who had been introduced as Orlov. He was the scientist who had worked on the calutrons and who had come to British Intelligence with the information.

"Once you get there, you turn right. You'll be able to move a little more easily. That's the good news. But I'm afraid this is where your problems begin, old chap. You're going to have to get through the exhaust fan."

Alex could already hear it. The fan was whirring at high speed, about fifty metres away. He felt the warm air rushing into his face. Alex grabbed the backpack and strapped it onto his shoulders. He was glad to have it behind him, out of the way. Then he started moving towards the next obstacle, supporting himself now with the palms of his hands. It was good to feel the space between his shoulders and the pipe as it curved over him. Briefly he wondered what had happened to Rafiq and the other Kochis. By now they should have worked their way around the mountains and onto the track leading down from Falcon's Edge. They must be reaching the Shuja cemetery, named after a famous Shah, but in fact, built by the British two hundred years ago for the soldiers who had died in the Anglo-Afghan war. Their instructions were to wait for him there but Alex wondered if he would ever see them again. He hoped they were still owed money. Then they might stay.

Something flickered ahead of him. There were two silver struts coming down from the ceiling, joining together in a V and they reflected back the light from the head torch. The struts were part of a larger machine, a fan sucking up the stale air from below. It was blocking the entire passageway, turning so fast that the blades had become no more than a blur. The engine that controlled it was set behind the struts. Even at a distance Alex could feel the power of the contraption. There was no way he would be able to stop it with his hand. He would simply lose the hand.

He continued forward until he was right up close, the breeze now battering his face and making it difficult to see. Automatically he reached up to a special pocket, built into the breast of his jacket, and unzipped it. He drew out a rectangular box, black metal, about the size of a TV remote control. It had an antenna which he unfolded and a simple on–off switch. Alex pointed it in front of him, wondering if it would actually work.

The technology was simple even if it was still top secret. It had been developed by the US Air Force as part of CHAMP: the Counter-electronics

High Power Microwave Advanced Missile Project. How Smithers had got his hands on it, he preferred not to say. The box was a radar transmitter. Alex directed it towards the engine management system that turned the fan. He flicked it on. Instantly, the machine sent a series of magnetic pulses that travelled through the wiring loom of the fan system, confusing the electrics and causing the entire engine to shut down.

The fan came to an immediate halt. Alex was impressed, despite himself. Smithers had told him that one day the same technology could shut down an entire city and now he believed it. Alex looked at each of the four blades, spaced out with enough of a gap for him to crawl through. He reached out to rotate them round so he could do just that.

If the creature hadn't moved, he wouldn't have seen it and, seconds later, he would have been dead. As it was, the beam of his torch reflected off some of its scales as they briefly twisted and that was what alerted him. He froze, his hand still outstretched, his mouth dry, his heart thudding against his chest. It was a snake and not just any snake. Crawley had shown him a picture during his briefing, just in case he happened to see one when he was crossing the desert. Alex recognized the ugly brown diamond shapes on its skin, the pear-shaped head, the bulging eyes. It was about half a metre long ... medium-sized. Its Latin name was *Echis carinatus*, but it was better known as the saw-scaled viper. It was one of the most dangerous snakes in the world.

How had it got here? It couldn't have crawled through when the fan had been turning. Either the engine had been switched off, perhaps for general maintenance, or it had reached this section of the pipe from another direction. It had been asleep but Alex had disturbed it and already it was uncoiling itself, preparing to strike. It was making a loud, hissing noise, which didn't in fact come from its mouth. It was rubbing its scales together to make the sound, a warning for its enemies. When it attacked, it could travel three times further than its own length. The fan wouldn't stop it. The blades were too far apart. Even if Alex began to back away, it would still reach him. The saw-scaled viper has killed more people than any other species of snake and he could already imagine it lunging at his throat, its fangs burying themselves in his flesh. After that, there would be a long, agonizing death. It might be months before his body was found.

How could he get past it? That was the next question. Alex knew that there was no other way round. If he turned back the way he had come, he would find himself alone in the Herat mountains and it was unlikely he would make it out of the country. But nor could he sit here hoping the snake would go away – there was no chance of that happening. The viper was angry, hissing more loudly, waiting for him to make his move. Alex remained perfectly still. One hand was on the propeller. The other, he realized, was still cradling the radar transmitter and suddenly he knew what he had to do. It was all a question of timing. There really were going to be just micro-seconds between life and death.

Very carefully, he adjusted his hand, feeling for the on–off switch. All the time, he kept his eyes on the snake, almost willing it not to move. For its part, the snake stared at him with all the evil in the world. The hissing was louder, more insistent, approaching the point of no return. It was about to strike. There could be no doubt of it. Alex weighed the transmitter in one hand. Then, quite deliberately, he slammed his fist into the side of the blade.

The snake believed it was threatened and leapt. It would have reached Alex before he could so much as blink but it had to manoeuvre its way through the gap between the blades and that slowed it enough for Alex to do two things. He twisted round, putting as much distance between himself and the snake as he could. At the same time, he flicked the switch that deactivated the transmitter, allowing the fan to start again.

The next two seconds disappeared in a chaos of hope and fear. The fan restarted, the blades reaching maximum speed almost at once. Alex felt the breath being knocked out of him as his back and shoulders slammed into the pipe. Out of the corner of his eye, he saw the viper above him, its eyes blazing, its mouth stretched open to reveal its curved fangs. The snake landed on him, its head on his chest, and Alex squirmed, barely able to stop himself from crying out in horror. Something splashed into his face. It tasted foul on his lips. He waited for the snake to bite him and it twisted away, as if more interested in something else. Another two seconds passed and in that time he saw that his plan had worked, that he hadn't been bitten. The fan had cut the saw-scaled viper in half. More accurately, about fifteen centimetres had made it through. The other thirty-five had been left behind. Some sort of signal must have reached whatever brain it had and it had lost interest in Alex, staring back at its own remains. Alex backed away, moving like a crab on the palms of his hands and the soles of his feet. He was feeling sick. He reached up with one arm and used his sleeve to wipe the snake's blood off his face. The viper was no longer moving. Alex reached for his water bottle and emptied it in three large gulps.

Snakes – and spiders – have a power that's hard to define. It's primal. When one comes close, human beings will react in the same way as any animal and that was what had happened to Alex. He had been submerged in pure, instinctive terror and it took him several minutes to recover, all the time staring at the severed head and the red, bleeding stub, wondering if the creature was really dead. Only when his heart was beating normally did he turn the transmitter back on, deactivating the fan once again. Then, carefully, he made his way through, trying to ignore the blood splattered on the pipe all around him.

After that, he moved as quickly as possible – both to make up time and to put the nightmare far behind him.

"When you get through the exhaust fan, there's about a hundred metres. It's pretty level and you should have nothing to worry about until you get to the main air shaft. That's when things begin to get interesting."

Smithers's voice guided Alex as he continued forward. The pipe was large enough to allow him to move freely but he still felt the weight of the mountain, the intense darkness, the isolation, and he had to fight to stay focused, to breathe normally. He had remembered to turn the fan back on before he left. He didn't want a maintenance engineer turning up to see what was wrong. Ahead of him he was aware of a soft, beating sound, some sort of machinery. He knew that he was getting close to the end.

"The plans show that the air shaft drops vertically – two hundred metres. That's about the height of the Gherkin, in London. It's one hell of a drop but unfortunately it's polished steel so you can't climb down. It's too far to lower you on a rope. And I'm afraid it's not quite wide enough for a parachute."

"So what do I do?"

"That's a very good question, Alex."

Alex reached the edge of the air shaft. The ground opened up beneath him and he lay, stretched out on his stomach, gazing down into nothingness. The beam of his torch was nowhere near powerful enough to reach the bottom and simply stopped in mid-air, illuminating the metal circle around it. The height of the Gherkin. It was as if he were lying on the roof of a London skyscraper, thinking about throwing himself off. Smithers had assured him that he had a plan and that it would work but Alex could only take his word for it. Was he reliable?

Well, there was only one way to find out. Alex swallowed hard, then reached behind him and found a cable poking out of his backpack. It had a jack plug that clicked into a socket built into one of the shoulders of his combat suit. He turned it and heard the safety lock engage. Then he waited for the computer that he had carried all this distance to boot up and do its work. Smithers had said it would only take five seconds but he waited half a minute just to be sure.

This was worse than the snake. What he was about to do went against every instinct. It was like committing suicide. But there was no other way.

Alex swung himself round and threw himself into the void.

A LONG WAY DOWN

Alex fell, feet first, hurtling to what felt like certain death. He couldn't see. The light was spinning uselessly around him, bouncing off the walls of the shaft and turning them into a dazzling blur. He could feel the wind punching up at him. He wanted to scream but it was as if iron bands had fastened themselves around his chest and his throat and no sound came. How fast was he falling? A hundred miles per hour? If he hit the ground at this velocity, every bone in his body would shatter. Everything depended on the equipment he had been given but even Smithers had sounded uncertain.

"Of course it'll work! I mean, I hope it'll work. But it is a prototype, you know..."

And now its moment had come. There was nothing for Alex to do. It all worked automatically.

First, the shoes. There were two miniature echo sounders built into the soles, behind the glass panels. They worked in much the same way as a depth finder on a boat. As Alex fell, they transmitted sound pulses which bounced back off the floor. The exact time of each pulse was recorded by the computer in Alex's backpack and – if Smithers had done his job – it would know exactly how far he had fallen.

Just three and a half seconds after Alex had launched himself over the edge, they registered that the end of the pipe was exactly one hundred metres away. One second later, the distance was just sixty metres. Instantly, the computer activated four tiny explosive devices in Alex's belt. Alex felt the suction pads being released, exploding outwards, trailing four lightweight cords. These were made out of the same super-strength nylon that Smithers had built into the yo-yo that Alex had taken with him on his first mission in Cornwall. The pads slammed into the metal wall and instantly stuck in place. The cords led back into a spool system concealed in the backpack and as they unravelled, they slowed down the rate of Alex's descent. He heard the gears turning and felt a lurch in his stomach as the cords took up more and more of his weight. Fifty metres, forty metres, thirty metres ... he was like a spider dropping out of a web. At ten metres, the rushing wind had stopped and Alex finally felt able to look down. He could see the floor below him. The cords lowered him the last few metres. His feet gently came to rest against the bottom of the next horizontal pipe.

He had arrived.

Alex took a deep breath. He felt as if he had left his stomach somewhere behind him and his head was throbbing, if only because of the change of pressure. With a shaking hand, he released the cords that remained, dangling from the edge of the pipe. Good old Smithers! He would be delighted to know that his invention had worked perfectly ... assuming, of course, that Alex got back in one piece to tell him.

The new pipe offered him another choice – left or right – and Alex turned left. A short crawl brought him to a maintenance hatch, locked from the outside. But once again, Smithers had prepared him. Alex drew a short, black cylinder out of his belt and weighed it in his hand. It looked like a flashlight but in fact it was a metal vapour torch fuelled by a mixture of copper oxide and magnesium to produce an astonishingly powerful flame burning at 2,500 degrees centigrade. He flicked it on and the flame leapt out, the carbon-fibre nozzle turning it into a blade that cut through the metal in a matter of seconds. Alex glanced at his watch. It was half past four in the morning. Everything had been timed so that he would arrive at Falcon's Edge when almost all the personnel would be asleep and security would be at its weakest. He waited until the metal had cooled, then pushed the hatch open and climbed through.

He found himself on the edge of a vast chamber, the size of an aircraft hangar ... and there was indeed a burned-out helicopter abandoned on one side. The place was like nothing he had ever seen before; nothing he could have imagined. It was as if the entire mountain had been hollowed out to make room for storage, weapons, ammunition and machinery. A night lighting system had been set in place, a series of neon tubes that cast a soft glow over everything and, looking around him, Alex saw half a dozen jeeps and other military vehicles parked in rows, some with anti-aircraft guns mounted on the roof. There were great piles of wooden crates, metal cylinders, half-dismantled pieces of machinery and, everywhere, a fantastic array of weapons including rocket launchers, bazookas, hand grenades and AK 47 machine guns ... enough to supply a small army. Alex began to creep forward, then ducked down, burying himself in the shadows, as something moved. A moment later, he relaxed. It wasn't a guard. There were three horses tethered to a rail. One of them had stamped its hoof on the stone floor.

The far end of the chamber was open to the night air. Keeping his distance from the horses – he was afraid of disturbing them and alerting any guards who might be passing – he made his way outside and found himself on a huge platform. He had plummeted two hundred metres down the pipe but he was still another three hundred metres above ground level. Now he knew how Falcon's Edge had got its name. The fortress was built into the side of the mountain, far above the empty plain that stretched out below, washed over by the light of the moon. Standing on the edge of the platform, Alex was surrounded by giant walls, ramparts and battlements. If he took one step forward, there would be nothing to stop him falling to his death. This was where the tribesmen had once executed their prisoners, throwing them into the abyss. Looking down at the ground, far away, he could imagine the terror they must have felt.

A massive archway stood to one side with a gate ... a portcullis that was closed and locked. The gate looked ancient but the CCTV camera mounted in the stonework was brand new and Alex made sure he kept out of its range. A rough track ran down the mountainside beyond it, but he couldn't possibly escape that way. He would have been seen at once. Even so, if all went well, that was how he would be leaving in a little over two hours' time. Somewhere, out in the darkness, the Shuja cemetery was waiting for him. It suddenly occurred to him what a grim meeting place Mrs Jones had arranged. He just hoped he wouldn't be needing it for all the wrong reasons.

He went back into the main body of the fortress, once again passing the horses. They were still restless, sensing his presence, but there didn't seem to be anyone else around. He had a job to do. Mrs Jones needed evidence that the calutron was there and that it was close to working. Back in England, he had studied the plans and he knew where he had to go – it meant crossing back through the storage area. He had got about halfway when he heard the unmistakable sound of boots on stone. Instantly, he crouched down behind one of the crates, noticing an expanse of white silk draped over the top. That was interesting. It was a parachute. Quite a lot of these supplies must have been dropped in by air, suggesting that Drake had friends in neighbouring countries. Pakistan, perhaps? Or China? Alex knew that Middle East politics were enormously complicated but it still might be in somebody's interest to support the new terrorist group and he made a mental note to mention it to MI6.

Two soldiers walked past without seeing him. They were dressed in loose-fitting, olive-green jackets and trousers with heavy boots, the uniform of ragtag armies all over the world. Both were bearded and young. They carried machine guns, slung over their backs. Alex waited until they had gone, then continued through the hangar, past the jeeps, making sure there were no cameras. Looking up, he saw iron gantries criss-crossing the ceiling with dozens of arc lamps hanging down. Huge fans were slowly turning, circulating the air. There didn't seem to be any CCTV.

He reached a staircase which he knew led up to the living quarters, contained within the fortress itself. Ahead of him, there was a corridor. It was exactly where he had known it would be. He followed it to the end. Five metal steps led into a second chamber. The calutron was right in front of him.

He had been shown photographs and knew what to expect, but even so, the size of it and its sheer ugliness surprised him. It was housed in a sort of cradle made up of concrete pillars, steel girders, walkways and ladders. It was shaped like a miniature athletics stadium with a wall of ceramic tiles and, above it, a platform and handrail which went all the way round. Alex guessed it would have taken him about five minutes to walk the complete circuit if he had wanted to. The whole thing was strangely old-fashioned but then it had been built back in the eighties. It looked dead and neglected. Smithers had given him a lecture about how the calutron worked – something to do with magnetic fields, ions colliding, uranium isotopes and all the rest of it. Was it actually working? It was making no sound at all. The truth was that Alex didn't really care. That wasn't his concern. He just wanted to take his pictures and get out of there.

He unzipped the backpack one last time and took out the camera he had been given. It was a Leica S 007 (the number had made him smile), one of the most advanced medium-format digital cameras in the world. Alex had been quite surprised that MI6 had provided him with such a stylish – and expensive – piece of kit. He knew that it was incredibly fast and responsive, with a capture rate of 3.5

frames per second. He also knew that it would have cost him fifteen thousand pounds if he'd gone out to buy one. Why did he need it? He wasn't out to win a photography competition. He was just there to take pictures of a lump of machinery. The camera concealed in his helmet would have done the job just as well.

Still, he wasn't going to argue. Quickly, he began photographing the chamber, the machine, the various wires and pipes, the dials and the gauges. Mrs Jones had asked him to capture everything he could. *"Take a thousand pictures if you have to. I want to know everything that's in that room."* Of course, it would all be useless if he couldn't get out himself. That was the problem. The great mass of the Herat mountains had prevented satellites from picking up any evidence of the calutron and, for the same reason, Alex was unable to send his images over the Internet. He would carry them with him, physically, when he left.

And that had all been arranged. He took a series of photographs of one of the control panels, then glanced at his watch. Quarter past five. At six o'clock, three supply vehicles would be arriving at Falcon's Edge, delivering fresh food from the market. One of the drivers had been bribed. Alex would be smuggled out in a crate and driven through the archway he had seen, then taken to the cemetery. When Mrs Jones had outlined the plan, it had seemed unlikely but she had been confident.

"You don't need to worry, Alex. They're only worried about people breaking into the complex, not breaking out. No one will have any idea you're there. The driver's name is Farshad and he'll be in a truck with a green cross on it. Just make sure you're not seen by anyone else..."

He had taken enough pictures. Alex had decided that, for once, Mrs Jones had got her intelligence wrong. None of the gauges that he had photographed had shown anything but zero. Some of the cables were disconnected. If Darcus Drake was planning to manufacture uranium, he wasn't going to start any time soon. Part of him was annoyed. Of course he was glad that Drake wouldn't be able to supply terrorist groups with nuclear material. But Alex was beginning to think all the effort of getting here had been a complete waste of time. Couldn't Mrs Jones have found out the truth before he left?

The camera was still hanging around his neck and he was just reaching up to turn it off when something metallic touched the back of his head and a voice, speaking with an Irish accent, said, "Please raise your hands very slowly, Alex, and don't try anything stupid or I'll blow your brains out."

Alex did as he was told. Without turning round, he lifted both hands, at the same time asking himself not how he had been caught, but how the man with the gun knew his name.

THE AWAKENING

"All right, Alex. You can turn round now."

Keeping his hands above his head, Alex did just that. He felt the gun move away from the back of his skull but as he turned full circle, he saw it pointing directly between his eyes, a silver TT-33 self-loading pistol, made in Russia, like the calutron. One twitch of a finger, and it would fire a 7.62mm bullet, travelling at four hundred metres per second, into his head.

The man whose finger was now curled between life and death was smiling. He had only just been roused from his bed. Alex could tell that from the stubble on his cheeks, the untidy silver hair and the grey eyes that hadn't quite shaken off their sleep. He was in his mid-thirties and reminded Alex of a long-distance runner, very slim and light on his feet. He was wearing a soft, grey tracksuit with a T-shirt. This had to be Darcus Drake. As he stood facing him, Alex's first thought was that this was an unusually handsome and very confident man.

It was only as the seconds ticked past that he realized something was wrong. Drake was still smiling. His expression hadn't changed, as if the photographer had been photographed himself. And the smile was only on his mouth, not in his eyes. There was nothing friendly about it, nothing humorous. It was simply there.

He was not alone. There were three soldiers surrounding him, watching Alex with deeply hostile eyes.

"So, at last I get to meet Alex Rider," Drake said.

"Yes." There seemed to be little point denying it.

"And you got in through the ventilation system?" He laughed softly but the smile remained the same. "I have to say, I really hadn't seen that one coming. It must have been a tight squeeze, even for you. Anyway, it's very early and you must be hungry. Why don't we have breakfast together?" He glanced at the guards and spoke to them rapidly in Farsi. Then he turned back to Alex. "I've told them to take everything you've brought with you and to give you a new set of clothes. I'm afraid we may not have anything very stylish but I'm not taking any chances, not when you've been kitted out by MI6. Once they've done that, they'll bring you to me."

"How did you know I was here?" Alex didn't expect Drake to answer but he had to know if he had made a mistake.

To his surprise, Drake seemed to be amused by

the question. At least, his eyes lit up even if the rest of his face refused to move. "Well, I suppose you deserve to know that after all your effort," he said in his lilting Irish accent. He gestured with one hand and a fifth man appeared, coming down the metal steps. Alex recognized him at once: the unpleasant white eye, the beard, the turban. It was Faisal, one of the tribesmen who had ridden with him into the mountains.

"You should be careful who you choose to trust," Drake said. "That's the trouble with the Kochis, Alex. They've been fighting so many different people they don't really care which side they're on. Whoever's got the money, that's all that interests them."

"Alex Rider. England spy," Faisal muttered, as if there could still be any doubt of it.

"I'll see you very shortly for breakfast," Drake continued, still addressing Alex. "And don't worry. I won't be inviting your friend. In fact, now I think about it, he probably isn't your friend any more. Take it easy. If you try to fight with my men, they'll break your arms and we wouldn't want that."

He turned and left. The soldiers closed in.

An hour later, escorted by two guards and wearing a dark green uniform that was too big for him, Alex was taken back through the great cavern beneath the citadel. His backpack, his belt, his camera, his shoes ... everything that he had brought with him had been removed. He had no socks and wore a pair of rough, leather sandals on his feet. He missed his combat boots more than anything else. He might get a chance to make a break for it – but there was no way he could make any fast moves the way he was dressed now.

Everything was very different. Sunlight was streaming in through the opening and the whole place had woken up with soldiers everywhere, many of them drilling on the outer platform, others carrying crates, cleaning weapons. Alex saw that the three supply vans had arrived. One of them was white with a green cross and he saw the driver, a dark, hooded man, staring in his direction. This must be Farshad, the man who was supposed to smuggle him out of here. Well, it wasn't going to happen. There was no way the two of them were going to make contact. More soldiers were helping to empty the vehicles, carrying fresh produce – meat, vegetables, sacks of grain – into the compound. The horses were kicking impatiently, anxious to be on the move.

The guards led him towards a stone staircase on the other side of a burned-out helicopter. Alex hadn't noticed it when he was there before. A hand shoved him hard in the back and he staggered up, climbing about fifty steps, and emerging in a vaulted hallway with brick walls and chandeliers filled with candles. The citadel was a strange mix of old and new. As Alex continued down a long, windowless corridor, electric light bulbs lit the way but the flagstones under his feet could have been medieval. They came to a curved wooden door and one of the guards knocked, then entered without waiting for an answer.

Darcus Drake had living quarters directly above the open terrace looking out over the plain. The room was huge and austere with a very old, solid table and twelve chairs, a stone fireplace and rough, Afghan rugs laid out on the floor. A fire had been lit but the room was cold. Alex noticed that there was no glass in the windows and although the sun was now well up in the sky, he could still feel the chill of the night. There were maps on the wall: the local area, the country, the whole Middle East. This was the sort of room where wars were planned. He wondered who had sat around this table and what horrors they had discussed.

The two guards waited by the door. Alex stepped forward.

Drake was alone, waiting for him. Breakfast had already been brought up and, despite everything, it looked good. There were eggs cooked with vegetables, sweet bread, pastries, cheese, dried fruit and black tea – or *chai* as it was called. Less welcome was the sight of his backpack with the contents scattered over the rugs. The computer, the vapour torch, the belt, the boots were all there. Drake was turning over the Leica camera in his hands. The smile was still on his face, exactly as before.

"This is a really fantastic camera," he said and

Alex remembered what Mrs Jones had told him. Before he had become a terrorist, Drake had been a professional photographer. "I'm quite surprised, MI6 giving it to a kid like you. No offence..."

"They wanted good photographs," Alex said.

"Of the calutron?" Drake laughed briefly. "Well, that's a waste of time, Alex. I can't get the bloody thing to work. Not that I need it. I've got much bigger plans." He set the camera down in front of him. "I'll keep this, if you don't mind. It'll be something to remember you by."

Alex didn't like the sound of that. "If you want to steal the camera, I can't stop you," he said. "And if it makes you smile..."

The jibe struck home. Drake's eyes darkened. "You've noticed that, have you?" He pointed to his mouth. "It's called Möbius syndrome. It's a very rare nervous disease, a sort of facial paralysis. I was born with it. It's funny, really. I've been smiling all my life even though I've never found very much to smile about."

"A bit like the Joker in Batman," Alex said. He was being deliberately offensive. He didn't want Drake to think he was scared.

"And what does that make you? Robin?" Drake shook his head. "I don't think so..." He gestured at the table. "Why don't you sit down? I promised you breakfast and you might as well enjoy it. It's going to be your last meal."

Alex felt a hollow in his stomach as he took

his place at the table. He had been threatened with death before. The last time, it had been Dr Grief who had wanted to cut him up in a biology class at the Point Blanc Academy. But now he was thousands of miles away from home. He had been betrayed. MI6 had no way of knowing what was happening. This wasn't looking good.

"I have to ask you some questions," Drake said. "I've already had most of the answers from Faisal, so if you lie to me, I'll know at once and then, I'm afraid, I'll give you to my men – they're trained in the art of cruelty."

"What do you want to know?" Alex asked. He helped himself to some bread and cheese. He didn't feel like eating but was determined to try.

"You know, I'd heard a whisper that MI6 had employed a teenager. Was it you who took out Herod Sayle?"

"Yes," Alex muttered the single word. The first time he had worked for MI6 he had been sent to Cornwall where the Stormbreaker computers were being manufactured and that was where he had come up against Herod Sayle. But he wasn't going to add any details if he could help it.

"That's very impressive. How many times have you worked for them since then?"

"This is the third time."

"Third time unlucky. You should have said no."

"They didn't give me much choice."

"That's a shame. Why did they pick on you?"

"They wanted photographs of the calutron. The only way in was through the pipes..."

"...and the pipes are too narrow for a fully grown man?"

"Yes."

"What were they going to do with the photographs?"

"They wanted to show them to the United Nations. They needed authorization. To bomb you."

Drake laughed delightedly. "It's very difficult to bomb me, Alex. First they have to find me and I move around a lot. You've done well, so far. I've got just one more question. Did they tell you I would be here?"

Alex hesitated. He didn't want to help Drake but nor did he want to be tortured. In the end, he decided that he had no choice. It probably wouldn't be that important anyway. "Yes," he said. "They thought you might be here."

"I'm surprised they didn't send you in to kill me."

"I wish they had," Alex said.

Drake laughed a second time. "You're a boy with spirit. I'll give you that! I'm very sorry it had to end this way. For you, I mean. But I've got no more questions. You can eat your breakfast now and while we're together, I'm going to tell you what's going to happen, although I doubt that you'll like it. What do you say?"

"I'll have some tea, if you don't mind."

"Of course." Drake poured. Then he began to talk.

"You were wasting your time, Alex. They can't bomb me, whatever they may have told you. The walls of Falcon's Edge are too thick and the caverns are too deep. They'd need to send a smart bomb in through the window, but I'm not sure they've got a bomb that's smart enough for that. What other options are there? A drone? I have two hundred men surrounding me; my own personal bodyguard. They'd shoot it down before it got anywhere near me. There's only one track that climbs up from the valley and I make sure it's well protected. And anyway, like I told you, I'm not here very often. I move around. That's what keeps me safe.

"I want you to understand who I am. I used to be a newspaper photographer. I'm sure they told you that. I was born and raised in Dublin and I spent five years working for the *Irish Times* before I moved to London. After that, I was sent to villages all over the Middle East, taking pictures after they'd been targeted by the British and the French and the Americans. Do you know what it does to you, after a while, recording all that misery? Dead people. Destruction. It gets to your head, Alex and, in the end, I realized that I couldn't do it any more; supplying nice people like you or your mum and dad with pictures to look at while you're having breakfast."

"I don't have a mum or a dad," Alex said. "You don't know anything about me."

Drake ignored him. "I'm doing something amazing.

I'm organizing an army. You see, the whole of the Middle East is crawling with freedom fighters – but there are too many of them, too many different groups. Every country has got half a dozen different factions and they're all too busy fighting each other to see that the real enemy is laughing at them. The West! The billionaires who sell the weapons and buy the oil. That's who they should be fighting. And here's the funny thing. They're listening to me. I speak their language and I understand their needs. They've accepted me as their leader and before long, they'll come together in a new organization that will stretch from here to Iran, Iraq, Libya, Pakistan and Syria. I've called it the Awakening. It has weapons. It has money. And quite soon it will launch a campaign of terror that will be unlike anything that has gone before."

"Why do you think killing people will make any difference?" Alex asked. "Don't you think enough people have been hurt already?"

"You're just a kid. You don't understand." Drake scowled, but only with his eyes. His smile remained frozen in place. "I can see I'm wasting my time talking to you, which is a shame because, you know, I'd heard so much about you. But you can still be useful to me."

He picked up a pastry and tore it in half.

"Here's what I'm going to do," he went on. "We'll wait until sunset. It'll be more dramatic then, with a red sky. And then we'll take you outside and put you in front of a shooting squad. We're going to execute you as a spy, Alex. And we'll film the entire thing. You'll be on the news. Your friends at school will watch you die. And the film will remind the whole world of the sort of dirty tricks that the intelligence services play ... sending schoolboys to do their work for them. It'll also show them that the Awakening is here and that we're in business. It's a win–win situation for us, Alex, although I suppose it's a lose–lose situation for you. Do you want some more breakfast?"

Drake gestured and the two guards came forward and grabbed hold of Alex before he could reply. As he was led out, Drake picked up the camera and took a couple of shots of him. As always, he was smiling.

BREAKOUT

Alex knew there was no way out of the cell. It was buried as deep in the mountain as it was possible to be. There was no window. But for the single bulb burning over his head, he would have been in the pitch dark. The door was a solid piece of wood about twenty centimetres thick. Alex had noticed that when he was led in. He had also spotted the two iron bars that would slide across on the outside. Even if he'd somehow got his hands on a pile driver or a battering ram, it wouldn't have done any good. And Alex had nothing. All his equipment had been taken away from him. The cell had a bunk, a table bolted to the floor and a plastic jug of water. Darcus Drake was taking no chances.

At sunset, he was going to be shot. Alex tried to force the image out of his mind. He was scared but he wasn't going to let fear weaken him. They still had to lead him from this cell, up two flights of stairs and through the main chamber to the stone platform outside, and somewhere along the way, an opportunity would arise. All it needed was one guard to make one mistake. Perhaps the man in the van – Farshad – was looking for him. After all, he had seen Alex taken prisoner. And what of Rafiq and the other tribesmen waiting for him in the cemetery? They would soon realize that something had gone wrong and they might try to help. Something would turn up. And Alex would be ready.

That was what he thought but as the day wore on and he was left alone for hour after hour he had to fight for control. He had no watch. He had no idea how much time was passing, how close he was to sunset. He kept himself active with press-ups, counting up to fifty before he allowed himself a rest. He paced from one wall to the other – six paces there and back – anything to keep busy. He sipped a little of the water. Nobody came with any lunch. He guessed that Drake was doing this on purpose. He wanted Alex to look worn out and defeated when he was taken out for execution. It would look better on film.

Three hours, four hours, five hours … Alex guessed it was close to midday when it happened. He heard a sound outside the door, metal scraping against wood. He had been resting, lying on the bunk and his eyes flicked open, instantly alert. Someone was drawing back the bars. Had they come for him already? He expected the door to open. It stayed shut but Alex was already on his feet, crouching down beside the wood, listening for any sound in the corridor outside. He heard soldiers march past, their boots stamping on the ground. Then silence. He reached up and grabbed hold of the iron ring that served as a door handle. He pulled. The door opened.

Looking out, he saw that the corridor was empty. Alex was puzzled. What was going on? Was this some sort of test? Was Drake playing a trick on him? He wasn't going to waste time wondering about it. This was the opportunity he had been waiting for. He slipped outside and found himself in a dungeon area with stone walls and doors. He watched the soldiers – there were four of them – disappearing into the distance and tried to work out his next move. He already knew that even if he was out of the cell, he wasn't out of trouble. Drake had told him there were two hundred men at the citadel. He was high up in the Herat mountains with a dizzying drop from the edge of the stone platform. The only way out was through the portcullis with the track beyond, but that would be heavily guarded. And if he did make it out of Falcon's Edge, where would he go next? The Shuja cemetery was beyond the plain, the Iranian border a lot further. He was on his own. As relieved as he was to be out of the cell, Alex knew that his position was almost hopeless.

He took the opposite direction that the soldiers had gone in. There were just a few steps until the passageway came to a corner and as Alex reached it a man suddenly appeared, walking towards him. With a shock, Alex recognized Faisal, the Kochi tribesman who had betrayed him in the first place. Faisal opened his mouth, about to call out, but Alex was already moving, running forward and lashing out with the front kick – *mae-geri* – that was one of the first moves he had learned at karate. Alex was half the size of the man he was attacking but that didn't matter; he had chosen his target carefully. The ball of his foot slammed into Faisal's solar plexus, knocking the wind out of him in one sharp breath. He followed through with a vicious back fist strike, targeting the man's throat. Faisal crumpled. Both his eyes had gone white although, of course, one of them had been that way already.

Which way? Before Alex took off, he reached down and removed the *shemagh* – the Afghan scarf – that Faisal had been wearing, winding it over his head and round the lower part of his face. In a way, Drake had done him a favour. By making him change his clothes, he had made him invisible ... now he looked like everyone else. He continued forward, leaving the unconscious man behind. He knew which way he had been brought here. He just had to retrace his steps and find a way out before Faisal – and the empty cell – were discovered.

He came to an old-fashioned lift. As he arrived, the gate opened and a chef came out, a man in a grubby white jacket, carrying some sort of skinned animal, perhaps a goat. There was no time to hide and Alex knew that any hesitation would finish him. He kept his head down. Without breaking his pace, he brushed past the man and went into the lift. As he had hoped, the man had his mind on other things and didn't even notice him. Alex pressed the top button and heaved a sigh of relief as the door slid shut.

He was carried upwards. The lift seemed painfully slow and Alex was already worrying about what he would see when the door opened again. In fact, he came out in an area behind the calutron and now he was doubly glad that the complicated machine wasn't working. There was nobody in this part of the complex. Alex hurried round the edge. He was already planning what to do next but he was also thinking back to the cell. Who had opened the door? Was there something he was missing? It occurred to him that he might have a friend somewhere in Falcon's Edge. After all, someone had opened the cell door. But if so, where were they and what had happened to them?

He was almost back where he had started. The main storage area was still a mass of activity with at least fifty soldiers moving around, going about their duties, all of them armed. The three supply vans had gone. Alex sneaked further into the chamber and hid behind one of the crates. It was attached to a parachute and he drew the silk fabric towards him, using it to conceal himself.

The outdoor platform where he was to be executed was right in front of him. He could actually see two men setting up a camera and a tripod. It made him feel sick that anyone could think of making a film like that and he certainly had no intention of being its star. But how was he going to get out of here? The portcullis was the only way. If it was open and if he moved fast enough ... but he still had to cross the plain. The moment they knew he was free, they would come after him. Stealing a jeep was out of the question. Even if Alex had known how to drive, he doubted they'd have left the keys in the ignition. Was there another way?

He remembered the horses. All three were still tethered to the railing and they looked sturdy and fast. Alex hated riding but at least they didn't need keys! The horses had been saddled and bridled. They were ready to go. Crouching beside the crate, measuring distances, Alex tried to work out a plan. He had no doubt that he could reach the horses without being seen. Everyone was too busy to notice him. It was when he mounted up and began to ride that his problems would begin. The alarm would be raised and they would either shoot him or shoot the horse. If they lowered the portcullis – and that would be the first thing they would do – he would be trapped. He needed the element of surprise. But how?

The idea came to him so suddenly that he almost gasped. It was impossible! He must be crazy. But he was alone, surrounded by an entire army. He was going to be executed at sunset. What other choice did he have?

He started at once. If he thought about this, even for a second, he wouldn't go through with it. It was early afternoon and the sun was at its hottest. That helped. A lot of Drake's men were unfocused, wishing they could have a siesta. They didn't notice the extra soldier making his way round the side of the cavern, carrying a bundle in his arms. Nor did they notice when he picked out one of the horses and got to work. The horse protested, snorting and stamping one of its hooves, but nobody came over. Alex was closer to the platform now and took stock of his surroundings. The camera was ready. Three more men were positioning a wooden stake in the ground, right next to the wall. That was for him. But Alex was grimly determined. Whatever happened, whether he lived or died, he wasn't going to play their game. He would go out fighting. He just wished he had been able to grab one of the AK 47 machine guns. Falcon's Edge was jammed with weapons of one sort or another. He was probably the only person in the entire place who was unarmed.

Alex's heart was thumping. His entire being recoiled at the thought of what he was about to do. A group of soldiers walked past and he leant down, pretending to busy himself with the horse he had chosen, in fact concealing himself behind it. He waited until they had gone. It was now or never. Once he climbed onto the horse, someone would be bound to see him. He couldn't hesitate, not for one second.

And then the alarm went off.

Someone must have discovered the unconscious man – either that or they had found the empty cell. The alarm was not a bell. It was a siren that tore through the air, screaming its urgency. Well, that might help him too. For a moment everyone was confused, wondering what the fuss was about. Alex untethered the horse. At the last moment, he noticed a riding crop on the floor and snatched it up, knowing he would need it. Even as he hoisted himself into the saddle, he felt the horse resisting. That was the whole secret of riding, that sense of understanding between the horse and its rider. Well, this horse would have realized at once that this Rider was not in control. It didn't matter. Alex was desperate. Somehow he would get the animal to do what he wanted.

He jerked on the reins and the horse tossed its head. At the same time, the scarf slipped and somebody cried out. They had seen him! Alex dug in his heels and for good measure lashed out with the crop. If the horse didn't move, they would both get killed. Sure enough there was a shot and a bullet ricocheted off the stone wall above his head. The sound of it frightened the horse more than Alex. He was almost thrown off as the animal reared up.

Alex heard a second shot and a bullet passed inches over his shoulders. Everything was happening at once. He felt the cavern spin around him. There were men running towards him. The siren was still blasting at full volume. The horse's front hooves made contact with the ground and then the two of them were off.

They were going the wrong way! The horse had set off at a gallop but it was heading back into the cavern, towards the jeeps and the helicopter. Alex pulled frantically on the reins and wheeled the horse round. He heard a series of shots and the windows of the jeep right behind him shattered, the glass crashing down. The sunlight was straight ahead of him. There was the arch of the cavern, then the stone platform and then, if he kept going, a drop of three hundred metres to the plain below. The gate with the portcullis was off to the right but the guards were already ahead of him. At least ten of them had grouped together to block his way. They were all armed, waiting for him to ride towards them.

Alex wasn't stopping now. With a yell, he whipped on the horse, propelling it out of the cavern and into the light. The soldiers were firing at him. He could feel the bullets scorching the air all around him. At this range, they shouldn't have missed but perhaps they were trying to hit him, not the horse, and anyway they had miscalculated because he wasn't riding towards them, he was going straight ahead. They stopped firing. There was no need to waste any more bullets. It was clear to them that Alex was committing suicide. He was heading straight towards the edge of the platform and the sheer drop beyond. Ten metres, five metres, three metres ... Alex covered the ground in no time at all. Out of the corner of his eye he saw the metal gate crashing down to block the archway and, nearer to him, the execution post, the waiting camera. He ignored them. He had made his decision.

The horse sensed what he wanted but only when it was too late. Alex whipped it one last time, hating what he was doing, knowing there was no other way. The soldiers stared. The horse screamed. The edge came rushing up towards them. And then they had gone, launching themselves into space. At that moment Alex was only aware of a great stillness, the sun blazing, the plain so far below that shrubs and boulders appeared only as tiny specks. He felt the wind in his hair. There was a sense almost of calm and he thought that, all in all, there must be worse ways to die.

But it wasn't going to happen. Not today. When Alex had crossed the cavern, he had been carrying the parachute which had been used to air-drop the crate. He had attached it, not to himself but to the saddle and to the horse, running the cords under its belly. When he had ridden out, he had been trailing the canopy behind him and, despite the alarms and the gunfire, his greatest fear had been that it would catch on something and tear. He had been lucky. The parachute had been intact as he urged the horse over the edge. The moment they cleared the platform, it was dragged upwards, opening out. It was above them now. It had formed itself into a fantastic flower, shading them from the sun. And the two of them weren't falling any more. They were floating down.

It was an amazing sight. The horse was terrified, its eyes bulging, its legs flailing as if it were galloping through the air. For his part, Alex was clinging on for dear life, too afraid to look down, vaguely aware of the cords stretching past him and the white silk billowing over his head. The parachute had taken their combined weight with ease. They were heading down towards the plain and being swept ever further away from Falcon's Edge. Alex risked a glance back and saw the soldiers on the platform, already miniature. One or two of them were shooting at them – he saw the flash of an AK 47 – but they were well out of range. Apart from the rush of the breeze in his ears, everything was silent. Even the horse seemed to have stopped panicking. Gently, they wafted down.

The next time Alex looked, the ground was rushing up towards them, far faster than he would have expected. He tensed himself, waiting for the landing – but already he knew that he had been lucky. He had rigged the parachute perfectly. If the cords hadn't been evenly divided, the horse could have tilted backwards or forwards and the two of them might have hit the ground as a twisting ball of animal and boy. Everything depended on the next few seconds. Alex had taken the horse with him because it wasn't enough to break out of the citadel. He also needed to be moving at speed. He had no doubt that once they had recovered from the surprise, Drake and his men would be after him.

This was the moment of truth. Once again the horse was pedalling, as if it understood what was about to happen. Alex tightened his knees and squeezed the reins. There was a thud as the four hooves came into contact with the ground. The horse stumbled and Alex was afraid that it was going to fall, that it might injure itself. But then it recovered and suddenly they were chasing across the plain, dragging the parachute behind. Alex couldn't stop himself. Like a cowboy in the Wild West he whooped with delight. He had done it! When escape had been impossible he had made the impossible escape.

It wasn't over yet. High above him, the portcullis gates of the citadel opened. Three jeeps with four men in each, came roaring out in pursuit.

THE SHUJA CEMETERY

The horse was behaving perfectly, streaking across the plain in a dead straight line. Alex had thought he would have to stop to release the parachute, but rocks and spiky plants had ripped the fabric to shreds in a few seconds so that only the cords were left trailing behind. It seemed to him that everything had changed. After its ordeal, plummeting through the air, the horse had decided that perhaps Alex knew what he was doing after all and was now obeying his every command. He felt more comfortable in the saddle. They were going so fast that when he looked down, the sand and wild grass swept past in little more than a vague green blur, but he no longer had the feeling that he was going to fall off. He had lost the riding crop as they came down but he had no need of it. He was clutching the reins, keeping his head low, feeling the breeze rush over his shoulders.

He had no real idea where he was going. Back in London, Mrs Jones had shown him a map with the location of the Shuja cemetery but at that time he hadn't thought he would need it. He was meant to be arriving there in the back of a van. He remembered her drawing a straight line with her finger, the direction south-west. She had also mentioned a village with a minaret, two miles on the other side. Alex couldn't be certain but he had seen where the sun had risen and had guessed that he was heading south-west. Also, there was definitely something tall and narrow on the horizon although he couldn't make it out yet. A minaret? He would know once he got closer.

He risked a glance back over his shoulder. The three jeeps were making their way down the winding track, going as fast as the hairpin bends would allow them. They already seemed a long way behind him, but Alex felt a tightening in his stomach. Once the jeeps reached the bottom, they would accelerate and it might take them five minutes to catch up with him. And he didn't really have anywhere to go. He doubted that Rafiq and his men would be waiting for him at the cemetery and it was unlikely that he would find a hiding place amongst the gravestones. There was always Mrs Jones's village – but why would anyone there want to help him? The plain that surrounded him could hardly have been more desolate. He had the mountains behind him, an almost empty horizon ahead. He seemed to be pinned down by the sunlight. He could already feel it burning the back of his neck.

Marino Branch 75
Brainse Marino
Tel: 8336297

The horse was doing its best and it was a miracle that it hadn't been hurt when it came into contact with the land. But it would soon get tired. Alex's earlier euphoria was wearing off. Things were looking hopeless once again.

He kept going. What other choice did he have? He heard the clanging of bells and turned in time to see a herd of goats scattering as he thundered past. There was no sign of any farmer or goatherd. There wasn't anyone for miles around. He looked back. The jeeps had already left the track and they were racing across the plain, sending up clouds of dust behind. He could even hear the engines. They could only be a mile away ... maybe less. He might have overestimated how much time he had left. He kicked in with his heels and he felt the horse jolt forward, doing its best. The poor creature had little energy left. Its flanks were shiny with sweat. There was a part of Alex that felt sorry for what he had put it through and the last thing he wanted was to see it gunned down. Even as the thought flickered through his head, he heard a gunshot. It was too far away to cause him any alarm but it was a warning. The soldiers had him in their sights and they were getting closer with every second that passed.

He saw the cemetery. As he approached, it seemed to shimmer, forming itself out of the heat-haze. It was just stuck there, out on its own. No roads led to it. There were no signs, no indication that anyone had even noticed it existed. Alex saw the remains of a low, square wall built out of mud-bricks. There were wide gaps where sections of it had collapsed, eaten away by the constant wind. About thirty or forty gravestones stood, grouped together, on the other side, with clumps of spiky, wild grass and shrubs growing between them. Even as he hurtled towards it, Alex saw that there was something terribly sad about the place. These were British soldiers who had been buried here, victims of a war that had long been forgotten. Who were they? How had they died? They had come here in their bright red tunics, their white belts and helmets, marching into a country they couldn't begin to understand and they had never returned home. This was where they lay and even their names had gone, fading away, wiped clean off their headstones by the relentless desert sun.

Nobody was waiting for him. He saw that at once. There were no horses, no men. Rafiq and the other Kochis had decided to go home. He glanced back and saw that the jeeps had halved the distance between him and them. If someone took a shot at him now, there was every chance he would be in range. What should he do? He could now see the village on the other side of the cemetery, a collection of dusty houses gathered round a crumbling minaret. Was there any point continuing or should he simply accept his fate and give himself up?

As if to answer the question, the horse stumbled and Alex was thrown off. There was nothing he could do to stop himself. He felt himself separating from the saddle and the next thing he was turning in the air, his arms in front of him, desperately trying to protect himself. He crashed down. Fortunately the ground was soft, a mixture of dust and sand. He rolled over twice and came up spitting and coughing. He knew at once that nothing was broken. The horse wheeled away and continued round the side of the cemetery and Alex wished it luck. At least it would be out of range when the soldiers arrived.

They were almost onto him. Alex heard the jeep engines and the sound of the wheels bumping over the plain. He saw the faces, bearded and angry, behind the windows. Faisal was with them! Alex saw him sitting in one of the front passenger seats. He must have joined them, wanting to take revenge on Alex for what had happened in the fortress dungeon. As the jeep slowed to a halt, he was the first one out, bringing up the pistol – old-fashioned, also Russian-made – that he had carried with him. Bruised and exhausted, Alex backed into the Shuja cemetery. He was surrounded by dead British soldiers. It was somehow fitting that, quite soon, a dead British spy would join them.

Darcus Drake's men came pouring out of the jeeps, moving more slowly now. They had caught up with him. Alex had expected Drake to come with them but he wasn't going to put himself outside the safety of Falcon's Edge. The commanding officer was a wiry, curly-haired man in his twenties. He had a broken nose and a beard sprouting unevenly on both sides of his face. He was holding a machine gun and Alex wondered if he had been ordered to finish it here or to bring him back so that they could make their film.

"Alex Rider," he said. He spoke the words as if for the first time, as if he didn't know what they meant.

The gunshot, when it came, was loud and incredibly close. Alex flinched, expecting to feel the pain – in his chest, in his stomach, wherever he had been shot. Then he realized that the bullet had come from behind him. A red hole had appeared in the commanding officer's head. He fell back, dropping the machine gun.

"Get down, Alex!"

The words, in English, were shouted out of nowhere. Instinctively, Alex obeyed. There were more shots. Two more of Drake's men died.

Alex twisted round and looked behind him, staring in amazement as dusty figures rose up, like zombies, climbing out of the graves. His first thought was that the ghosts of the nineteenth-century soldiers were rising up to save him, but he knew at once that it was simpler than that. Rafiq and his men had been waiting for him after all. They had used the old graves as hiding places, covering themselves with a thin layer of sand. Now the four of them revealed themselves, firing at the soldiers with guns they had been clutching all the time. Surprise was on their side. Another six men had been shot and killed before they had understood what was happening.

Faisal was not one of them. Alex saw that he had not fired yet although he too was armed with an AK 47 and could have taken out Rafiq and the others with a single burst. Could it be that he was reluctant to turn on his former friends? There was the click of a gun being loaded. Alex twisted and saw, just a few steps away, another of Drake's men pointing a pistol directly at his head. He knew what was about to happen. He saw it in the man's eyes. Somehow the tables had been turned. Alex had reached the cemetery and his friends were here, waiting for him. Half of Drake's men had been killed. But whatever happened, the English boy was not going to get away. This man had decided it. He was going to kill him now.

The commanding officer had dropped his machine gun. It was lying on the ground just inches away. Alex dived for it. But before he could reach it, Faisal stepped forward and Alex saw the white flame as his machine gun spat out its thirty rounds in a matter of seconds. But he wasn't aiming at Alex. He wasn't aiming at Rafiq. Impossibly, he was shooting Drake's men, including the one who had been about to finish Alex. Alex saw him blasted off his feet.

And then it was over, as suddenly as it had begun. All the Kochis – including Rafiq and Faisal – were alive. So was Alex. Only one of Drake's men was moving. Alex turned away as Rafiq finished him with a single shot.

Faisal was on his side?

It couldn't be true. But as Alex got to his feet, he saw Rafiq embracing Faisal, the two men laughing. The other Kochis had gathered around in the Afghan equivalent of a group hug. And Alex had seen it for himself. Faisal had just saved his life. He had taken out half a dozen of Drake's men. What was going on?

"English boy!" Faisal exclaimed, seeing him. He was beaming, which was odd, because the last time they had met, Alex had kicked him hard, where it hurt.

"Can someone explain what's happening?" Alex asked.

"Ask no questions, my friend." It was Rafiq who had spoken. And suddenly he was speaking perfect English. "We have a long journey to the border and there is a helicopter that waits. Ask your questions when you are home."

Questions. Yes. The more Alex thought about it, the more he had to ask.

SPECIAL DELIVERY

The Tornado GR4 looked deadly even before it left the ground. Officially described as a day or night, all-weather attack aircraft, it certainly looked the part with its sleek fuselage and V-shaped variable-sweep wings. The plane was waiting for clearance, sitting in the baking sun at the end of the runway at RAF Akrotiri at the southernmost tip of Cyprus. The Tornado GR4 is not a new aircraft. It was developed during the Cold War with Russia. But it remains a favourite of the RAF: fast, quiet and easy to fly. Normally, it might have been armed with all manner of missiles: up to five Paveway IV smart weapons, for example, or Storm Shadow cruise missiles. But this aircraft carried just two weapons. They were Brimstone ground attack missiles and they had been specially primed. There was no chance that they could miss.

"Go!"

The single word came from the control tower.

The pilot, anonymous in the dark blue meta-aramid flight suit and helmet that would provide thermal, chemical and radiation resistance, raised a thumb in acknowledgement. Seconds later, the two Rolls-Royce 199 Mk 103 turbofan engines flared and the plane began to roll forwards, picking up speed. Each engine provided a thrust of sixteen thousand lbf. By the time it reached its cruising altitude of thirty thousand feet, the Tornado would be travelling at around one thousand miles per hour.

The sun glinted off its metal carcass. In seconds it was gone, clearing the airport and arcing over the Mediterranean Sea.

It was on its way to Afghanistan.

In London, Alex was sitting opposite Alan Blunt, the chief executive of MI6 Special Operations. Mrs Jones was with him. Less than twenty-four hours before, he had been facing certain execution in the Herat mountains. He had broken out of prison and ridden a horse over a ledge with a drop of three hundred metres to the ground. He had been involved in a gunfight at a cemetery. Finally, he had crossed the border into Iran, where a helicopter had been on standby to fly him on the first leg of his journey home. In all that time, nobody had explained to him what had really happened – but Alex had begun to work it out for himself. He knew that, once again, he had been used. He wasn't surprised.

And now, here he was on the seventeenth floor of the building in Liverpool Street with the traffic rumbling past outside. Blunt had welcomed him with tea and chocolate digestive biscuits, brought in on a trolley. There was something about the normality of it all that really shocked Alex. He was still waiting for answers. It was as if he had been invited onto a stage to take part in a play – but no one had remembered to give him his lines.

"I don't want you to blame yourself, Alex," Blunt was saying. "We're very grateful to you. The mission may not have gone quite as we hoped but you really couldn't have achieved any more."

Alex examined the spymaster who had sent him on three missions. Each time he had been lucky not to get killed. Blunt really did look like a bank manager. He was the sort of man you would forget instantly ... assuming you had noticed he was there in the first place. He was about fifty years old – maybe older – with grey hair, glasses, thin lips. His eyes gave nothing away. Nor was there anything in his office that said anything about him. There were no photographs on the desk, no personal items. Even the pictures on the walls had been deliberately chosen. A view of a field. A vase of flowers. A ship at sea. They were the sort of art you buy to fill a space, not because it is something you want to see.

"We're very glad you weren't hurt," Blunt continued. "And I understand Brookland is opening again tomorrow. You haven't missed any school, which is excellent. I'm sure you'll be quite pleased to be back."

"What about Darcus Drake?" Alex asked.

"You brought us very useful intelligence, Alex. This calutron of his doesn't seem to be working after all. He's not quite as much of a threat as we thought."

"He's still gathering an army," Alex said. "He still wants to attack the West."

"There are plenty of people who want to attack the West. We were afraid of a nuclear attack but, thanks to you, we know that's not going to happen."

"Forget about Darcus Drake," Mrs Jones said. She was sitting with her legs crossed and her hands folded on her knees. There was no expression on her face. Alex guessed that she wanted him out of the room. He had got that feeling the moment he walked in. "We'll deal with him in due course. He's got nothing to do with you."

"He nearly killed me," Alex reminded her. "He wanted to execute me by firing squad. He was going to film it and put it online. Jack would have seen it. So would all my friends."

"We're just relieved that you escaped."

"No!" On the last two occasions when he had been in this room, Alex had done what they wanted. He hadn't argued with Blunt or Mrs Jones. This time was different. He knew something was wrong. There was something he hadn't been told. "It doesn't make any sense," he went on. "The whole thing ... from start to finish. It doesn't add up."

Blunt twitched his lips in the sort of smile that could have been drawn with a pencil as a single line. "I don't know what you mean, Alex."

"Then let me tell you." Alex took a breath. "First of all, you send me all the way to Afghanistan to take photographs of a machine that isn't even working. I don't believe you didn't know that. You've got spies. You've got satellites. You knew everything about Darcus Drake. You must have known he didn't have the ability to make nuclear weapons."

"That's what we sent you to find out," Blunt said.

"I don't believe you," Alex said. He was surprised how easily the accusation slipped out. "I think you sent me there for another reason. I've gone over what happened. You paid a bunch of Afghan tribesmen to take me up into the mountains and I crawled through the pipes like you said. But while I was doing that, one of them – a man called Faisal – rode into Falcon's Edge and told Drake I was on the way. That's how I was captured."

"Faisal was bribed," Blunt said. "You can't really trust these people. They'll work for the highest bidder."

"That's what I thought. But here's the funny thing. When I was in my cell, someone came down and unlocked the door. I never found out who it was – but now I think about it, Faisal was right outside. I saw him in the corridor and I assumed he was going to raise the alarm. I was wrong, wasn't I? It was Faisal who unlocked the door. He must have been about to open it and let me out when a group of soldiers came along and he was forced to hide. As soon as they were gone, he came back for me but by that time I was already on my way and before he could explain that he was on my side, I'd knocked him out. That was my mistake, but how was I to know?"

"Are you saying that he changed his mind?" Mrs Jones asked.

"I don't know, Mrs Jones. But he certainly helped me when I got to the Shuja cemetery. He shot a whole load of Drake's men. And Rafiq and the others were delighted to see him. They didn't think he was a traitor. They were all pleased with what he'd done. And while I'm at it, here's another question. Why were they waiting for me in the cemetery? I'd missed the rendezvous but they were all there, buried in the graves. They knew I'd be coming eventually and they were there to help me."

"Did they tell you anything?" Blunt asked.

"They wouldn't talk about what had happened," Alex said. "They were very friendly. They got me back over the border and when I left we all shook hands like we were the best of friends. Even Faisal embraced me and called me his brother. But they knew something and I think you know it too. So why don't you tell me?"

Alan Blunt coughed. Alex noticed that he and Mrs Jones were carefully avoiding each other's eyes.

"I'm afraid I can't help you, Alex," he said, eventually. "The Kochi people are a law unto themselves and I don't know what was going on in their minds – although I'd say you're reading too much into it. It sounds like they got paid twice. We paid them to take you to Falcon's Edge and Drake paid them to hand you over. You're just lucky that they decided not to leave you behind."

There was a file on the desk in front of him. He drew it towards him.

"I can understand that you're disappointed," he went on. "The Stormbreaker business went extremely well and you followed that by taking out Dr Grief at the Point Blanc Academy. But if you're going to be a spy, Alex – if you're going to work for us – you've got to learn that you can't be successful every time."

"I don't want to be a spy and I don't want to work for you," Alex said.

Blunt ignored this. "The calutron isn't working. There was no need to penetrate Falcon's Edge in the first place. It's no longer our business." He had a rubber stamp. He pressed it against a red ink pad, then brought it down onto the cover of the file. Alex saw he had printed two words: MISSION FAIL.

"You did extremely well, Alex," he concluded. "The failure is entirely ours, not yours. I'm sure we'll see you again very soon. If we need you, we know where to find you."

"Yes," Alex said, gloomily. "You do."

The Tornado was closing in on its target, maintaining a high subsonic cruise speed. Its route had taken it through the air space of Jordan, Saudi Arabia and Iran before it had curved up into Afghanistan, but nobody had protested. There are times when governments and intelligence agencies, even the ones that are supposedly hostile to each other, will work together for the common good. This was one of them. It had been decided that the mission was so important that the Tornado had been given "invisible" status. As far as the world was concerned, it had never taken off. Its flight path hadn't been recorded. If anyone ever asked, the mission had never taken place.

Inside the cockpit, the pilot prepared to fire the two missiles. There wasn't even any need to take aim. The Brimstone had originally been developed as part of a system known as "fire and forget". The two weapons had been programmed in Cyprus, before the plane took off. Even if the pilot didn't know the target, they did. The Herat mountains were coming up ahead of her now. There was white snow glistening on some of the peaks. The great plain stretched out below. The Tornado cast a shadow as it swept forward – but so quickly that it was literally gone in the blink of an eye. The pilot flicked off the safety switch, then made final checks on the computer screen. There was no need for further authorization.

The pilot fired.

The two Brimstone missiles disengaged and at once their independent solid propellant rocket motors fired up, taking them in a matter of seconds to supersonic speed. The millimetric wave radar seekers built into the missiles fed back images of the target and precise information such as the exact time to detonation, while digital autopilot ensured that they stayed rigidly on course. The missiles weighed just fifty kilograms. They were 1.7 metres long. They cost one hundred-thousand pounds each.

The pilot did not wait to see the explosion. Long before the Brimstones hit, he had expertly brought the aircraft round 180 degrees and was on his way home.

Neither Alan Blunt nor Mrs Jones spoke until Alex had gone. It was only after the door had closed that Blunt turned to his second in command. "That went very well," he said.

"He knows that we used him," Mrs Jones remarked.

"He's unusually bright for a fourteen-year-old," Blunt agreed. "That's what makes him so valuable. But I don't think he'll guess the whole truth."

"You mean, that you turned him into an assassin?"

"That we entrusted him with what you might call our special delivery. Alex was an excellent postman.

It was so unlikely that we'd use a child that Drake didn't ask too many questions ... not the right ones, anyway."

"You mean, he bought that business about the pipes."

"Well, it was true. No adult would be able to get through." Blunt picked up the file that he had stamped when Alex was sitting in front of him. He tore it up and dropped it in the bin. Later, it would be shredded. The true file, the actual record of Alex's mission, was on its way to Number Ten, Downing Street. "Darcus Drake had to die," he went on. "With or without nuclear weapons, he was a major threat to world security. If he had succeeded in uniting all the different terrorist groups in Afghanistan and elsewhere, there's no way of knowing how dangerous he might have become or how much damage he might have done. He had to be taken out."

"And Alex did that for us."

"Exactly. He delivered the package and he got out of there in one piece. He really is remarkable." Blunt paused. "Did you know that John Crawley has asked permission to use him?"

"Really?"

"Yes. Something to do with Chinese triads wanting to sabotage the Wimbledon tennis championships. He thinks Alex would make a good ball boy."

"And what do you say?"

Blunt smiled. "I don't see why not..."

* * *

Darcus Drake was also thinking about Alex Rider. He was smiling, of course. This was the smile that never left his face.

He was sitting at the table in his living quarters, the same room where he and Alex had talked. He still didn't understand quite what had happened. He had sent twelve men out into the plain following Alex's astonishing escape. None of them had come back. How was that possible? The boy was unarmed. There must have been people waiting for him but even so he was surprised that all his people had been killed.

Well, it didn't matter. Alex had learned that the calutron was useless – but Drake had never pretended otherwise. It made no difference to his plans. Later that afternoon, the leaders of seven terrorist organizations were coming to Falcon's Edge. Only he, Darcus Drake, could have persuaded them to come together. They were the Awakening and they were going to discuss their first operation, an act of violence so shocking that the whole world would sit up and take notice. He had already worked it out. There were just the details to be discussed and they would go ahead and, together, they would change history.

All in all, it wasn't such a bad thing that Alex had come here. Drake had been alerted to the lack of security in the ventilation system and he had already taken measures to ensure that nobody else would ever break in that way. And there was something else he was grateful for. As he sat at the table, he examined the camera that Alex had brought with him, raising it to his eye and taking a couple of shots. The Leica really was a fabulous piece of kit. It reminded Drake of his early days in Dublin, when he had worked for the *Irish Times*. Well, it would come in very useful. He would take wonderful photographs of the death and the suffering that he himself would cause. He would even send them to the newspapers. How marvellous it was that MI6 should have allowed the camera to fall into his hands.

He didn't know, of course. MI6 were determined to deal with him once and for all. The RAF needed a precise target. Falcon's Edge was almost impenetrable and Drake himself was difficult to locate. But Alan Blunt had guessed he would keep a beautiful and expensive camera if it was delivered to him, and so he had had a miniaturized homing beacon built into the Leica; a beacon that was even now transmitting a signal to the two Brimstone missiles which swept down almost joyously, picking out the actual window of the room, closing in at the speed of sound and then vaporizing their target in two giant balls of flame.

THE MAN WITH
ELEVEN FINGERS

MARMITE SOLDIERS

Jack Starbright was making breakfast, carefully cutting the toast into fingers before arranging them around Alex's egg, which was still bubbling away in a pan. She glanced at her watch. There was no sign of Alex although it was already half past eight and they had to be out of the house by nine.

She walked over to the door and called up the stairs. "Alex!"

"I'll be one minute, Jack!" The familiar voice came from the bedroom on the first floor.

Jack smiled and went back into the kitchen. As she lifted the egg out of the boiling water, she asked herself – for the thousandth time – how she had managed to get into this situation. And what would anybody think, looking at her? She was fast approaching her thirties. This Christmas she would be twenty-nine. When she had first arrived in Chelsea, she had been a law student, looking for a part-time housekeeping job to support herself. Now, seven years later, she was still living there, sharing the place with a fourteen-year-old boy. It was an unusual arrangement, to say the least.

When Jack had first met him, Alex had been seven, a little boy with messy fair hair, brown eyes and plenty of attitude. He had come into the room with his hands in his pockets, his shirt out of his trousers and one shoelace trailing and she'd had no idea that he was going to completely change her life.

"This is Alex," Ian Rider had said. "Alex, this is Jack."

Alex had stared at her. "Jack's a man's name." Those were the first words he had ever spoken to her.

"Well, it's my name and you'd better get used to it," Jack had replied.

They had become friends almost immediately.

Jack may have had a place at one of the best colleges in London – but what she didn't have was money. She had answered an advertisement in *The Times*:

Room in Chelsea available plus living expenses in return for some housekeeping duties and childcare. Would suit a student or part-time professional.

The advertisement had been placed by Ian Rider, who had introduced himself as Alex's uncle, a banker working in the city. She could still see him now, a darkly handsome man dressed in an expensive suit, sitting with his legs crossed and a glass of red wine in his hand.

"Let me explain, Miss Starbright. Alex's parents died when he was very young and I've looked after him pretty much since then. Alex's father was in banking ... the same as me. The trouble is, I'm having to travel more and more these days – Zurich, Luxembourg, Singapore. That's the joy of international finance! I don't want Alex to have a nanny or anything like that. I try to spend as much time as I can with him when I'm home. What I really want is for someone to live here part-time and to become a sort of friend to him so he won't notice it so much when I'm away. You'll find that Alex is very good at looking after himself. He goes to school just down the road and I'm sure the two of you will get along well. You're much closer to his age than I am and he's a very easy-going chap. What do you say?"

How could she have possibly known that almost everything Ian Rider had told her had been untrue? He wasn't in banking. He was a spy. Alex's father had been a spy too. Both Alex's parents had been killed by a bomb planted on a plane and Alex would have died with them but for the chance ear infection that had forced him to stay at home. Sometimes Jack hated Ian Rider for the way he had deceived her. But that hadn't been the worst of it. He had also lied to Alex just about every day of his life, cold-bloodedly preparing him for a destiny that had been chosen for him the day he was born. How could anyone do that to a child?

The climbing trips, the martial arts classes, the trips abroad and the different languages that Alex spoke ... they had all been nothing more than basic training. Ian Rider had moulded Alex into an image of himself.

And then he had been killed. The police had said it was a car accident but Alex had found the car and discovered that it was riddled with bullet holes. Another lie. After that, everything had happened very quickly as the entire construction that had been built around Alex's life collapsed in on itself. Alex had met Alan Blunt and Mrs Jones on the day of the funeral and almost immediately afterwards he had been recruited by MI6 and sent for two weeks' intensive training in the Brecon Beacons. It had included assault courses, unarmed combat, forced marches and survival in the so-called Killing House, a mock-up of an embassy used to practise techniques in hostage release. Alex had found himself up to his eyes in freezing mud and water, stumbling up and down hills being shouted at by sergeants in khaki whose entire vocabulary seemed to be made up of four-letter words, swallowing down meals out of mess tins and desperately snatching a few minutes of sleep when the exercises ended in the middle of the night. He was a child! Nobody seemed to have noticed.

Over the years, with Ian Rider away more and more, Jack had become Alex's closest friend and there could be no secrets between the two of them.

She knew everything about his first mission, when he had been sent to the headquarters of Sayle Enterprises. Alex had almost got himself killed but what really worried Jack was that it wouldn't end there. MI6 needed Alex Rider. And she was certain that one day, soon, they would be back for more.

What should she do? Jack sighed to herself as she unscrewed the Marmite and searched for a knife. She had questioned Alex when he had finally got home in one piece. The two of them had talked until late in the night. Alex didn't want to be a spy but, the truth was, he had no choice. Ian Rider had already made the decision for him. Jack had considered going to the newspapers. Part of her wanted to stop this madness before it went any further. But she knew that she couldn't protect Alex by exposing him. All she could do was support him and try to stop him getting into trouble again.

She cut the toast into strips and smeared each one with Marmite, then arranged the pieces on the plate. Looking down, she was annoyed with herself. What did she think she was doing? Alex was fourteen, not four – and she was behaving exactly like the nanny she had never wanted to be. She was tempted to throw the whole lot into the bin and start again. At the same time, Alex liked being looked after. And she knew that he wasn't looking forward to this morning, to what lay ahead.

"Hi, Jack!" Alex appeared at the door and slouched,

bleary-eyed over to the table. Like every other teenager, he wasn't at his best first thing in the morning. He was wearing his school uniform (the tie was spectacularly crooked) but he wouldn't be in school until after eleven. He had an appointment. It had been in the diary for weeks.

"Good morning, Alex." She examined him. "You look a bit of a mess today."

Alex yawned. "That's what you said yesterday."

"No. Yesterday I said you were a total mess. Today is definitely an improvement." She slid the plate in front of him. "Breakfast!"

"Thanks, Jack."

She went over to the fridge, took out a carton of orange juice and poured a glass. When she brought it over to the table, she was absurdly pleased to see that he had lopped the top off the egg and dipped the toast in. What had happened in Cornwall hadn't changed him. At heart, he was still just a kid. "We need to leave in fifteen minutes," she said.

"I can go on my own."

"No. I'm coming with you."

Alex hesitated. "Jack," he said. "I've been thinking about this. Do I really need to go today? I mean, couldn't we wait until the holidays? I've missed enough school as it is."

"One more morning won't make any difference, Alex."

"But it's not hurting any more. Honestly, I think I'm going to be fine. Let's just cancel."

Jack couldn't hide her smile. "You're not afraid, are you?"

"No!"

"Then what's the problem?"

"There is no problem..."

"Then forget it, Alex. We were lucky to get an appointment. Finish your breakfast and then go and clean your teeth. If you can remember what a comb looks like, you might also think about doing your hair."

"Jack..."

"I mean it!"

Jack went over to make herself a cup of coffee. She wondered what MI6 would have made of it all. Alex hadn't been afraid of the SAS. He'd been dumped in a tank with a giant jellyfish and survived. He'd parachuted out of a helicopter over London and smashed through the roof of the Science Museum.

But he was still scared of the dentist.

A tiny little filling.

Jack flicked on the kettle while, behind her, Alex finished his egg.

CRUNCH TIME

It had begun, like all toothaches do, with a twinge. Alex tried to ignore it but very quickly it had got worse. Hot drinks were bad. Ice cream was worse. In the end he had been forced to mention it to Jack and she had phoned the dentist right away. Alex needed an emergency appointment and that meant missing a few hours of school. He wasn't happy about that either. Thanks to Alan Blunt and Mrs Jones, he had missed plenty enough school already.

The two of them set off together, walking down the King's Road to Sloane Square tube station. The dentist – his name was Wiseman – had offices just off Oxford Circus. Alex had only been there half a dozen times but he remembered every detail, from the nasty, striped wallpaper to the fish tank with its depressed-looking fish and the old magazines on the round table in the waiting room.

"Cheer up," Jack said as they passed through the ticket barrier and made their way down to the platform.

"What's there to be cheerful about?" Alex growled. "You're not the one having a drill in the top of your mouth…"

"You should have thought of that before you ate all those sweets."

"I don't eat sweets." Alex glared at her. "And you didn't need to come with me. I could find my way there on my own."

"Of course I had to come with you, Alex. And if you don't stop complaining, I'm going to insist on holding your hand when we go in."

They waited in silence until the train arrived, then climbed on together. Alex didn't feel like talking and snatched one of the free newspapers that someone had left on the seat. He glanced at the headline: "FREDDY FINGERS GOES ON TRIAL." It had been on the breakfast news on television too. Freddy Fingers. Everyone knew who he was. There had been enormous publicity about the trial which was to take place at the Old Bailey. It began today.

His real name was Sir Frederick Meadows. Until recently, he had been the chairman of City Capital, one of the biggest banks in the country. The Queen was actually one of its customers and he had often been photographed coming in and out of Buckingham Palace, a small, bald man with a round face and a nervous smile. Everyone trusted him. He had been knighted for services to banking and had frequently appeared on television, talking about the economy. He was always cheerful.

He was easy to understand. And so it had come as a real shock when, after a two-year investigation, the police had arrested him for the theft of one hundred million pounds.

It was well known that Meadows had been born with a very unusual condition. He had an extra finger on his left hand – and of course that had been a gift for the journalists. There were plenty of headlines that described him as being light-fingered or having his fingers in the till. He had become known to the whole country as Freddy Fingers.

Alex read the story in the paper he'd picked up.

Meadows used his position in City Capital to hack into the bank's computer system. Every time a payment was made, one pound was transferred to a secret account he'd set up for himself. This went on for ten years, by which time it is estimated he had stolen at least a hundred million pounds. Last summer, Meadows announced his retirement and was on his way to Heathrow Airport when a sharp-eyed accountant realized what had happened and telephoned the police. Meadows was arrested as he tried to board a flight to Mexico.

Experts have been unable to locate the missing funds and Sir Frederick has refused to co-operate. It is believed that he had concealed the money in secret bank accounts in Switzerland and the Cayman Islands. The trial, which will take place at the Old Bailey, will have maximum security. More than a hundred policemen will surround the court as there is a real fear that he may try to escape. Somewhere, there's a huge fortune waiting for him. And you can bet that Sir Freddy will want to give justice the finger!

Alex finished the article, then turned to the sport. He supported Chelsea and had watched them tie with Barcelona in the International Champions Cup over the weekend. He read the match report, putting everything else out of his head.

They reached Oxford Circus in good time and climbed the escalator back into the daylight. The strange thing was that Alex's tooth wasn't hurting any more – but he was still feeling a little queasy. It wasn't just the drill. He could see Mr Wiseman with his huge eyes magnified behind his protective goggles, bending over him. He hated the thought of the man's hand with its latex-covered fingers, poking around in his mouth. Still, there was no point arguing. It was ten to nine and the intersection, where Regent Street met Oxford Street, was packed with commuters. The dentist was about a five-minute walk away.

"Free snacks! Try a Cadbury's Choco Bar. They're free today. Try one now...!"

There were half a dozen men and women on the pavement, dressed in jeans and mauve jackets, covering all the station entrances. They were handing out little bars of chocolate and Alex guessed there would be more of them in other parts of London. It was quite common for big companies to give away free samples at all the main stations when a new product was being launched. Almost without thinking, he reached out and took one.

"Forget it, Alex," Jack said. "You can't eat chocolate five minutes before you go into the dentist."

Alex was annoyed. When he had been training with the SAS, he had been treated almost as an equal. Certainly nobody had made allowances for his age. But here he was in the middle of London with Jack and she was treating him like a child. "I'm not going to eat it now," he protested. "I'm only taking it for later."

"You may not be able to eat it. Your mouth will be numb."

"Then you can keep it for me." He was about to hand it over when he stopped and looked at it more closely. The chocolate bar was in silver foil with the name in bright red. All around him, people were grabbing their free samples. Even as they stood there, a hundred or more bars must have been given away. "That's really weird," he said.

"What?"

"The wrapper..." He held it out so Jack could see. "Read what it says."

"Cadbury's Choco Bar." She read the words out loud. She didn't understand what he was getting at.

"It's wrong," Alex explained. That's not how you spell it. It ought to read 'Cadbury' without the apostrophe and the s."

"Are you sure?"

"I think so. It doesn't look right."

Jack shrugged. "They must have made a mistake," she said. "New product, new typing error." She took the bar and slipped it into her pocket. "We'd better get a move on, Alex. I don't want to be late."

But Alex was puzzled. He examined the man who had given him the sample and who was still working his way through the crowd. He was very muscular, clean-shaven with his hair cut short. Alex noticed that he only had one hand. He turned his attention to the others. There was something quite similar about all of them – and it wasn't just the mauve jackets and jeans. They were all fit. They all had short hair. All of them – the men and the women – carried themselves in a certain way. It was in their body language, the way they stood. And they were nervous, as if they knew something bad was about to happen.

A white van pulled in across the road and parked on a double yellow line. The driver got out and went round to open the back door. If Alex hadn't been on the alert he would barely have noticed him but as he watched, he felt a sudden shock. He recognized him!

In his twenties with close-cropped hair. Well built. The cold eyes of a mercenary. Alex couldn't believe what he was seeing. It was impossible that the man should be here, in the middle of London, but he knew he wasn't making a mistake. You never forget the face of someone who has threatened to kill you – and that was just what this man had done ... in the secret research centre under Sayle Enterprises. He had been a guard, employed by Herod Sayle, and he had grabbed Alex just as he had come out of the disused mine.

"If you make any sudden moves, I'll shoot you in the head."

Alex remembered the voice. The guard had been over-confident. After all, he had a gun in his hands and this was just a fourteen-year-old boy. He had also been stupid. He had looked away long enough to allow Alex to take him out with a single karate move, an *empi uchi,* or elbow strike, behind the ear.

Why was he here?

Alex watched as the driver picked up a cardboard box and walked to the area where the pavement widened in front of the Niketown store. There were two distributors here, hard at work. One of them had a black eye patch slanting across his face. They nodded at him, took the box and began to unload more of the bars. Alex tried to make sense of it all. A hired killer from Sayle Enterprises had now become a delivery driver in central London. Well, that wasn't as crazy as it sounded. Herod Sayle was dead and Sayle Enterprises had been closed down. He would need another job. But there was something else. The chocolate bars were supposed to be made by Cadbury but somebody had made an elementary mistake with the spelling.

Perhaps it was something he had inherited from Ian Rider. Or maybe it had been knocked into him when he was with the SAS, moving through the dark and silent passageways of the Killing House. But Alex had learned to trust his instincts and right now there was a warning bell jangling madly in his head. It might be that he was about to make a complete fool of himself. But that didn't matter. He knew he had to act.

"Jack," he said. "I need you to contact Alan Blunt."

"What?" Jack stared at him. "What are you talking about?"

"Alan Blunt and Mrs Jones. You need to call them."

"I can't call them. I don't have their phone number."

"It doesn't matter. Find them somehow. Or call the police. But I think there's something going on."

"Alex. If you're trying to get out of going to the dentist..."

"I'm not. These chocolate bars they're giving out. There's something wrong with them. I'm sure of it."

"Because they made a spelling mistake?"

"Just do it, Jack!"

Alex didn't have time to explain. He already knew what he had to do. The man with the cardboard box, the man who had tried to kill him, was waiting for the distributor to finish emptying it. Without saying another word, Alex ran across the road, weaving between the traffic. There was the

111

blare of a horn and a dispatch rider on a black Kawasaki swerved round him, the driver swearing beneath his helmet. Alex reached the white van. He looked inside. It was empty. This must be the last delivery. There were some old blankets lying on the floor. They were perfect. He took one quick glance around, then climbed in and pulled them over himself.

For Jack, it all happened too quickly. She had heard what Alex said and had watched him race across the street, almost getting mown down by a motorbike. She had seen him climb into the back of a white van and now she watched the driver return. Was he going to look inside? No. He casually closed the doors and returned to the front. He climbed in and a moment later the van drove off.

Once again, Alex had put himself in danger. Jack was left there, still holding the free sample and with Alex's words ringing in her ears, *"Alan Blunt and Mrs Jones. You need to call them."*

She didn't doubt him. How could she? He had been right before.

MI6. They worked in a building that called itself the Royal and General Bank in Liverpool Street. That was where she would start. She could still see the men and women handing out chocolate bars. Quickly, she took out her mobile and made the first call.

THE MEAT MARKET

There was a rough wooden panel dividing the back of the white van from the driver's seat, but fortunately, there was a knot in it, which provided Alex with an eye-hole, directly over the driver's shoulder and out of the front window. It felt strange to be only inches away from a man who had once held him up at gunpoint and Alex had to be careful not to shift his weight while the van was standing still. Any movement would have told the driver that he was carrying an uninvited passenger.

In fact, Alex was beginning to question the wisdom of what he was doing. Could it be that he had imagined a danger that didn't in fact exist? The driver had once worked for Herod Sayle. That didn't mean he was involved in anything criminal now. And had there really been a spelling mistake on the chocolate bars? Now that Alex thought about it, he wasn't quite so sure. Cadbury's or Cadbury? There wasn't such a huge difference between the two.

It was too late to back out now. He was in the

back of a van being carried across London. Jack would be trying to contact MI6. It was quite possible he was making a complete fool of himself but he might as well see it through to the end.

They were heading east. They stopped at a red traffic light and Alex was able to make out another tube station: Holborn. There were more distributors in mauve jackets, more Choco Bars being handed out. The men and women looked exactly the same as the ones that Alex had seen at Oxford Circus: military haircuts, fit, quite young. And the samples were just as popular here. Before the lights had gone green they must have handed out another twenty or thirty bars. Was that so surprising? The truth is that chocolate is one of the rare things that unites adults and children. There are very few people who don't actually like it.

The van continued past the huge building site that Farringdon had become with the construction of all the new office blocks and luxury flats springing up around Crossrail. The driver slowed down and turned into a narrow street that threaded its way between offices and fast-food restaurants. Ahead of him, Alex saw a strange building, almost like a railway station, made out of stone, brick and iron, decorated with statues of dragons and knights. There was a great archway and the road – which was cobbled – continued straight through it and out the other side. The whole thing looked like something out of Sherlock Holmes and it took Alex a minute or two to realize where he was.

Jack had brought him here once. The meat market at Smithfield. He remembered her telling him that there had been a market here for over eight hundred years. It was one of the oldest in London and unlike the fish market at Billingsgate and the fruit and vegetable market in Covent Garden, it had refused to move out. Huge lorries would arrive in the middle of the night, unloading hundreds of carcasses, whole pigs and sheep, dangling on hooks. They would trundle slowly forward on the next stage of a journey that would finally take them to restaurants or supermarket freezers.

With his face still pressed against the eye-hole, Alex watched as a couple of workers crossed the road, wearing bloodstained white overalls. A huge lorry – PETERSFIELD ORGANIC MEAT – pulled away. Several sections of the market had been closed. They stopped in front of an ugly building with a green, sliding door. This was one of the storage facilities that had been built just after the war. Alex remembered Jack telling him that they were empty and that there were plans to knock them down. The driver had pressed the button on a remote control and the door slid open. It seemed that they were going inside. They drove into a wide, empty space that led directly to a solid brick wall. There was absolutely nothing there, just dust and debris, a few planks of wood, rusting oil drums and scraps of cloth. It was obvious that nobody had been here for a long time. Alex heard the sound of an electric motor and the door slid shut behind him. The driver didn't move. What the hell was going on?

And then there was another click and, in front of him, the brick wall began to sink into the floor, carried by hidden hydraulics. The whole thing was fake. There was a huge space behind it, brightly lit, spread over several floors and illuminated by powerful spotlights. It was hard to make out very much through the small hole cut in the wood but Alex was aware of some sort of control centre with several television screens, a digital communications system, computers, ticking clocks. Unlike the rest of the meat market, everything was clean and modern. The white van swung round to the right and parked. As the driver turned off the engine, Alex heard a voice, being relayed over a loudspeaker.

"Fourteen minutes until outbreak."

Outbreak? What did that mean? Normally, if you used the word "outbreak", you'd be talking about a disease. The more Alex saw, the less he liked it. He needed to tell Jack where he was and get someone over here ... ideally in the next fourteen minutes. He began to reach for his phone, then silently cursed. Mobile phones weren't allowed at Brookland. He had left his at home.

The driver got out of the van. Alex heard him walk away, then hurried over to the back door. He was lucky. It could be opened from inside. Gently, he eased down the handle and slipped out. He saw at once that the van had been parked next to another vehicle: an ambulance. That was another question. What was it doing here? Being careful to make no sound, Alex moved forward. Nobody could see him. But crouching down between the two vehicles, he could see everything.

There were four men grouped together, surrounded by metal tables with computers, maps, radio transmitters and various weapons. Their attention was fixed on a bank of television screens, which were showing fuzzy, black and white images of London streets; the traffic moving slowly in different directions. Alex guessed that they had somehow hacked into the CCTV cameras that were all over the city. A fifth man sat in a leather chair with his back to Alex. The driver walked up to them and stood to attention. The chair swivelled round and Alex saw that it was occupied by an enormous man, well over six feet tall with square shoulders, muscular arms, dressed in loose-fitting combat fatigues. The man had a strangely babyish face with blond hair and blue eyes so intense that even at this distance Alex found himself staring. The driver saluted and suddenly Alex understood what he should have known all along. They were all military. He remembered the man he had seen, missing a hand. He must have been wounded in action. Just an hour ago, Jack had been serving him Marmite soldiers for breakfast. Now, somehow, he had stumbled onto the real thing.

"Welcome back, Charlie." The blond man smiled. Somehow Alex wasn't surprised that he had perfectly white teeth too. "Report?"

"Distribution proceeding smoothly, Colonel."

"No interference from the police?"

"No, sir. In fact, a couple of them even came over to ask for some of the samples."

"That's very good."

"Will it kill them?" Another man, darker-skinned, had asked the question.

"Don't worry, Khyber. I've already told you. It's a hallucinogen, not a poison. Extracted from toads in Peru! They're not going to feel well. They may think they've had a heart attack. But they'll be fine."

"That's him! There's our man!" One of the other soldiers had spoken. The blond man spun round again and looked at the screen.

This television was tuned to Sky News and there was a report about the banker who Alex had been reading about on the tube. Sir Frederick Meadows was being taken to the Old Bailey. Alex saw a security van driving into the famous court with a scrum of journalists and photographers firing off their cameras into the blacked-out windows. Was Meadows somehow involved in this? Was that what this was all about? None of it made any sense.

"Thirteen minutes until outbreak."

The amplified voice sounded again.

Alex couldn't hang around any longer. He had to get out of here before he was discovered – or at least find a working phone so he could contact Jack. The men were all gathered in a group. They had no idea he was here. Keeping close to the ambulance, Alex backed away, then slipped round the side of the chamber, staying in the shadows.

He came to a metal staircase and crept down. The complex – he thought of it as an operations centre – was all metal and glass with just a few of the older brick walls painted white. Once it must have been part of the meat market. Alex could imagine live animals being kept here before they were sold. Someone had come in, hollowed the place out and then created this modern construction inside. It must have cost millions – but then maybe that was what this was all about. Sir Frederick Meadows had stolen more than one hundred million pounds. The newspaper had said he might try to escape. Alex had just seen him being taken to court. He could have planned this before his arrest.

There was an open doorway and he went through it, into a room which turned out to be a kitchen with a coffee machine, a gleaming aluminium fridge, a table with six chairs and a cupboard. His eye was drawn to a photograph on the wall. It was a newspaper clipping showing a man in a morning suit, holding up a medal for the cameras.

Alex recognized the fair-haired man he had seen upstairs. The headline read: "MEDAL FOR WOUNDED IRAQ HERO." He read some of the text:

Colonel Aubrey Sykes, who was badly wounded in Operation Telic in Iraq, today visited Buckingham Palace, where he received the Distinguished Service Order from the Queen. Colonel Sykes saved eleven of his men when he came under fire in an ambush near Mosul – even though he himself had suffered major shrapnel injuries...

He was right. They were all soldiers, the whole lot of them. Or ex-soldiers. And whatever they were up to, they were treating it like a military operation. They saluted each other. They called their senior officer "sir". The whole thing was hard to fathom.

He crossed the kitchen to a second door which led into a larger space. Alex found himself surrounded by machinery: some sort of industrial oven, a conveyor belt, a printing press, a great cylinder of silver paper. The smell of sugar and cocoa hung heavy in the air. Of course! This was the factory where the chocolate bars had been produced. Alex went over to a metal counter and found one of the samples, discarded with the wrapper torn. Cadbury's Choco Bar. He couldn't help smiling. All this planning and then someone had made a stupid mistake because they didn't know how to spell.

He continued through a frosted-glass door which

slid open to allow him into a third room, this one a laboratory with scientific apparatus spread out across a sanitized work surface. He walked past glass flasks and test tubes. Ahead of him there was a shelf lined with about twenty or thirty identical bottles, most of them empty. He picked one up. This one still had two or three centimetres of some sort of colourless liquid. There was a label with the name – BUFOTENINE – and a picture of a crouching frog. Alex unscrewed the bottle and sniffed. The liquid had no smell.

"Eleven minutes until outbreak."

The voice, booming out over the loudspeaker, reminded Alex that time was fast running out. He needed a phone. He put the bottle down and headed back to the kitchen. He went through the factory and had reached the door when he heard the clang of footsteps on the metal stairway and ducked back just in time to avoid being seen. It was one of the soldiers from upstairs. He was dressed in the dark green trousers and short-sleeved shirt of a paramedic. He wore tinted glasses and he had a moustache and thick, black hair, neither of which looked quite real.

Alex watched from the doorway as the man opened a cupboard and took out a selection of cups, filling them with coffee from the machine. He wasn't sure what to do ... he needed to get out of here, but that meant going back upstairs. He was also painfully aware of time running out.

A moment later, the decision was made for him. The soldier twisted round. "Who the hell are you?" he demanded.

Alex froze. How had the man known he was there? He hadn't made a sound. He glanced left and right, then understood. It was the fridge. He had been given away by his own reflection in the aluminium door. Alex didn't hesitate. Smiling, with his hands raised to show that he was unarmed, he stepped into the kitchen. The man didn't move. All he saw was some crazy fourteen-year-old boy who had appeared out of nowhere. It was the same mistake that many of the guards had made at Sayle Enterprises. As soon as he was close enough, Alex twisted round and lashed out, hammering his fist with all his weight behind it into the man's stomach. It was the fastest and easiest way to make sure that he went down and stayed there but, just to be sure, Alex followed through with an elbow strike to the side of the head.

The man collapsed. As he slid to the floor, the wig he had been wearing came loose from his head. The moustache was fake too. Alex understood. The man had been in disguise. When this operation was over, he wouldn't want to be recognized. But what exactly was the operation?

Somehow, in the next few seconds, Alex managed to piece it all together. The chocolate bars, the ambulance, the laboratory, Sir Frederick Meadows. Yes. Of course. He remembered what Colonel Sykes had said. *"It's a hallucinogen, not a poison."* He must have been talking about the liquid that Alex had just seen. They were planning to poison London! The bufotenine – or whatever it was called – wasn't lethal. They weren't planning mass murder. But there was going to be mass panic as people all over the city thought they were having heart attacks. And the ex-soldiers were going to drive an ambulance right through the middle of it all. They would get into the Old Bailey and grab the banker before anyone knew what had happened. One hundred million pounds! It was a huge risk but the reward made it more than worthwhile.

"Eight minutes until outbreak."

What was he going to do? The soldiers were waiting for their coffee. If it didn't arrive soon, one of them would come down to investigate. Alex searched through the pockets of the unconscious man. There was no phone. Moving quickly and silently, he went over to the cupboard and opened it. It was empty and there was plenty of room inside. He remembered seeing parcel tape in the room where the samples had been manufactured. That provided part of the answer – but the rest of it? He picked up the wig and the glasses. The man was short, only a few inches taller than Alex himself. Yes! If he was lucky, it might work.

Three minutes later, dressed as a paramedic, wearing the wig, moustache and glasses, Alex climbed the metal staircase and went over to the television screens where the men were still waiting. He just hoped they wouldn't look at him too closely. The man he had attacked was still downstairs, stripped to his undershorts, tied up and locked in the cupboard. Keeping his head down, Alex placed the tray with the coffees on one of the tables and moved away.

"You took your time, Sarko," Khyber muttered.

Sarko. Some sort of nickname. Alex realized this must be the man he had knocked out. He grunted and moved to the far corner of the room, trying to keep himself out of sight.

The men drank the coffee. They studied the images on the television screens, the various roads of London, as if they were searching for a single vehicle in the endlessly moving traffic. And all the time, the pre-recorded voice continued the countdown until a red light glowed on the control panel and the announcement came:

"Outbreak commencing..."

Colonel Aubrey Sykes, the man who had been given a medal by the Queen, got to his feet. He towered over the other men. "Gentlemen," he said. "We are about to see something that has never happened before in London, something that has never happened in any European city. Let's have no illusions. We haven't set out deliberately to kill anybody but nonetheless people are going to die today. Maybe a lot of people. I understand that you may not be too happy about that. We're not criminals. We're not killers – even though all of us have killed for our country.

"What we are today is victims. I don't want any of you to forget that. Khyber, you were driving a Snatch Land Rover in Afghanistan when you drove over a landmine. It wasn't a suitable vehicle and that's why you're missing a leg. Charlie, you were put on trial, accused of killing people in Iraq. The judge seemed to forget that was why you were sent there. Sarko..." Alex straightened up. The Colonel was addressing him. "You watched your best mate blown to pieces right next to you and you have nightmares every night but nobody cares about you any more. Danny and Gareth—" these were the last men in the group, also dressed as paramedics— "after you were wounded in Helmand Province, you both spent six weeks in a mixed NHS ward. Nobody gave a damn about your dignity."

He paused.

"Today is all about payback. No more. No less. We are going to get what we deserve and because the British Army wouldn't give it to us and the British government forgot about us, we're going to take it for ourselves."

"Colonel. Sir...!" Khyber pointed at one of the TV screens.

Alex looked. There had been some sort of accident. Two cars had collided with each other. It was difficult to see exactly what had happened: the image was so fuzzy and in black and white. But a tailback had already built up. The cars were at different angles to each other. None of them were moving.

Sykes nodded. "We called this operation London Down," he said. "And as you can see, it's started. So let's get out there and do it!"

EMERGENCY SERVICES

It had begun near Blackfriars Bridge.

Later on, the newspapers would identify the first victim as Frank Smith, a black-cab driver. He had started work at six o'clock and had continued until half past eight when he had stopped for a break. He'd gone into a Starbucks which happened to be next to a tube station and when he came out he'd noticed a couple of young men giving away samples of some sort of chocolate bar. He'd taken one without even thinking about it and had eaten it with his coffee.

Just after ten o'clock, he had been approaching the bridge when it hit him. First, there seemed to be too much saliva in his mouth. He couldn't understand it. He had a pet dog back home, a bulldog, and he had often seen it dribbling when food was about to be served. Now he was doing the same! Then he realized there was something wrong with his eyes. They were hurting and his vision was going in and out of focus. Frank should have stopped driving then and there but he decided to keep going. He was sure that whatever was wrong with him would pass in a minute – and if it didn't, he could always pull in at St Thomas' Hospital on the other side of the river. He could feel his heart beating. It was pounding inside his chest as if it was trying to break out. Ahead of him, the lights changed. Thinking about the hospital, he pressed down on the accelerator.

He didn't even make it onto the bridge. In pain, frightened and out of control, Frank went the wrong way round a roundabout and didn't even try to stop himself as he smashed head first into another car. Neither he nor the other driver were badly hurt but almost at once a traffic jam built up around them. As it happened, there were two policewomen on foot patrol nearby. They saw the accident and came running but, before they reached the scene, one of them clutched her stomach and fell to her knees. On the other side of the road, a newspaper seller collapsed on the pavement in front of his kiosk. The wind snatched a newspaper out of his hand, sepa-rated it and blew the pages across the cars which were already backing up all the way to St Paul's.

The same sort of scene was being repeated all over the city. The free samples had been distrib-uted all around the West End, the City and the Docklands and there were hundreds of people who hadn't even waited to get to work before they had tucked in. The sickness, when it came, was sudden and violent. It was like being punched in the stomach. One after another, they found themselves doubling up in pain: secretaries, shop assistants, cleaners, office workers, security guards, construction site workers, traffic wardens, police officers ... even the poor homeless people who had spent the night out on the pavements and thought they had been lucky enough to get something for nothing. Soon the streets were filled with people staggering blindly, throwing up and desperately calling 999.

It got worse. Tube trains had come to a halt as the drivers crawled out onto the platforms and waited for help to arrive. Many of the paramedics were themselves out of action. In the hospitals, nurses and doctors staggered into each other, helpless and frightened, more aware than anyone that something terrible had happened, that it was impossible for so many people in the city to fall ill at one time. The ambulances were going nowhere. Half the streets were blocked. Drivers were collapsing at the wheel. Cars were colliding with each other. Smoke was rising in a cloud over Piccadilly: a van had crashed into a shop and burst into flame. Less than a mile away, a lorry had swerved into the side of Waterloo Bridge and was hanging, suspended over the Thames.

Although the public know very little about their exact workings, there are in fact a number of rules or "protocols" in place in case London is hit by a terrorist attack. The police, the intelligence services, the army, the fire brigade and many other organizations have secretly planned exactly what to do. Less than twenty minutes after Frank Smith fell ill, the prime minister, the home secretary and a dozen other politicians and civil servants were being rushed to a secure room in Whitehall for an emergency meeting. Soldiers armed with sniper rifles and machine-guns were taking up positions at strategic points around the capital. And the BBC was already transmitting a message which had been recorded a long time ago – just in case it was ever needed.

"This is a terrorist alert. Do not panic. If you are driving, stop your car and wait for assistance. Police and medical authorities will be with you shortly. If you are at home, do not leave the house. News will be broadcast as soon as it is available. The government is aware of the situation and is doing everything in its power to make the city safe."

But people were panicking. Rumours were spreading so fast that even the news channels were unable to keep up. London had been the victim of a dirty bomb. Someone had poisoned the water supply. There had been an attack with chemical weapons. Piccadilly had turned radioactive. Nobody remembered the little bar of chocolate they'd eaten a few hours ago – or if they did they failed to put two and two together. Everywhere now there were people writhing on the ground, crying out for help. Huge queues had built up outside hospitals and chemist shops. There were cars everywhere – on the roads and on the pavements – many of them empty. Mobile phones weren't working and that only added to the sense of fear. So many people had tried to make calls that the entire network had reached capacity.

The enemy was invisible. That was the worst of it. London was under attack but it was impossible to say who by. Nobody knew who had started it. Worse still, they didn't know what might come next.

Alex Rider was able to glimpse some of this, sitting in the back of the ambulance as it pulled away from the meat market. But it was the sounds all around him that told him more. Helicopters buzzed overhead. Sirens screamed. Car horns blasted uselessly. It was obvious that London was in the grip of something it had never seen before and their progress was slow, with countless stops and starts.

The five of them had climbed into the back of the vehicle, all of them dressed as paramedics. Charlie was once again driving. Colonel Sykes was next to him. It was interesting that neither of them had bothered with a facial disguise. The other three were in the back with Alex. The man called Danny was short and very muscular, smoking a cigarette. He had a tattoo, a broken heart, on the side of his neck. Gareth was watchful, a little older than the others. Khyber was next to him. Alex was terrified that one of them would address him. So far, nobody had given him so much as a second glance, but his voice would be certain to give him away. Fortunately, no one seemed inclined to talk.

He looked out of the back window and saw a woman, kneeling beside a pram, holding on to it with one hand. A chef in a white hat and apron was sprawled outside his restaurant. Many of the roads seemed to be blocked. A fire engine, with its complete crew, had come to a halt at a crossroads. A motorcyclist lay unmoving, trapped beneath his own bike. Alex could imagine these scenes repeated all over the city and could only stare in silent horror.

Colonel Sykes had created the perfect conditions for any crime he wanted to commit. London had come to a standstill. The police were going to be too sick or too busy to do anything. He and his men could choose any bank or museum and just walk in. There were millions of pounds' worth of paintings waiting to be lifted off the walls at the National Gallery. Or how about the gold bullion kept in the Bank of England? Alex knew that none of these was their target. In fact, they wouldn't be driving far. The meat market was barely half a mile from the Old Bailey – presumably that was why they had chosen it as their base of operations. Sir Frederick Meadows had to be behind this. Get him out of prison and out of the country and the prize would add up to a hundred million pounds; more than enough for all of them.

The ambulance passed St Bartholemew's Hospital

with hundreds of frightened people crowding round the main doors. Next, it turned into Newgate Street. St Paul's Cathedral was just behind them. There were more crowds on the steps and Alex could imagine the priests and the congregation cowering inside. After all, what had happened was like some biblical plague. They swung round to the right and for the first time he saw it: a handsome, domed building made out of grey stone with, high up, a statue of a woman carrying a sword and scales. The Central Criminal Court. Also known as the Old Bailey.

He was right.

The ambulance stopped outside a thick, modern wall made of reinforced concrete. The bulk of the Old Bailey was many hundreds of years old but Alex knew that parts of it had been added more recently. They had come round to one of the side entrances.

Charlie turned off the engine. The Colonel twisted round. "All right, gentlemen," he said. "Let's get kitted up."

The other soldiers moved into action straight away. Alex saw guns being taken out, tested, then concealed. He had no weapon himself – Sarko hadn't been carrying one when he'd knocked him out – and now he hoped that nobody would notice. Both Charlie and Colonel Sykes had put on surgical masks that completely covered the lower halves of their faces. So that was why they hadn't needed disguises! It was perfectly reasonable for para-medics to be protecting themselves against any contagion and there was no chance of their being recognized.

Everyone was ready. Sykes glanced one last time at his men. "You all know what to do," he said. "Good luck. Ten minutes maximum and we'll be on our way."

He nodded. Charlie stayed in the driving seat. The other men threw open the doors and climbed out. Alex hesitated. He hadn't been there when they discussed the plan. He didn't know what to do.

"Get a move on, Sarko," the shorter man – Danny – called to him.

Alex knew he had no choice. Operation London Down had entered its second phase and like it or not he was part of it. Gritting his teeth, he climbed out of the ambulance and joined the rest of them in the street.

PHANTOM LADY

On a normal day, the Old Bailey would have been surrounded by security. During high-profile trials it was quite common to see police officers strolling along the pavements with gas-operated Heckler & Koch G36 assault rifles cradled in their arms and even an ambulance would have been unable to park anywhere near any of the main entrances without proper authorization. But there was nothing normal about this day and, as the Colonel had rightly guessed, a working ambulance with a healthy crew would be welcomed with open arms.

Alex followed Sykes, Khyber, Danny and Gareth across the pavement and in through a modern door, complete with metal scanners and CCTV. They found themselves in a bare, brightly lit reception area where there were two security guards on duty. At least, one of them was. He was about fifty years old, grey-haired, with the name TRAVIS written on a badge on his jacket. He had the look and the manner of a retired policeman. The other guard was sitting on a chair, bent over, with his hands clutched across his stomach. It was instantly obvious which one of them had eaten a chocolate bar on his way to work.

"What took you so long?" Travis demanded. "I dialled 999 an hour ago." He was exaggerating. An hour ago, the outbreak hadn't even begun.

"I'm sorry..." the Colonel began, speaking from behind his surgical mask.

"It's madness here. We've got lawyers, judges, half the juries ... they're all sick. Look at Johnson!" He pointed at the other guard. "He doesn't know what to do with himself!"

"I feel bad," Johnson groaned.

"We'll deal with your friend as soon as we can," Sykes responded. "But we've been called here to deal with one of the prisoners. Sir Frederick Meadows. He's had a major heart attack. He's critical."

Travis had been trained to never allow anyone through the doors, no matter what the circumstances. Normally, he would have demanded to see the paramedics' ID. But he had never encountered anything like this. Everyone around him seemed to be dying. Even Johnson, his closest friend in the building, had been brought down. Finally, help had arrived. He was in no mood to argue.

"All right," he said. "But you're not leaving until you've looked after my mate."

A second door, solid with a small glass window,

led out of the reception area. The guard used his electronic key card to open it and the Colonel, followed by his three men and an increasingly uneasy Alex, passed through. Should he raise the alarm now, while they were inside the building? No. He remembered the various weapons he had seen when they were in the ambulance. Both Travis and Johnson were unarmed. If he started a gunfight inside the Old Bailey, he might end up getting them both killed. He still had no idea where this was going or how he was going to get out of it, but for the time being, he had no choice but to play along.

Travis took them down a long, empty corridor with white-tiled walls and a wooden floor, being taken ever further into the building. They walked down a flight of stairs to another locked door with a third guard outside, slumped in a chair, sweating.

"Are you all right, Jim?" Travis asked.

"No." It was all the guard could manage, to spit out the single word.

"I've brought help. Open the door..."

Jim was as unquestioning as Travis had been. This door had a keypad and needed a six-figure combination before it would unlock but he managed to do it, fighting his pain to focus on the right numbers. Ahead of them, a second corridor stretched out, this one with cell doors spaced out at regular intervals, facing each other on both sides. A fourth and final guard sat at a small table with a number of files in front of him. He was a young man with a neat beard. He looked up as they approached.

"What is it?" he demanded. He looked past Travis at the group of fake paramedics and Alex saw at once that he was smarter than his colleagues and that if he'd picked up a free chocolate bar, he hadn't eaten it.

"They've come to help," Travis explained. He made it sound obvious. "They want to see Meadows."

"They can't just walk in here!" The younger guard was astonished. "Have they got authorization?"

"Everyone's sick!" Even as Travis spoke, Alex understood what had happened. This new guard had been inside the building all morning and he was completely unaware of what was happening outside. "It's crazy out there," Travis concluded. "You've got to let them in!"

"I'm sorry!" The guard was only in his twenties but he knew what he was doing. "You've got to follow the procedure. Anyway, I saw Meadows five minutes ago. He's fine!"

That was as far as he got. The Colonel stepped forward and Alex saw him slip a handgun out of his pocket. It was a Mauser M2, self-loading and semi-automatic and Alex knew he had to act even if it meant giving himself away. He couldn't just watch as the guard was shot in front of him. But before he could do anything, the Colonel swung the weapon through the air, using it as a club. The guard grunted and collapsed. At the same time, Khyber brought out his own gun and held it against Travis's neck.

"What—?" Travis began.

"Shut up," Khyber whispered. "Make a move and I'll kill you."

Travis had gone white. Meanwhile, Danny had stepped forward and searched the unconscious man. He found a bunch of keys and tossed them to Alex. Just for a second, Alex hesitated. "Get on with it, Sarko," Danny growled.

Alex nodded, then, keeping his head down, hurried forward, examining the cells. Each one had a number but there were no names attached, perhaps for reasons of security. Fortunately, the doors had peep-holes. The first two cells were empty. The third contained a red-haired woman, reading a magazine. The fourth was empty again. Alex found what he was looking for in the fifth.

Sir Frederick Meadows was sitting on the edge of his bunk, his hands resting on his knees. He was dressed in an immaculate charcoal suit with a white shirt and a dark blue tie. His shoes were brightly polished. Alex recognized him from the photograph that he had seen that morning. The banker was perhaps a little neater than he had imagined, with a perfectly round head and a moustache that could almost have been drawn on with a pencil. He was wearing round, rather school-boyish glasses. There was a slight smile on his face. Looking at him, it was hard to believe that he was sitting in London's most famous court, about to go on trial for the theft of a hundred million pounds.

Alex's eye was drawn to a gold signet ring on one of Sir Frederick's fingers. One of his six fingers. It was strange but absolutely true. There were five fingers next to the thumb on his left hand. Alex blinked. If he hadn't read about it in the newspaper, he might not even have noticed because actually – if you didn't bother counting – the hand looked completely normal. Quickly, Alex searched through the keys, found the right one and used it to open the door.

Sir Frederick looked up. He didn't seem surprised to see Alex. "Yes?" he asked.

Alex wasn't sure what to say – and the less said the better. He had, after all, the voice of a fourteen-year-old boy. "Sir Frederick?" he asked.

"That's right."

"It's time to go."

"I see..."

The banker got up. He pushed past Alex and emerged into the corridor where Sykes was waiting. It took him only a few seconds to assess the situation. One guard unconscious, the other being held at gunpoint. He nodded briefly. "You've come for me," he said.

"That's right, Sir Frederick," Sykes said. He stepped forward and spoke a few words in the

THE MAN WITH ELEVEN FINGERS

banker's ear, talking quietly so that only the two of them could hear.

Meadows nodded. "Right," he said. "Let's go."

The Colonel gave a signal and Danny led Travis into the cell that the banker had just left. Gareth and Khyber followed, carrying the unconscious guard. Once the two security men were inside, Alex closed the door and locked it, still doing his best to keep his face turned away. Unlike the others, he had no surgical mask. Sir Frederick was standing beside Sykes, waiting patiently, and Alex wondered how the two of them had managed to organize all this. How had they even communicated? Another question occurred to him. When this was all over how much would Colonel Sykes and his men be paid?

They were already making their way back to street level, the Colonel first, the banker beside him. Nobody challenged them. As they reached the entrance hall, a policeman rushed towards them and for a brief moment Alex thought they were going to be stopped. But the policeman hadn't even seen them. He was making for a toilet. Alex heard the door slam and the sound of retching from the other side.

The ambulance was exactly where they had left it, waiting in the street with Charlie behind the wheel. This time, Alex and Khyber sat in the front. Sir Frederick was loaded into the back with the Colonel, Gareth and Danny. As they set off, Charlie turned to Alex.

"All OK, Sarko?" he asked.

"Yeah." Alex muttered the single word without looking up. It was the last thing he wanted ... a conversation, but, a moment later, Charlie turned on the siren, drowning out any sound the two of them might have made.

The roads of London were still jammed. If anything, they had got even worse in the last ten or twenty minutes. Ahead of them, Holborn Viaduct was an unmoving wall of traffic. There were sirens going off everywhere. But they didn't have far to go. Charlie steered the ambulance through a series of side streets, heading back towards St Paul's. Alex had a front-row seat and saw them dipping down between a series of office buildings which suddenly parted to reveal the wide expanse of the River Thames. They had only been driving for less than five minutes but they had arrived. Across the river, the Tate Modern – once a power station – stood out against a clear blue sky. The Millennium Bridge, silver and slender, curved across the water. Charlie stopped the ambulance and they all climbed out, Alex feeling more exposed than ever in the bright, open air. Any minute now, someone would surely see through his disguise and realize that the real Sarko had been left behind. And what would he do when the moment came to remove the wig and shaded glasses?

"This way, Sir Frederick," the Colonel said.

He led the banker down to the water's edge. And

here was the final phase of the operation: a ship moored at a private jetty. It was a sixty-foot, white motor cruiser with a luxurious drawing room and dining area opening onto the back deck. A wide staircase led down to a lower area. There could have been half a dozen bedrooms below. The ship was called *Phantom Lady* and Alex noticed that it was equipped with a sophisticated satellite dish and radio mast. Every part of the plan had been thought through. The roads might be snarled up but the river wasn't. They could transport the banker past Greenwich and out to sea. Before the sun had set he would be abroad – in Holland, Belgium or France. And the next day, presumably with a false passport, he would be on his way to anywhere in the world.

The fake paramedics had already torn off their surgical masks. Alex guessed that they would have a change of clothes on board so that if they were stopped they would look like wealthy businessmen or maybe members of the crew. Was this the right moment to make a break for it? Once he was on the ship, he would be trapped, with nowhere to run. As soon as they discovered he wasn't Sarko, they could shoot him and drop him overboard. He thought briefly of Jack and wondered if she had managed to contact MI6 yet. She certainly wouldn't be too happy when he was found, floating face down in the Thames.

He wasn't given the chance. It was almost as

if the other men knew what he was thinking. They surrounded him as they all climbed up the gang-plank, giving him no room to move. Sir Frederick was sitting down inside the main living area, out of sight. Charlie had taken his place, once again, behind the wheel. Danny and Gareth were on the deck, on either side of Alex, both of them towering over him. Khyber untied the ropes and climbed on board. Almost at once, *Phantom Lady* was away, travelling down the river, helped on by a strong tide. Charlie pressed down the throttle. The sound of the engine rose. They headed east, past the Globe Theatre, passing underneath Southwark Bridge.

Alex didn't like this. Nobody had spoken to him since they had left the Old Bailey. Had he somehow given himself away? He was weighing up his options when he realized that, actually, he didn't have any.

Colonel Sykes walked over to him. He really was a huge man, he towered over Alex. "What's the matter, Sarko?" he demanded. "You've been very quiet."

Alex waited, knowing what was coming. The Colonel reached out and snatched off his wig, then tore the glasses away from his face. Alex didn't wait for the rest of it. He removed the fake moustache himself.

The Colonel stared at him. Then, slowly, he took out his gun. He pointed it straight at Alex. "I'm going to give you three seconds to answer this question," he said. "And if you're lying to me, I'm going to shoot you where you stand. Who are you and what are you doing here?"

"That's two questions," Alex said.

The finger tightened on the trigger. "Then give me two answers," the Colonel said. "And give them to me now."

DOWN RIVER

Phantom Lady continued its journey down the Thames, its two 1,050 horsepower diesel engines propelling it effortlessly forward. Sir Frederick Meadows was still sitting on his own in the main saloon. He had found a bottle of white wine and had poured himself a glass as if this was just a river cruise and he was an invited guest. Charlie was steering, perched on a high stool behind the wheel. Alex was standing in the middle of the deck. Colonel Sykes was in front of him, surrounded by Khyber, Danny and Gareth, who were all armed. Meanwhile, the famous landmarks were flashing by, one after another ... HMS *Belfast*, City Hall, the Tower of London. It occurred to Alex that tourists would have paid a fortune to be on this boat. He would have happily paid anything to get off it.

"Who are you?" Colonel Sykes repeated the question.

"He's just a kid!" Khyber couldn't believe what he was seeing. After months of planning, the operation had been a complete success. But at the final moment, something inexplicable had happened. The group had been infiltrated ... not by a policeman or an undercover agent, but by a schoolboy!

"My name is Alex Rider," Alex said. Things were bad and with every second they were getting worse. Tower Bridge was already far behind him. London was slipping away. It felt like his chances of survival were going with it.

"How did you get here? What happened to Sarko? What do you think you're doing, sticking your nose in our business?" The Colonel seemed to have shrunk. All the confidence and good humour had left his face. His hand tightened on the Mauser. He was aiming it directly between Alex's eyes.

Alex didn't know how to answer the questions. Where was he even supposed to begin? Looking back at the events that had taken place since he got off the tube train that morning, he saw that any explanation would be too complicated, too unbelievable. It was easier just to remain silent.

But then Charlie answered, twisting round briefly on his stool. "I know who he is!" he exclaimed. "He works for MI6. He's a spy."

"He's a teenager!"

"I know, Colonel. But he was there when I was working for Sayle Enterprises. He's had special training ... martial arts. He knocked me out. I swear to you. I recognize him." Charlie was torn between staring at Alex and keeping his eye on the river. "He was responsible for that whole operation going pear-shaped. That's why I ended up working with you. Nobody believed it. But it's true. MI6 sent him in."

Sykes turned to Alex. "Did MI6 send you after us?" he demanded.

"No." There was no point lying. "I saw your driver. I recognized him. He led me to you." He paused. "Also, you don't know how to spell Cadbury."

There was a long silence. Alex felt the breeze whipping over his shoulders, tugging at his hair. Despite the bright sunshine, it was cold on the boat. He looked at the grey water rushing past and wondered if he could make a break for it. He could dive into the river and swim for the shore. The trouble was, there were too many guns. He was surrounded. He knew he would be dead before he could even reach the side.

The Colonel had been examining him, struggling with himself. What was it that he had said, back in the meat market? *"We're not criminals. We're not killers."* Alex hoped he'd remember that now.

"We've got to get rid of him," Khyber said. "He knows who we are. He can identify us."

The Colonel nodded slowly. "You're right, Khyber." The bright, blue eyes settled on Alex as if seeing him for the first time. "You shouldn't have come here, Alex," he said. "You shouldn't have interfered.

I don't like the idea of killing children, but you're not a child, are you? You're a child soldier. That's not the same." He was working himself up into a fury, driving himself towards what he had to do. "I want you to understand something. What we're doing, we're only doing because we had to. Our country wouldn't look after us, so we had to look after ourselves. And I'm not going to let you or anyone else stop us. Not now, when we're so close." His finger tightened on the trigger. "You brought this on yourself, Alex. I'm sorry…"

And then the soldier called Danny cried out and jerked forward as if he had been punched in the stomach. His face had gone white. The heart tattoo on his neck seemed to be beating with a life of its own. "Colonel…" He gasped. He ran to the side of the boat and threw up.

The other men stared at him.

"What…?" Sykes began.

"Wait!" Khyber stared.

And then it was his turn. One moment he was standing there, utterly confident, waiting for Alex to be gunned down. The next he was twisting on his feet, reaching out for support. He was sweating. A pulse was throbbing on his temple. His eyes were glazed and out of focus.

"What is it?" Sykes demanded.

"I'm not well." Khyber gasped out the words. "The coffee…!"

Sykes stared at Alex. Suddenly he understood.

When Alex had made coffee for the five men back at the meat market, he had come to an instant decision. He had no gun, no gadgets, nothing he could defend himself with. Somehow he had to turn the situation to his advantage and he had come up with the one option that was available to him. He would attack the men with their own weapon. Leaving the five cups of coffee to cool on the tray, he had rushed back to the laboratory shelves and to the plastic container that he had opened: the one with the crouching frog. He knew that it was fast-acting. He knew that the liquid was non-lethal. He had heard the Colonel describing it. Shortly after you'd drunk it, you'd think you were having a heart attack. That was fine. That would give him the opportunity to get away.

Alex had taken the container back into the kitchen and added a dose to each of the cups. Then he had carried them upstairs. He had been waiting for the poison to take effect ever since ... and it had certainly chosen the right moment. Another few seconds and it would have been too late.

Khyber and Danny were out of it. They had completely forgotten Alex. Even if they had wanted to kill him, they would be unable to shoot straight. Colonel Sykes had frozen, taken by surprise. The bufotenine hadn't worked on him yet. He was so huge that presumably it would take longer to work its way through his bloodstream. Alex was already moving. Even as Sykes swung round to take aim at him again, Alex rushed towards him, covering the short distance in a matter of seconds. His left elbow crashed into his stomach. At the same time, his right hand shot out, grabbing hold of the Colonel's wrist, forcing the gun away. The Colonel fired. Charlie screamed and fell off the stool with a bullet in his shoulder. Immediately, *Phantom Lady* spun out of control.

Alex almost lost his balance as the powerful cruiser veered to one side, then swung round in a giant horseshoe, heading back the way it had come. Danny was less fortunate. He was still leaning over the side of the boat and, taken unawares, he tumbled forward. He cried out and then he was gone, his round head bobbing in the water like a buoy, already far behind. Well, at least that reduced the odds. Now it was only four against one.

Or three against one. Charlie was writhing on the deck, blood seeping out of a wound in his shoulder. The older soldier – Gareth – was bringing his gun round on Alex. Perhaps he hadn't drunk any of the coffee. He didn't seem to be affected. But it was almost impossible to aim straight with the boat rocking from side to side and, anyway, Colonel Sykes was in the way. Alex was still holding on to his arm, trying to keep the gun away. But the Colonel was slowly, steadily bringing it round and Alex knew he didn't have the strength to stop him.

He felt the deck swaying beneath him. Charlie must have had his hand on the throttle when he was hit and he had dragged it down as he fell. The boat was rocketing forward, doubling its speed with every second that passed. Tower Bridge with its two mighty turrets and sixty-metre span was straight ahead. Would they go under it or crash into one of its massive concrete piers? Right now that was down to luck. *Phantom Lady* would make the decision for herself.

The boat jerked to the right and for a moment Alex and the Colonel were like dance partners, locked together as they fought for balance. Alex saw the gun out of the corner of his eye. Inch by inch it was edging towards his head. Sykes was much taller and stronger than him and Alex knew that he was going to have to play dirty if he was going to survive. He made the one play available to him, suddenly dragging the gun down, leaning forward and sinking his teeth into the man's wrist.

Sykes howled and dropped the gun. Alex kicked it away across the deck, then brought his knee up into the man's groin. *Phantom Lady* was zig-zagging crazily along the Thames. Surely someone would see it and realize it was out of control. The water was roaring past. Tower Bridge was looming over them. Alex had to reach the wheel before they smashed into it! And what about Sir Frederick Meadows? What had happened to him? All these thoughts were tiny fragments, spinning through his head as the boat surged on.

Gareth had lost interest. He had drunk the

coffee after all and now he was slumped on the deck. Charlie was unconscious. Khyber was groaning. Danny had gone overboard. But Sykes hadn't given up. He lashed out and Alex was thrown backwards. He felt his shoulders slam into the deck and for a moment everything swam in front of his eyes. Before he could get up, Sykes was on him, his hands around his throat.

"You've ruined everything!" he screamed. He had forgotten everything he had ever said. He was no longer a soldier, a war hero who had received a medal from the Queen. He was a killer. He was going to take his revenge.

His hands tightened. Alex tried to suck in air but the man was too strong. Nothing was reaching his lungs. The world seemed to shudder all around him. No. That was what was actually happening. *Phantom Lady* was careering round on the water. The steering wheel, with no one to hold it, was spinning so fast it had become a blur. The bridge was shooting towards them. Alex knew that he was about to black out. The Colonel was strangling him. He tried to fight back but he no longer had the strength.

There was the sound of a gunshot. The Colonel's face was inches from his and he saw the shock and pain in the man's eyes. His hands loosened and he fell to one side. Alex looked past him and saw Sir Frederick Meadows, standing in front of the cabin, holding the Colonel's gun in both of his hands, the second of his eleven fingers around the trigger.

Smoke was rising from the nozzle. The banker looked dazed.

There was no time to talk. Alex dragged himself to his feet, then staggered over to the steering wheel and grabbed it just as the huge bulk of Tower Bridge rose up, right in front of him. He wrenched the wheel down with less than a second to spare. *Phantom Lady* spun sideways with water jetting out. Even so, the starboard side hit concrete and there was the terrible sound of splintering wood as the entire length of the luxury cruiser was torn apart. Alex was sure they were going to capsize. The engines were screaming. He reached for the throttle and rammed it up, reducing their speed. And then they were out, on the other side of the bridge, slowing down, part of the cabin crushed and the gleaming handrail twisted and broken. Far behind him, Alex heard sirens. The river police had finally arrived.

Sir Frederick Meadows hadn't moved. He was standing there, small and neat, staring at Alex as if he couldn't quite work out what had just happened, but disapproved anyway. Alex was equally puzzled. The banker had just shot one of his own men and saved his life. Why?

"Are you all right?" Meadows asked.

"Yes," Alex said, although it wasn't quite true. His throat had been crushed. It still hurt to breathe.

The banker lowered the gun. "Well, that's that," he said. He didn't sound too happy, but then he had no reason to be. The police boats were drawing closer. In just a few minutes, he would be under arrest once again.

"Why did you do it?" Alex asked.

"I'm sorry?"

"You saved me."

"That man was going to strangle you."

"Yes. But didn't you want him to? He was helping you get away."

"Is that what you think?" The banker smiled. Alex got the impression that it was something he didn't do very often. "You think these men were working for me?"

"Weren't they?"

"They kidnapped me. I had never seen them before in my life. At first, I thought you were genuine paramedics. That's why I went with you. But the Colonel told me the moment I came out of my cell that they were going to force me to give them my money. They would have tortured me to find out where it was. So actually, I was quite glad to stop him."

Alex looked around him – at Charlie, stretched out on the deck. Sykes wasn't moving. He might be dead. Khyber and Gareth were both whimpering, gasping for breath. Two police launches had reached the boat and he saw Danny sitting in one of them, soaking wet and handcuffed. And finally there was Sir Frederick Meadows in his expensive suit, blinking behind his glasses, still holding the gun.

"Did you really take it?" Alex asked. "The money?"

"Yes, I did. A hundred and twenty million pounds! More money than you can begin to imagine."

"What were you going to do with it?"

"Well, you probably won't believe me, but I wanted to give it all to charity."

"Really?" Alex was amazed.

"Absolutely. The fun of it was actually stealing it, doing it under everyone's noses without getting caught. I didn't particularly want it for myself." Meadows smiled again, a little sadly this time. "Of course, that won't make any difference. They'll still put me in prison – but it won't be so bad. I was at boarding school for ten years so I know what it's like."

The first of the policemen climbed on board, followed by several others. Alex watched as the gang were arrested and Sir Frederick was led away. One of the officers came over to him. "You're Alex Rider?"

"Yes."

The policeman shook his head in disbelief. "We were told you might be on board. We're to take you back downriver. You have an urgent meeting."

"With MI6?"

"No. With a dentist."

So there was to be no escape after all. Alex climbed down into the police launch and a moment later they were skimming across the water, heading back the way they had come.

HIGH TENSION

It was another perfect day in the South of France. Once again, the mistral – that irritating wind which blasts in from the north-west – had decided to stay away and the sky was a dazzling blue. In London, the summer had got off to its usual shaky start. It was pouring with rain and with Wimbledon just a week away, everyone was watching the forecasts with a mixture of gloom and resignation. But the French Riviera, the famous Côte d'Azur, knew nothing of that. Here the sun rose early, shone all day and only crept behind the horizon reluctantly and with the promise that it would soon return.

Alex Rider stood on the terrace of the villa at Mont Boron, just outside Nice. From here he had a stunning view of the entire bay with the beaches of the Promenade des Anglais sweeping round in a great curve that reached all the way to the airport at the far end. Even as he watched, a private jet took off, tiny in the distance, rising steeply before banking left, corkscrewing up into the sky:

some billionaire returning home. It was a reminder that tomorrow he too would be on his way back to England. The visit would be over all too quickly.

The whole trip had come out of the blue. A friend of his from school had invited Alex to join his family for a weekend in the South of France. His name was Wilfred Sutton and every year his parents rented the same villa, perched on the rock face. It had a huge living room, four bedrooms and a series of terraces, one above the other, with a circular swimming pool at the bottom and a vertical drop to the Mediterranean far below. Alex didn't hesitate. It would mean three days of luxury and he knew that it would give Jack a chance to have a break too.

Wilf, as he liked to be called, was a year younger than Alex but the two of them had always got on well. He was quiet and made friends easily with his scruffy appearance and easy-going smile. He had a brother, a sister and a dog, a black retriever called Olly, which he had once smuggled into school for a whole day in order to win a bet. His mother was a doctor and his father worked as an editor for the BBC.

Alex quickly fitted into the family routine starting with croissants for breakfast and then an early dip in the sea. There was just one fly in the ointment. An elderly French woman lived next door – her name was Célestine – who acted as an unofficial nanny, housekeeper and general nuisance while the Suttons were there. She had already decided that Alex and Wilf were a danger to themselves and everyone around them. She watched in horror as they jumped off the terrace and into the pool. She didn't want them to go out on their own – she was afraid they'd get lost. When they went snorkelling near the old port, she had been hunched up on the beach, certain they'd be run over by one of the ferries heading out to Corsica.

And much to his horror, Alex found himself alone with her for three hours on the Sunday morning. Wilf's parents were visiting some old friends in Villefranche just down the coast and there wasn't going to be room for everyone in the taxi.

"You don't mind being left behind?" Alex hadn't heard Nicholas Sutton step out onto the terrace behind him. Wilf's father was wearing a white jacket and a panama hat. "We'll be back in time for lunch."

"I'll be fine," Alex said. "I can hang out by the pool."

"Nonsense!" Nicholas came over and stood beside him. "This is your last day. You ought to do something memorable." He thought for a moment, then a gleam came into his eyes. "Have you ever been parasailing?"

"No."

"Well, it's great fun. You're not scared of heights, are you?"

"Not really."

"Then you should give it a go." He called back into the kitchen. "Célestine! Why don't you take Alex down to the Blue Beach?" Célestine appeared in the doorway. She was holding a plate, wiping it dry. "He wants to go parasailing," Nicholas explained.

This wasn't quite true. But that was the way with Wilf's father. Once he'd got an idea into his head, he always assumed that everyone would agree.

Wilf had heard this and frowned. "Why can't I go parasailing?" he demanded.

"I'm afraid you're coming with us."

Célestine was unhappy too. "Is it necessary always to suggest these dangerous sports?" she scolded. Her English was good but not perfect and she spoke with a heavy French accent.

"It's not dangerous." Wilf said. "It'll give him a laugh – if it doesn't scare the socks off him first."

Somehow, Alex didn't think that being dragged behind a motorboat while attached to a half-sized parachute would be particularly frightening ... not after what he had been through just a couple of months before, when he had been forced to launch himself out of a cargo plane thousands of feet above London, crash-landing through the glass roof of the Science Museum. And there had been a second parachute jump here in France – storming the Point Blanc Academy high up in the Alps, near Grenoble. Not of course that he could tell the family anything about it. He hadn't even told Wilf ... or anyone else at Brookland School, for that matter.

At eleven o'clock that morning, the family set off with a grumpy-looking Wilf ("Visiting old people I don't even know isn't my idea of a holiday") and a few minutes later, Célestine drove Alex down the steeply winding boulevard Carnot that led into the old port of Nice and then round the headland into the city itself. The beaches were already busy as the holiday season had begun.

They parked near the Opera House and crossed the main road with the sea in front of them. Alex had noticed two or three facilities offering parasailing and other water sports. From his balcony, he had watched the miniature figures dangling underneath the wisps of brightly coloured silk as they were towed up and down the bay. He was looking forward to trying it for himself. He imagined how peaceful it would be, hanging over the water in his own little space between the sea and the sky. At least nobody would be trying to machine-gun him.

It was also going to be expensive – sixty euros for around ten minutes. But Jack had given him plenty of money before he left and so far the Suttons hadn't let him pay for anything. He and Célestine reached a makeshift hut on the beach where two slim and permanently suntanned Australians were getting everything ready while a third man, on a speed boat, waited to launch the ride. The parachute that would lift Alex into the air was already spread out on the shingle. A narrow strip of carpet led down to the edge of the water. The runway.

"You gonna give it a try, mate?" The Australian had somehow guessed that he was English.

"Sure. Why not?" Alex handed over three twenty euro notes.

"OK. My name's Jake." He pointed at the other man. "That's Gary. Who are you?"

"Alex."

"Good to meet you, Alex. Let's get you kitted out."

Célestine watched suspiciously as Alex was given a lifejacket, which he buckled across his chest. Gary, the younger and quieter of the two men, held up a sort of harness ... it was nothing more than a strong canvas belt, shaped like a figure-of-eight with two industrial hooks like the ones used by mountain climbers – carabiners – one on each side. The harness was fastened around his waist.

"This way, Alex..." Jake led him across to the carpet. At the same time, Célestine came over to him.

"Alex, you will not mind if I do not watch? This makes me ... *très nerveuse* ... you understand?" She searched for the English. "Very nervous! If you like, I will buy you an ice cream for when you come down." She nodded at some shops on the other side of the Promenade des Anglais.

"Thank you." It made no difference to Alex if she was there or not.

"What flavour would you prefer?"

"Lemon."

"Very good." Célestine took one last glance at the tangle of ropes, the waiting parachute. "Enjoy yourself," she said, but without much conviction.

Jake was in a hurry to get Alex airborne. The sooner he was finished, the sooner he might be able to sell another ride. "When the boat starts, you take three or four steps," he explained as he handed Alex a black, metal bar with about a dozen different cords leading back to the parachute. He snapped the two carabiners into place. The parachute was now securely attached to Alex's waist. When he took off, the metal bar would be pulled above his head. A long rope led from the bar to a pole in the motorboat, just behind the driver's seat.

Alex noticed that the driver of the motorboat was smoking. It seemed slightly odd given that this was meant to be a healthy, outdoor activity. The driver was old and overweight. He was hunched over the steering wheel and didn't seem happy at all.

Jake must have seen the look in Alex's eyes. "That's Kristof," he said. "The usual guy's got the day off. But don't worry. He'll give you a good ride." Jake stepped back and took hold of one corner of the parachute. The other Australian, Gary, did the same, the two of them holding it up so that it would catch the wind. Jake gave a signal. Kristof sat down and gunned the engine. Alex saw the boat move forward and the rope began to go taut.

Marino Branch
Brainse Marino
Tel: 8336297

He took three steps and rose effortlessly off the beach. He could barely even feel the parachute pulling him – all the strain was taken by the harness and divided equally between his thighs. As the boat picked up speed, he climbed faster until he was about twenty metres above the water. He noticed the various swimmers watch him go. There must have been forty or fifty people in the sea and maybe a couple of hundred more on the public beach, some of them spread out on towels, others lying sardine-like on the blue and white sunloungers on the private Neptune Plage next door. There were children building sandcastles and paddling. A couple of them waved at him as he soared above them.

The speedboat was an American-built Tige 21V Fox Racer, six metres long with a single 315 horse-power outboard engine. It was speeding down a narrow channel between two lines of buoys with the open sea ahead. Alex was surprised by how high up he was. From this height, even Kristof seemed to be doll-sized. Alex watched as the driver flicked his cigarette into the slipstream. That surprised him too. The butt of a cigarette is made of cellulose acetate, a type of plastic, and would take years to biodegrade. It would also leak tiny amounts of formaldehyde, cadmium and arsenic straight into the Mediterranean. As if dumping plastic in the sea wasn't bad enough!

He put it out of his mind. He was actually enjoying this. They were still heading out to sea, leaving

Nice behind them, and Alex felt a strange sense of both calm and exhilaration. The sun was sparkling off the sea, the wind rushing through his hair. He would be sorry when Kristof turned round and headed back but he knew that the ride would last ten minutes at the most.

And then Kristof stood up. Alex wondered what he was doing. It was as if he had been stung by a wasp. Still standing, he turned like he was about to shout out to Alex. Then he clutched at his chest and toppled sideways, landing on the steering wheel.

He lay still. The boat surged on towards the horizon. Dangling high above, Alex couldn't quite believe what he had just seen. From the look of it, Kristof had just suffered some sort of stroke or heart attack. It was hard to say if he was dead or alive, but he certainly wasn't moving. His whole body was crumpled, his hands hanging limply above the deck. Alex almost wanted to laugh. This could only happen to him! Well, it looked as if he was going to get a rather longer ride than he had bargained for.

Kristof wasn't moving.

Alex took stock of the situation. He was in no real danger. Provided the Tige kept moving forward, he would continue to fly behind it. It wouldn't take very long for the two Australians to realize that something had gone wrong. They would raise the alarm and send another boat after him. Somehow they would have to climb onto the Tige and bring it back to shore, slowing it down so that Alex could descend. Then they would call an ambulance for the unfortunate Kristof. Perhaps, after this, he would think of quitting cigarettes.

The boat, left to itself, was still speeding in a more or less straight line. Alex glanced back. Nice was now a long way away, the sun glinting off the long row of flats and the hotels which were all packed together, facing the sea with the mountains behind. Despite his first thoughts, Alex was getting a little uneasy. He didn't like being out of control and right now there was absolutely nothing he could do. He really was a puppet on a string.

Should he unhook the carabiners? It might be possible if he shifted some of his weight onto the metal bar, which was now above his head. Then he would be able to let go and drop down into the water. But that wouldn't help. From this height, he would probably break both his legs.

And then the speedboat must have been hit by a little wave. Kristof slid off the steering wheel and fell back, slumping against the rope that connected Alex to the boat. The movement caused the wheel to turn. The Tige cut a complete circle in the water and began to head back the way it had come. Alex felt himself being pulled round. Suddenly he was facing Nice and saw, with a jolt of horror, exactly what was going to happen next.

Unless Kristof recovered consciousness, which seemed unlikely, the boat would keep going until it hit the beach, slamming its way through any swimmers who happened to be in the way. Alex would be all right – he was safe so long as he was up in the air – but other people would be injured or even killed. And what about the dozens of sunbathers on their beach towels? Unless the boat was stopped, it would plough across the shingle and into them too. Alex was four, or maybe five minutes away from a bloody catastrophe. Perhaps the most horrible part of it was that he had been given a grandstand seat.

And there was nothing he could do.

Or was there? If Alex could get into the boat, he could take over the controls ... slow it down and stop. But how was that possible when he was twenty metres up in the air? The carabiners! Alex reached up and grasped the metal bar, using both arms to drag his weight upwards. That took the strain off the hooks connecting him to the parachute and, struggling to stay steady, he managed to free one of them, contorting his body and reaching back with one hand. Then he did the same on the other side. This was more difficult because the moment the second hook was unfastened, he would be hanging free, with all his weight transferred to his wrists and hands. If he let go, he would fall.

The beach was getting closer. The boat seemed to be rushing gleefully towards it. Why couldn't another wave hit the damned thing and turn it back again?

The second hook came free. Now Alex was clinging

to the bar with the harness hanging uselessly off his thighs. He could imagine the crushing impact if he let go and fell. Even if he managed to save himself, it would be at the expense of everyone else. He would be responsible for the carnage as the boat smashed into the beach.

He had to get down to the level of the water. That was the only reason he had unhooked the carabiners. And he had worked out how to do it. On his first mission, he had been given parachute training by the SAS in the Brecon Beacons, and part of it had involved emergency procedures. He remembered what he had been taught. If he could fold the edge of the parachute in against the wind, he would be able to force a controlled descent. He looked up and caught sight of two coloured cords. They were exactly what he was looking for.

It wasn't easy. Having unhooked himself, he was now supporting himself with both hands. He let go with one and immediately felt the strain as his entire bodyweight transferred itself to the other. There was no time to rest. No time to hesitate. Nice was looming ahead of him. He could already see the swimmers – dots in the distance – bobbing up and down in the water, close to the shingle. The Tige was heading straight for them, as if it wanted to do as much harm as possible before it crashed into the beach. Alex still hoped that Kristof would regain consciousness, get up and see what was happening. But he wasn't moving. He was as still as a corpse.

Somehow, Alex's flailing hand caught hold of the rope. With the breeze beating at his face, he pulled with all his strength, expecting the parachute to fold in on itself and then flutter down. But it didn't work. With a sense of dismay, he realized that as the boat ploughed forward, the rush of the wind was too great. He couldn't fight it. He was stuck in mid-air. He could still save himself. All he had to do was let go and he would fall. He might break a few bones but the life jacket wouldn't let him drown. The people on the beach would be less fortunate. Alex remembered the two young children he had seen paddling in the water. What if they were hit?

Ahead of him, the buildings were getting closer and closer. He could make out the improbable pink and green roof of the exclusive Negresco Hotel ... he could even read the letters of its name. How much longer did he have? A couple of minutes. Not more. He pulled again. The cord didn't give an inch.

He was saved by the unlikely help of an EasyJet Airbus coming in to land at Nice airport. All the parasailing companies were aware of the blowback from the jet engines and the danger they could pose to their clients but it was far too high up to be any threat to him. In fact, Alex never even saw the plane but he felt the blast as the blowback hit the parachute. He knew it was now or never and pulled one last time. The silk folded and suddenly he was plunging down, the water rushing up.

He hit it feet first, not hard enough to do himself damage but even so, he was shocked by the impact. One moment he had been floating in the air, the next he was soaking wet, being dragged at speed through the sea, saltwater lashing into his face. He was blinded. He could barely keep his eyes open. At the very last moment, he had let go of the parachute, which was instantly swept away behind him, and transferred his grip to the tow rope. This was the critical moment. Time was running out. He only had a few seconds left.

Alex forced his eyes open. The Tige was in front of him. Fighting against the rush of the water, he began to pull himself forward, one hand over the other, desperately seizing hold of the rope. He bounced violently up and down, the water pounding into him. He could hardly breathe. His arms were being torn out of their sockets. He was being tortured a dozen different ways.

He was getting nearer to the boat. Alex didn't have time to congratulate himself. He had become aware of a new, last danger. The Tige's propeller was chopping up the water, turning it into a vicious white froth. If he tried to drag himself over it, his hands and then his arms would be chopped up. Gasping for breath, he hoisted himself above the surface, peering through the curtain of water that hammered into his face.

He'd had one piece of luck. When Kristof had fallen, he had snagged the rope, carrying it slightly over to one side. As Alex drew himself towards the back of the boat, the propeller was horribly close. He could feel it, churning the water, inches from his stomach and legs. But it wasn't directly in front of him. By twisting his body to one side, he was just able to avoid it.

There was a duckboard at the back of the boat. Alex reached it and caught hold of a stanchion at the very corner. He had used up almost all his strength. He was choking. He felt he had swallowed half the Mediterranean and the salt water was burning the back of his throat. The roar of the engine was in his ears. He cried out and pulled himself up. Somehow his body came clear. He felt the wooden deck under the life jacket across his chest. He wriggled forward. He was on board!

He looked up and realized with despair that he was too late. The Tige was travelling at about thirty miles per hour and the first swimmers were only metres away. Alex could see the horror in their eyes as they took in what was about to happen. On the beach, sunbathers were rising out of their loungers, staring open-mouthed, watching the disaster unfolding in front of them. Someone screamed. Alex could pull back the throttle, cut the engine. But even that wouldn't help. Propelled by its own momentum, the boat would still shoot forward, its prow crashing into the swimmers before it hit the beach and stopped. People would die. He had no doubt of it at all.

In the last remaining seconds, Alex threw himself forward. Ignoring Kristof, who was still lying there unconscious, he grabbed hold of the wheel and wrenched it to one side. The prow swung round, missing the first of the swimmers by inches. There were people everywhere. Alex spun the wheel the other way, weaving through the swimmers. He heard more screams, rising even above the roar of the outboard motor. Somehow, he managed to avoid them all.

The Tige reached the beach. The shingle was right in front of him. He heard the bottom of the boat grinding against the shallows and knew that the propeller would be next. Alex pulled back on the throttle even as the metal blades came into contact with the seabed and shattered. He felt the whole deck shudder.

And then the entire boat left the water. Alex was in the driving seat, on dry land, sunloungers and umbrellas on one side of him, beach towels on the other, a blur of astonished faces watching him as he shot past. At the very end, he wrenched the steering wheel one last time. There was a narrow gully with boulders on both sides and straight ahead, directly underneath the Promenade des Anglais, a dark tunnel with a wire fence blocking the entrance. Some sort of storm drain. The boat was slowing down, dragging against the ground. The prow hit the wire. The boat stopped.

Alex heard shouting behind him – a gabble of

French voices. Quickly, he unfastened the life jacket and the harness. Someone else would look after the unconscious driver and he had no desire to answer any questions. Before anyone could reach him, he dropped out of the boat and ran up a flight of steps leading to the main road.

He had no sooner reached the top than he saw Célestine on the other side, coming out of an ice-cream shop with a cone in each hand. Alex was dripping wet. He was only wearing his swimming shorts. Fortunately, in Nice, he didn't look out of place. Dodging the traffic, he ran over to her.

"Alex!" She was surprised to see him. "What happened? Are you all right?"

"I'm fine." Alex had no intention of telling her what had happened. He looked back. He had moved so fast that nobody had seen where he had gone.

"Where is your T-shirt? And your sandals?"

"They were stolen."

"Stolen? But that is terrible!"

"It doesn't matter. I've got more back at the house." Alex took one of the ice-cream cones. He needed something to cool him down. "Can we go home?" he asked.

"Of course. But how was the parasailing? Did you enjoy it?"

Alex glanced back one last time. He could hear the scream of an approaching ambulance. He could imagine the pandemonium on the beach. "Well," he said, "it was certainly quite a ride."

SECRET WEAPON

SKODA

The man with the two missing teeth had thought a great deal about killing Alex Rider. He had imagined it. He had planned it. And quite soon he was going to do it. There was just one problem. At the moment he was locked up in a maximum-security prison in South Yorkshire. He had only been there for two months. He had been sentenced to twenty years.

That would make him forty-eight when he came out. Middle-aged!

His name was Brian Smith although it had been a long time since anyone had called him that. Right now he was prisoner A8793WS. His skin had already gone pale from the amount of time he had spent inside: twenty hours a day, locked up in a cell with two bunks and a toilet, which left just four hours divided between the prison workshop, the education centre and the exercise yard. The prison food hadn't helped either. He had been thin and unhealthy-looking when he went in but now his own mother wouldn't have recognized him. Not that she would have anyway. She had walked out when he was three years old.

Brian had been fostered and brought up on an estate in Dagenham, East London. His new parents had done their best for him but it was as if there was something in his blood. At school he had been difficult and disruptive. Though small for his age – smoking hadn't helped – he knew how to use his fists and the other children were careful to keep their distance. By the time he was ten he had become the head of a gang of bullies and misfits who enjoyed hurting anyone unlucky enough to get in their way. He had stopped even pretending to do any work. Why did he need school? He had been excluded from two of them and knew that there were plenty of ways to earn a living that didn't involve maths or science or reading or any of the dreary things that were thrown at him in class.

He was eleven years old when he first became involved in drugs. There was a gang – a real gang – in the neighbourhood where he lived and Brian was thrilled when he was asked to join them. A small, sickly boy was exactly what they needed. This was how it worked. The customer would draw up in their car and hand over the money to the dealer. They would signal to Brian, who was waiting at a corner, usually smoking. The dealer would walk away and only then would Brian come forward with the product. That way, the dealer was protected if there was a police ambush and because Brian was underage, there was a limit to the amount of time he could spend in jail.

Brian sold drugs. He took drugs. As far as he was concerned, it would have been stupid not to. When he reached his teens, his two front teeth had rotted away, his eyes had gone a strange shade of yellow and he had lost most of his hair. As if to make up for the collapse in his appearance, he had become interested in body piercing. He had five studs in his ear and others in his tongue, the side of his nose and his nipples. He really liked this new image even though to everyone else, including his horrified foster-parents, it simply looked as if his body was falling to pieces and he had made a desperate attempt to pin it back together again. He started seeing a girl called Lucy and had LOOSIE tattooed on his arm. It was a shame that he had never learned to spell.

Brian did well as a criminal – certainly better than he had ever done at school – and he was lucky. One summer, when he was sixteen, all his bosses got wiped out in a gang war and this left him free to go into business for himself. He started selling drugs on his own behalf although he was smart enough to keep well clear of his old stamping ground, moving his operation to the other side of the city. He settled in Putney, south-west London. His customers were the kids in the local schools, the young men and women on their way to

181

the clubs ... anyone actually who wanted what he had to sell. Nobody knew him as Brian any more. He was known by the name of the car he drove when he did his rounds.

People called him Skoda.

And Skoda had one remarkable idea that would serve him well for years to come. He needed a base where he could prepare the drugs he was selling. The various white crystals that came into his hands had been smuggled all the way from South America and once he had them, he added glucose, baking powder, dried milk, even rat poison ... anything to make them go further. By this simple method he could double or treble his profits and what did he care if he was ripping off his customers, threatening their health at the same time?

His brainwave was to buy a boat, a barge called *Blue Shadow* that happened to be moored on the River Thames, close to Putney Bridge.

Working quietly and using suppliers from all over London, he converted it into a floating laboratory with glass flasks, weighing machines, Bunsen burners ... everything he needed. It was the last place the police would have thought of looking, which was actually ironic because it was quite close to a major conference centre that they often used. It amused Skoda to think that while they were all gathered there, going on about the "War on Drugs", he was actually continuing the war right under their noses.

Everything went well for Skoda until the day Alex Rider came along. Even now he wasn't quite sure what had happened. He'd been enjoying a glass of gin with a friend of his – Beckett – the two of them measuring out the next batch of drugs when suddenly, without warning, the barge had begun to rise out of the water. It had been a moment of complete insanity with cups and plates, jars and test tubes, pipes and burners all tumbling and smashing on the floor. Desperately, the two men had tried to get out onto the deck, only to find that the door was locked. Skoda's world had been turned upside down – for real. He and Beckett had found themselves tangled together at the bottom of the cabin, screaming in fear as the entire boat was lifted out of the river into the air.

It was only much later, when he was recovering in hospital, that he had found out what had happened. Skoda had been selling drugs at a school in Chelsea – a place called Brookland. It turned out that one of the boys who went there had followed him back to *Blue Shadow* and somehow hooked it to a crane. The boy had climbed up to the control cabin at the top of the crane, started it up and lifted the four-tonne barge sixty metres into the air. And that wasn't the end of it. The chain had snapped. The boat had plunged down – through the roof and into the conference centre. The next thing Skoda knew, he was lying on his back with a broken arm, a broken leg and a fractured pelvis, surrounded by about five hundred policemen and women queuing up to arrest him.

All because of a fourteen-year-old boy!

That was the worst of it. Strangely enough, nothing had been written about it in the newspapers and the kid's name hadn't been mentioned at all. But as he recovered in hospital, Skoda used his contacts on the street to begin making enquiries of his own. Apparently there was a boy at Brookland who had been involved in something strange just a few weeks before, a shoot-out at the Science Museum. Nobody knew who he was but there was a whisper he was connected in some way to the security service. Skoda pushed a little harder. Someone knew someone who knew someone and finally a name came up. Alex Rider. Skoda checked. Yes. There was an Alex Rider at Brookland and he had been absent for a large chunk of the summer term. Skoda managed to get a photograph smuggled into the hospital and found himself examining a good-looking boy with fair hair and dark brown eyes. It was him. Somehow he knew it. And that was the moment he began to plan his revenge.

The story of his humiliation had followed him to HMP Doncaster, which was where he was being held. That was how it was in the criminal world. People knew things. It didn't matter how they found out – they just did, and they never forgot. Skoda was mocked from the day he arrived. He wasn't the big deal drug trafficker that he pretended to be. He was the guy in the boat who had allowed himself to be beaten by a kid. Even the warders laughed at him and at night, lying in his bunk, Skoda would feel hot tears of anger trickling down his cheeks. It wasn't being in prison that upset him. It was how he'd got there.

He also knew how he was going to get out. Skoda wasn't stupid. After all, the *Blue Shadow* idea had worked brilliantly until Alex Rider came along. Breaking out of a maximum security prison wouldn't be easy – not with steel doors, CCTV, sensors in the walls and the floors, guards patrolling every hour of the day and the night. But he'd worked out a way.

It was four o'clock in the afternoon and Skoda was out in the yard, along with another thirty men, all strolling around in the cool air, trying to catch a glimpse of a bird or a plane or anything that might remind them of normal life outside. The walls blocked out any view and even the blue sky was framed by a twisting coil of razor wire. Armed guards in observation towers looked down on the prisoners as they walked aimlessly backwards and forwards with nowhere to go. Prison really was a horrible place, Skoda thought to himself. He would get out even if it killed him.

He glanced up at the nearest tower, then casually reached into his trouser pocket and took out a bright green object about fifteen centimetres long. It was a makeshift knife that he had created for himself ... a horrible-looking thing, made up of a toothbrush with the handle melted and the blades from three safety razors embedded in the plastic.

This was going to hurt. But it had to be done. Skoda drew his head back and let out a blood-curdling scream. Then he drew the knife across his own chest.

SPIDER

He hadn't cut himself deeply, although there was a lot of blood. The moment he had screamed, alarms had gone off all over the yard and guards had come running out, herding the prisoners back to their cells. Skoda had collapsed. His hands were crimson. There was a bright stain spreading on his shirt. The knife lay on the tarmac, nearby. Several guards came running over to him and soon he was surrounded.

"Help me!" he screamed. "I've been attacked! I'm dying! I can't breathe! Someone tried to kill me!"

"Who was it?" The first guard to reach him was crouching down, examining the wounds. They didn't look life-threatening at all.

"I didn't see, sir. I was just walking, minding my own business. The next thing I know ... they hurt me!" Skoda was weeping. Tears were also oozing out of his nose. He was squirming on the ground.

"You must have seen them!"

"No, sir. Honest! I just felt this terrible pain and then these horrible cuts in my chest..."

There is, of course, a code in prison. No matter what happens, nobody tells the guards anything. Nobody snitches. The guards knew that so they didn't ask any more questions. They scooped Skoda up and carried him over to the hospital wing.

It was exactly what he wanted. So far, his plan was working.

Two days before, another prisoner had been admitted into hospital – and this was the man that Skoda wanted to see. His name was Harry Baker but he was known to everyone as Spider because of the huge tattoo he had on his forehead. Harry had created it himself, using a sharpened paperclip to make the punctures and soot mixed with shampoo for the ink. It was a hideous thing, a great, black tarantula that sat between his eyes with the front legs stretching out towards his ears. Harry had killed a policeman during a bank robbery and he was in prison for life, but that life had almost run its course. Only a week before he'd had a major heart attack and the prison chaplain had assured the governor that he would be dead by the end of the week.

Skoda and Spider were not friends. The two men had barely spoken – but as soon as he heard what had happened, Skoda had known what he had to do. He had made the knife out of a toothbrush. He had stolen a black felt-tip pen from the education centre. He had bribed a prisoner who worked in the hospital wing to tell him what he needed to know. And now everything was going according to plan.

Skoda was examined by the prison doctor. His cuts were hardly more than scratches and he wouldn't even need stitches but he was given an injection, just to be on the safe side. His chest was wrapped in bandages. And because he was still in hysterics, it was agreed that he should spend the night in the hospital wing. He was placed in the same ward as Spider. There were six beds but only two patients, which was exactly what he had expected. The hospital was still part of a maximum-security prison. The windows were barred and the doors kept locked. But there were fewer guards. The atmosphere was more relaxed. After all, sick and dying men are unlikely to try to escape.

At six o'clock, Skoda was seen by the doctor and given a bowl of soup and some bread. The lights in the ward went out a few hours later although a single bulb was left on. It would glow all night. Skoda settled back, his head nestling against a pillow which was much more comfortable than the one in his cell. There was an ugly smile on his face. His smile was always ugly, thanks to his missing teeth. Slowly, he turned his head and examined the other man who was lying two beds away. He could hear Spider wheezing. His chest was rising and falling but very slowly, with difficulty. He hadn't spoken when Skoda arrived. Nor had he had anything to eat or drink. It was obvious that the end was fast approaching but Skoda was relieved that he wasn't dead yet. If he had been, it would have been impossible to murder him.

Skoda waited until the night was at its darkest and the silence at its most complete. Then he got out of bed and tiptoed across the ward. He stood looking down at the other man.

"Cheerio, Spider," he muttered. "Forgive me, mate. It's nothing personal..."

He had carried his pillow with him. He took one quick glance at the door, then slammed it down on Spider's face, holding it in place with all his strength. Spider reacted at once, his body jerking, his hands desperately clawing at the fabric. But there was nothing he could do. He was lying on his back. Skoda was much stronger than he was. It was all over very quickly. Skoda stepped back. The man in the bed lay still.

There could be no going back now. Skoda returned to his bed, replaced the pillow, then hit the alarm button set in the wall. There was one beside every bed, connected to the medical office just down the corridor. A few minutes later he heard the rattle of a key in a lock, the lights went on and the door opened. Two men stood there, one a prison guard, the other a young doctor.

"What is it, Skoda?" the guard demanded. He looked suspiciously at the prisoner. There didn't seem to be anything wrong with him. "I hope you're not wasting our time," he added.

"No, sir!" Skoda jerked a thumb. "It's Spider, sir. Just a moment ago he woke up. He was coughing and spluttering and then he made this horrible gurgling noise and now he's gone quiet. I went over and had a look at him but I don't think he's breathing..."

The doctor hurried over. First he looked into Spider's eyes, then he felt for a pulse at the side of the neck. He knew at once it was over. "He's dead," he muttered.

"Dead?" Skoda's voice was high-pitched and trembling. "Poor old Spider! He was my mate, sir. I can't believe it!"

"You don't need to upset yourself," the guard muttered. "He didn't have much time left anyway..."

"You're not going to leave him in here, are you?" Skoda sounded terrified. "I can't share a room with a dead man."

The doctor and the guard exchanged a look. "I'll call for an ambulance," the doctor said.

"I can't bear it!" Skoda climbed back into his bed and pulled the blanket up to his chin. "I don't even want to look."

"You go back to sleep, Skoda," the guard suggested. "We'll get a stretcher and we'll move him out of here."

The doctor and the guard left the room, once again locking the door. Skoda made sure he was alone. Then, at once, he leapt out of bed. It was time to put the second part of his plan into operation. First of all, he grabbed hold of Spider, dragged him out of his bed and threw him into his own. Then he covered him with the blanket so that none of his face was showing. He took out the black felt-tip pen that he had stolen and went over to the corner of the room. There was a mirror hanging there. As carefully as he could, he drew a spider on his own forehead, placing it right in the middle with the legs pointing at his ears. Finally, he got into Spider's bed, closed his eyes and waited for his heart to beat a little more slowly. The secret now was to relax. He had to look dead.

Skoda knew exactly what he was doing. He and Spider were bald, thin and unhealthy. They were wearing the same prison pyjamas. There wasn't much light in the ward and they looked fairly similar to begin with. But it was the tattoo that actually clinched it. When people looked at Spider, all they saw was the ugly black decoration on his forehead and they recognized him instantly. The same would have been true if he'd had a peculiar moustache or even a birthmark. When you look for someone in a crowd, you start with what's obvious.

Sure enough, when the guard and two paramedics arrived about half an hour later, they didn't look twice. They simply lifted the man with the tattoo onto a stretcher and carried him out. They didn't need to check that he was dead. The doctor had already done that when he'd first come in. Nor did they glance at the other prisoner who was still hiding under his cover and seemed to be asleep. They just wanted to get this over with as quickly as possible so they could all get to bed.

The supposedly dead man was taken out of the prison in an ambulance and left on a trolley in the morgue at Doncaster Royal Infirmary. It was well after midnight when a nurse noticed that the trolley was empty and an enquiry began to find out who had moved the body and where it might be. By then, Skoda had stolen the wallet and a complete set of clothes belonging to one of the patients in the hospital along with a car, parked outside that belonged to a doctor. By the time the alarm was raised, he was already on the M1 motorway, heading for London.

He didn't know where Alex Rider lived.

But he knew where he went to school.

NINJA

Alex was late. It was one of those days when nothing had quite gone right. His alarm hadn't gone off and Jack had to drag him out of bed with breakfast getting cold on the table. He couldn't find two pages of homework – an essay on renewable energy which had taken him an hour the night before. Then he missed the bus and had to run all the way to Brookland, the local comprehensive which, today, wasn't local enough. He was crumpled and sweaty but even so, he might have made it to assembly on time except, at the last minute, he was stopped in the corridor.

"No running!"

Hearing the voice, he stopped and turned. There was a woman standing behind him and although he hadn't met her yet, Alex knew at once who she was. Everyone had been talking about the new supply teacher who had turned up just a few days before. She taught chemistry and suddenly half the boys in the school were saying it was their favourite subject. Miss Maxwell was young, still in her twenties, with shoulder-length blonde hair, blue eyes and movie-star lips. She dressed like a teacher in a grey, tailored jacket, serious shoes and glasses. But she walked like a model.

She wasn't smiling as she examined Alex. "You're late," she said.

"That's why I was running," Alex replied.

"Mr Bray has made it clear that he won't tolerate running in the corridors." Henry Bray was the head teacher at Brookland. Everyone liked him but it was true that he had his occasional crusades. It could be running, hands in pockets, chewing gum, mobile phones. It depended on the time of the year. "You have to understand," she went on, "it's a health and safety issue. If you slipped, you could hurt yourself quite badly."

For a moment, Alex felt a sense of unreality that he knew only too well. Only a couple of weeks before, he had been fighting for his life on Air Force One, the presidential plane, with a mad pop singer trying to strangle him. And now he was being warned that he might hurt himself running down a corridor! Sometimes it was impossible to connect the two worlds he inhabited, one minute a schoolboy, the next a very reluctant spy.

"What's your name?" Miss Maxwell asked him.

"I'm Alex Rider."

"Oh yes!" She'd obviously heard about him. "You've been missing quite a lot of school recently."

"I've been away ... sick."

"You seem to get sick quite a lot."

Alex shrugged. He didn't enjoy telling lies. That was the worst part of what had happened to him. It was easier to say nothing at all.

"Well, just be careful. This is the only warning you're going to get, Alex. Remember – I'll be looking out for you."

Alex wondered how anyone so pretty could be so severe. As a result of his confrontation with Miss Maxwell, he was late for assembly and was given a detention. That was just the start of it. Geography, maths, biology ... Alex found himself struggling to keep up in every class. The trouble was, Miss Maxwell was right. He had missed so much school that he was falling far behind and the only bright spot in the day came when he got an A+ for an essay he'd written on Russian politics and the collapse of the fleet at Murmansk. Alex couldn't help smiling. What he'd learnt about Murmansk hadn't come out of a book. If it hadn't been for him, Murmansk – along with half of Russia – would no longer exist.

He was glad when lunchtime arrived and after wolfing down his food he strolled outside for a breath of fresh air. He was joined by Tom Harris, who was his best friend at Brookland. The two of them were almost exactly the same age – their birthdays were two days apart – and they had fallen into a friendship on the day they had met. Tom was small and skinny, with messy black hair and freckles. Most of the teachers had given up on him ... he came bottom in every subject. But everyone liked him. He was good at sport. He was funny. He'd been brilliant in the school play and even if he never got a single A-level, everyone agreed he had a future as an actor.

Tom was in a gloomy mood. "It's not fair," he said, as he slouched on a bench at the bottom of the schoolyard.

"What isn't?" Alex said.

"This trip we're having to do this afternoon. We won't be back until five thirty. It's like having two extra hours of school. And it's not as if we're going anywhere interesting."

"We're going to the V&A," Alex said.

"Exactly! What's the point?"

It was a history trip to the Victoria and Albert Museum. They were leaving at three o'clock. Alex had been looking forward to it although he didn't like to say so now.

"I hate museums," Tom went on. "My mum and dad used to take me all the time. Old paintings, old dresses, old bits of stone. They once took me to a museum of knitting. You probably think I'm making it up but it was there, I swear to you, in Nottingham. I was so bored. It was like having a knitting needle driven into my brain. When they told me they were going to get divorced, you know what my first thought was? No more museums! But then I got worried that it would mean twice as many. They can take me alternate weekends..."

"This one may not be so bad," Alex said.

But Tom was still complaining. "They could have taken us in the morning. Or not at all. It makes you think, Alex. Being at school, you have no human rights at all."

The bell went for the next lesson and Alex and Tom began to move towards the main door. Alex certainly didn't want to be late a second time. But as they went, something made him look back. There was a man standing close to the gate, on the other side of the fence that surrounded the school. Although Alex couldn't be certain, he was fairly sure that the man had been there twenty minutes ago, when they had come out. Why had he noticed him now? Perhaps it was because he was so still, unmoving. His eyes seemed to be fixed on him. He was dressed in a shabby coat with his hands in his pockets but he was too far away for Alex to recognize him and even as he looked, the man turned and walked away.

Well, you got all sorts of weirdos hanging around outside schools. If the man really was up to something, he would have been spotted on CCTV and security would have asked him to move on. Alex put him out of his mind.

But Skoda had seen him. Skoda had already made enquiries and knew where he was heading. Skoda had decided what he was going to do.

SCHOOL TRIP

The Victoria and Albert Museum in South Kensington is so huge that you could spend a week there and still not see everything it contains. In fact there are about three million objects on display in an area larger than ten football pitches. As Alex followed the long, underground passageway that led from the tube station to the museum entrance, he was actually thinking that this made a welcome break from ordinary school. There were thirty of them in the group, escorted by Mr Kydd, who taught history, and Miss Maxwell. Alex wondered how she had managed to tag along. After all, she had barely been at the school for forty-eight hours. But at least she hadn't told him off again.

They were here to visit an exhibition called "SEVEN HUNDRED YEARS OF WAR". It was basically about weapons and there were hundreds of them on display: from medieval bows to ultra-modern semi-automatic Air Burst grenade launch systems. The collection had been drawn from many different cultures. It seemed that there wasn't a country in the world that hadn't gone to war at some time in its history. Japan had provided samurai swords, razor-edged fans and battle pipes. There were spears from Africa, tomahawks from America, clubs and boomerangs carved by the Aboriginal people of Australia, silk garrottes that the Thuggee cult had used to strangle their victims in India. The First and Second World Wars each had a room to themselves with models and photographs of planes, rockets, tanks, frigates and destroyers. There were glass cases filled with hand grenades, gas masks, pistols, knives, bayonets and flame-throwers. It really was incredible how many different ways human beings had thought up to kill each other.

The exhibition was arranged in a warren of rooms, spread out in the basement of the museum. Each room had a different theme and Alex found himself fascinated as they moved between them. Even Tom seemed to be showing some interest, although he complained that all the weapons were locked away or fastened to the wall and that it would be much more fun to see some of them being demonstrated ... particularly the flame-thrower. They had arrived at three thirty and had a full hour and a half before the exhibition closed for the evening, after which they would return as a group to Brookland before they went home.

"The next room is dedicated to spies," Mr Kydd announced. "Can anyone name a real-life spy?"

A boy with dark blond hair put his hand up. His name was Sam King and he was another of Alex's friends. "Mata Hari," he said.

"That's right. Well done, Sam. She spied for Germany in the First World War."

Sam found himself next to Alex as they passed through the door. "I wish I could meet a spy," he said.

For a moment, Alex wasn't sure what to say. "They probably wouldn't tell you if they were," he muttered.

"That's true."

Alex particularly liked some of the secret weapons that were on display. These had been designed so that at first sight they didn't look like weapons at all. There was a torch from Korea that fired a bullet at the touch of a switch and an umbrella from Bulgaria that shot a poisoned pellet from the tip. It had famously been used to kill a dissident writer in the middle of London back in the seventies. Back in the nineteenth century, someone had come up with another tiny gun that could be worn around a finger, like a ring. It was called the Dyson LePetit Protector Ring Pistol. And there were all sorts of devices invented by the British Special Operations Executive during the war: a spring-loaded cosh that leapt out of the sleeve, a dagger concealed in a pencil, a lipstick that fired tear gas. Alex couldn't help but think of Smithers who had supplied him with all sorts of bizarre gadgets for his various missions. Would they be on display here one day he wondered. The exploding ear stud, the book with a concealed knockout dart, the stun grenade keyring?

Alex was so wrapped up in his thoughts that he didn't notice that he had lagged behind. He was in a room dedicated to ninja weapons – the ninjas had lived in ancient Japan and were famous for their fighting methods. He looked up just in time to see the remaining members of his party leaving the room. It was almost five o'clock and this section of the museum was closing for the day. The last thing he wanted to do was hold everyone up when they were in a hurry to get home and he moved quickly to catch up, only to find his way blocked by a museum guard.

"What is it?" Alex asked. He had barely looked at the man who was wearing the white shirt and dark trousers of all the museum staff. There was a radio transmitter hanging from his belt.

"Are you with the Brookland School group?" the man asked.

"Yes."

"I'm afraid I'm going to have to ask you to wait here a minute."

"Why?"

"There's been some damage done in the World War Two gallery. The museum director is on his way down."

"I had nothing to do with it," Alex said.

The guard nodded briefly. "In that case you've got nothing to worry about. I won't keep you long."

A whole minute went by and Alex was aware that the basement was suddenly very quiet. He was tempted to push past the guard and rejoin the group but he was nervous about making a bad situation worse. The man might claim he'd been attacked or something ... and if it came to that, someone in authority versus a schoolboy, who would be believed? At the same time, he knew there was something wrong. The guard was looking at him strangely and now it occurred to Alex that his uniform didn't fit. The shirt and the trousers were both one size too large. His face was also unnaturally pale. It had all the colour of a corpse. He was missing two teeth. Alex only noticed because his lips had curled into an unpleasant smile. The man was enjoying this.

Alex realized he was in danger before he understood why. Suddenly he remembered the man he had seen standing outside the school and knew that this was the same man, that he had been held back on purpose. He was angry with himself. It was something he should have learned by now. Just because someone is wearing a uniform – a policeman, a fireman, a nurse – it doesn't mean that's what they are. He'd seen the clothes. He hadn't examined the person inside them.

It was too late now. The guard was already moving towards him, his face no longer concealing a grimace of pure hatred. Alex didn't hesitate. He kicked out, his right foot lashing through the air. The guard had been expecting it. His hand swung down, catching Alex's ankle. He twisted hard, then jerked upwards. Alex lost his balance and was thrown backwards. His shoulders slammed into one of the display cases, smashing glass which rained down over him. He slipped to the ground and lay there, momentarily dazed. Some of the ninja weapons had tumbled out: a length of chain; a blowpipe; a handful of *shuriken*, the five-pointed stars with razor-sharp edges designed for throwing. As he watched, the guard strolled to the other side of the room and drew a curved sword off the wall. Alex watched, fascinated, as the smooth, silver blade came clear of its mountings.

The guard weighed it in his hand. He stepped forward so that he stood over Alex, who was lying on his back, surrounded by broken glass. "You don't remember me," he said. His voice was trembling with excitement. There was insanity in his eyes.

"Yes..." Alex was fighting for time, trying to work out what to do next. "You were at Madame Tussauds."

"What?" The guard frowned.

"The Chamber of Horrors. Third from the left, next to Jack the Ripper..."

The guard swung the sword in front of him. The blade was so sharp that Alex could almost feel it, cutting the air. He knew he had made a stupid joke but he didn't care. He wanted to annoy his attacker, to throw him off guard. That way he would be more likely to make a mistake.

"I was in Putney," the guard said. "On the *Blue Shadow*..."

The *Blue Shadow*! Alex remembered the canal boat, the crane, the police conference and at that moment everything made sense. "Skoda!" he muttered.

"That was what people called me. I had a business. I had money. I had everything going for me – and then you came along! You tipped up the boat. You hooked me on a crane. How did you do that? Why did you do that?" The words were pouring out. "And because of you, I was in hospital for weeks with several broken bones. You ruined me."

"You ruined a lot of people ... the drugs you were selling."

"I gave people what they wanted!" Skoda stopped. His eyes were wide. There was a vein beating in his forehead.

Alex looked around him, wondering why nobody had come. Surely they would have heard the breaking glass. But it was late. The museum was emptying and they were far down in the basement. And what next? What happened now? It seemed to him that Skoda had been so intense, so determined to explain himself, he had forgotten the sword he was holding. He remembered it now.

"This is all I want," he rasped. "This is all I've

dreamed about. Alex Rider." He spoke the name with contempt. "I'll go back to prison. I'll be in prison for the rest of my life. But I won't mind, knowing that you're dead."

"You're too late, Skoda," Alex said and then continued, speaking to someone in the door behind him, "I'm glad you're here. You can take him now."

Skoda turned. It was the oldest trick in the book. There was no one there. He was distracted for just one second but that was enough time for Alex to make his move, snatching up the chain and rolling to one side. Skoda knew he had been deceived, spun round and slashed down with the sword. It missed Alex's arm by an inch, the blade thudding into the wooden floor. For another precious few seconds it stuck fast and by the time Skoda pulled it free, Alex was on his feet.

And armed. The chain was actually known as a *manrikigusari* and in the hands of a ninja warrior it was said to have ten thousand uses. The word *man* means "ten thousand" in ancient Japanese. The weapon that Alex was holding had a handle at each end. It was like a steel skipping rope. But Skoda's sword was even more lethal. It had left a deep gouge in the floor. If Alex hadn't rolled away in time, he would have lost his arm.

"That's not going to help you," Skoda said. He was juggling with the sword, looking for an opening. "Put that down and I might make it easier for you."

"Why don't we talk about this...?" Alex had no intention of giving up his weapon. He gripped it more tightly. He was still waiting for someone to come. Surely Mr Kydd or Miss Maxwell would have noticed he was missing?

"We've talked enough!"

Skoda edged towards him and then everything happened in a blur. Skoda attacked, jabbing forward with the tip of the sword. Alex avoided it easily. He was fitter, faster and lighter on his feet than Skoda, who still hadn't completely recovered from his broken bones. Skoda missed. Alex swung the chain. There was a great thud as it made contact with Skoda's hip. Skoda howled and fell to one side. That left the entrance free. Alex made for it. Six steps and he'd be out of the room. He wouldn't stop running until he had reached the ground floor and found someone to help him. But for once in his life he was unlucky. His foot came down on the blowpipe that had fallen out of the case. He felt it roll beneath him and before he could stop himself he had lost his balance and once again crashed down to the floor. The chain was knocked out of his hand. The next thing he knew, he was lying on his back, unarmed and Skoda was standing over him, holding the sword in both hands.

"Not quite so clever any more, are you?" Skoda giggled. "This is where it ends, Alex Rider. Shall we do it slowly or shall we do it quickly? Which bit of you shall we cut first?"

"Look behind you, Skoda," Alex said. He could taste blood. He must have bitten his tongue as he fell. "We're not alone."

"You think I'm going to fall for that one again?"

"He's telling the truth."

The voice had come from the door. Skoda spun round, his eyes widening in shock. Miss Maxwell was standing there, her blonde hair hanging loose and something deadly in her eyes. Alex realized that she wasn't wearing her glasses. She didn't need them. Perhaps she never had. There was a gun in her hand and Alex was as surprised to see it as Skoda. "Put the sword down and step aside," she ordered. "I'm telling you now, I won't give you a second warning." The strange thing was, her voice was exactly the same as when she had been telling Alex off for running in the corridor.

"Wait a minute, lady..." Skoda's voice was a whine but he lowered the sword.

"Are you all right, Alex?"

That was her mistake. In the moment that she had looked at him, she had taken her eyes off Skoda and that was when he swung the sword ... not at Alex but at her. She fired and Skoda spun round, screaming. He had been hit in the shoulder. But the teacher hadn't escaped injury either. The tip of his sword had cut through her grey jacket, drawing blood. Alex heard her gasp. Skoda barrelled forward, shoving her aside. And then he was gone, out of the room, leaving the two of them alone.

THIRTY MINUTES

"I'm sorry," Miss Maxwell said. "That was clumsy of me. Mrs Jones won't be pleased."

She had examined the wound made by the sword. Fortunately, it wasn't very deep. She seemed more annoyed about the damage to her jacket.

"You work for MI6?" Alex asked.

The supply teacher nodded. She took out her phone and pressed speed dial. "This is Maxwell. I'm at the V&A. Subject was here but he managed to get away. You'd better hand over to the police." Quickly, she added a description of Skoda and what he had been wearing. "Alex is unhurt," she added. "I'm with him now."

"What exactly is going on?" Alex asked, when she'd rung off.

"Brian Smith escaped from prison a few days ago," she explained. Alex had never actually known Skoda's real name. "Mrs Jones was worried he might come looking for you so she sent me to keep an eye out."

"That's very nice of her." But Alex knew that being nice had nothing to do with it. He looked around him. Here he was in an exhibition called "SEVEN HUNDRED YEARS OF WAR" but in a way he wasn't just visiting. He was part of it and had been ever since his uncle had died. MI6 had made him their secret weapon. They had put him into a glass case of their own and they were the ones with the key. Miss Maxwell had been sent here to protect him because he was valuable to them. That was all it came down to.

"I noticed you weren't with the rest of the group when we reached the exit," she continued. "So I came back to look for you."

"So what happens now?" Alex asked.

"You heard me say on the phone. Smith has no money and nowhere to go. He has a bullet in him. He's not going to be difficult to find. We need to get you back home. And of course, nobody else from Brookland must know what happened."

Alex understood why that was important. He was only useful to MI6 while nobody knew about him. "Where is everyone?" he asked.

"They're outside with Mr Kydd. He's waiting to take everyone back to the tube station."

"Are you going to be all right?"

Miss Maxwell flexed her shoulder. "I'll get a medic to take a look at it when I'm back. I'm still annoyed that I allowed myself to be distracted. And I should have aimed at his head!" She put her jacket back on. "It's such a great pleasure to meet you, Alex," she said. "I've heard so much about you – and that business with General Sarov really was extraordinary."

Alex tried not to think about it. Sometimes, at night, he was woken up by the sound of gunfire, shattering his dreams.

"I know Mr Blunt thinks very highly of you," she continued. "By the way, I'm sorry I had to tell you off for running in the corridor."

"I'll try not to do it again," Alex said.

His mobile rang. He took it out and looked at the display. The call was from Tom Harris. "Alex..." Tom began.

Even that single word told Alex that, somehow, trouble had returned. There was a gasp at the other end as the phone was torn away and then he heard Skoda's voice, ugly and excited. "I have your friend," he said. "Your best friend."

"What do you want?" Alex asked quietly.

"You know what I want. Is it going to be you or is it going to be him? If you want to see him again, come back to where we first met. I'll send you a signal. You'll see where I am. Come alone. Come unarmed. If I see anyone with you or if I believe anyone is with you, your little friend is going to have a horrible time. Do you understand?"

"Yes."

"You have thirty minutes. After that, it'll be too late."

The phone went dead.

"Who was that?" Miss Maxwell asked.

Alex hesitated. He should tell her. If Skoda had snatched Tom, she would find out soon enough anyway. She could summon MI6. They could send in cars, helicopters ... the works. But at the first sign of trouble, Tom Harris would die. Skoda had nothing to live for. He had said as much already. And would MI6 care too much about the death of an unknown schoolboy? They were interested in Alex. No one else.

"It was Jack," he said. "She was wondering when I'd get back." He leaned down and brushed a piece of broken glass off his trainer.

"You'd better join the others. I'll wait here and talk to the museum authorities. We're going to have to explain all this damage."

"Thanks, Miss Maxwell."

Alex hurried up the stairs and into the main reception hall, where Mr Kydd was lining up the students, preparing to leave. He found Sam King. "Can you call out my name if there's a roll call?" he whispered.

"Sure."

That was what Alex liked about Sam. He didn't ask questions. He was happy to help.

Alex took one quick look around and slipped out of a side door. It was early evening and the sky was beginning to darken. The rush-hour traffic was heavy, thundering down the main road.

Alex didn't wait for the lights to turn red; he dodged between the traffic, ignoring the horns as different drivers jammed on their brakes to let him pass. Skoda had given him thirty minutes. He didn't intend to be late.

THE CRANE

It was strange to be back in Putney. It felt as if years had passed since Alex had sneaked onto the building site close to the River Thames – his first encounter with Skoda. In fact it had been a matter of months. He saw the wooden jetty jutting out into the water. That was where *Blue Shadow* had been moored, but it was empty now, the brown water churning sluggishly past. And there was the brand-new conference centre that he had accidentally destroyed when he dropped the boat. It was covered in scaffolding now. They were building a new roof. The building site was exactly as he remembered it. They hadn't actually done a great deal of building since the last time he was here. Alex guessed that the arrest of Skoda, the police enquiry and the confusion surrounding what had actually happened would have slowed things down. The area was still surrounded by a tall, wire fence with a gate giving access from Lower Richmond Road. The gate should have been locked. It was hanging open.

Alex had run down from Putney Bridge tube station. He still had five or six minutes in hand but he moved warily, looking around him. The clouds had closed in and darkness had come quickly. Skoda could be anywhere. There were half-built walls, scaffolding towers, deep trenches and vehicles parked all over the compound. Alex examined the mechanical diggers, the bulldozers, the compactors. In the hands of a maniac, any one of them could become a weapon as dangerous as those he had seen in the V&A. Where was Skoda? He thought about calling out to Tom but decided against it. He didn't want to put him in any more danger than he was already in.

He saw something out of the corner of his eye. A light had blinked on and off: a torch. Where was it? The beam flashed a second time and Alex looked up, his eyes travelling to the control cabin of a crane that loomed high over him, in the very centre of the building site. He waited a moment to be sure. Yes. There it was. Skoda knew exactly what he was doing. This was the same crane that Alex had climbed when he had followed the drug dealer to his river hideaway. He had sat in the control cabin and used the two joysticks to hook *Blue Shadow* and lift it out of the water as if in some fantastic arcade game. Well, Skoda had invited him back. The fight was going to end where it had begun.

Alex was being watched. He was in full view of Skoda and he guessed that Tom would be up there with him too. He hadn't enjoyed climbing the crane the first time: a metal tower with three hundred rungs and nothing to stop you if you lost your grip and fell. This time it was worse. Skoda was waiting and Alex knew exactly what he intended to do. Skoda had taken the samurai sword with him when he escaped from the museum and he would certainly have it with him now. As he took hold of the first rung and began to climb up, Alex found himself thinking of Miss Maxwell. She'd saved his life but Skoda was still on the run.

The ground was disappearing behind him, the vehicles and building equipment getting smaller and smaller. Just to add to his troubles, it had begun to rain, a thin drizzle that stung his face and the backs of his hands and made the rungs slippery. Part of him wondered if he was doing the right thing. Maybe he should have told Miss Maxwell the truth and let MI6 deal with it. No. Tom was his best friend. Skoda must have seen the two of them together when they were in the schoolyard. This was his fault. He would deal with it.

His arms were aching. His clothes were damp. His hair hung down in his eyes. But finally he reached the top, nearly one hundred metres above ground level. He was effectively in the middle of a gigantic T. The cubicle with the controls was right in front of him but there was no one inside and the door seemed to be locked. Over to the left, he could make out the massive cement blocks that kept the whole thing balanced. Looking the other way, he saw the operating arm stretching out into the darkness with the hook dangling below. There were two figures waiting for him about halfway along. Tom Harris was on his knees. Skoda was standing over him with the sword pointed at his neck.

Alex looked down. The ground was a long way down, the drizzle suspended in the air. Skoda was about four or five metres away. To reach him, Alex would have to walk along the arm, steel struts criss-crossing each other and wide gaps beneath his feet. Worse still, the safety railings on each side only came up to his thigh. It was hardly safe at all. If he slipped, he could all too easily fall over the edge. And that, of course, was exactly what Skoda wanted to happen. Preferably, after he'd stabbed him.

"So you came!" Skoda said. It was as if he couldn't believe his luck.

"That's right, Skoda. I came." Alex examined the other man. He was in a bad way. Miss Maxwell had shot him high up in the shoulder and his shirt was hanging off him, already made damp by the rain and saturated with blood. Shock and pain were distorting his face. His eyes were wide. His skin had no colour at all. It was extraordinary, really, that he was still conscious.

Meanwhile, Tom was slumped in front of him, refusing to look up. He had started crying. Now that Alex was closer, he could hear the boy gasping for breath. Everything about him suggested that he was terrified.

"I'm here now," Alex said. "So you can let him go."

"I'll let him go when you're dead!" Skoda almost screamed the words. "I want to see you jump. That's how it works. You do what I say or I'll cut off his head ... I swear to you."

"Alex!" Tom sobbed. "He grabbed me at the museum. He made me come here."

"It's all right, Tom." Alex looked Skoda in the eyes. "How do I know I can trust you? Let him go first. Then it'll just be you and me."

"I don't care about him. It's you I want. Climb over now. Do it or watch your friend die."

"Alex...!" Tom was wailing like a little child.

"Now!" Skoda tightened his grip on the sword.

And then everything happened at once.

Tom suddenly straightened up, slamming his fist hard between Skoda's legs. Skoda gasped and doubled up in pain. Alex knew that Tom had been faking the tears. His friend was a brilliant actor and there was no way he would have allowed a thug like Skoda to humiliate him. And Alex had been waiting for exactly this moment. Even as he had talked, his hand had been behind him, searching in his back pocket for the weapon that he had concealed there. It was one of the five-pointed stars, the ninja *shuriken* that had fallen out of the display case back at the museum. With a single movement, he took it out and threw it. The star didn't have very far to travel. It spun through the air and buried itself in Skoda's hand. Skoda screamed and dropped the sword. The sword slipped through one of the gaps in the floor and disappeared.

With a scream that was more animal than human, Skoda threw himself at Alex, half tripping over Tom. Somehow his hands found Alex's throat. For a moment the two of them were close together and Alex saw the man grimacing at him with the dark gap where his front teeth should have been. Tom had got to his feet and threw himself at Skoda. At the same time, Alex lashed out and felt Skoda's hands lose their grip. That was when Skoda lost his balance. He let out a final whimper and toppled to one side. The railing wasn't high enough to save him. He plunged into the darkness.

Neither boy watched him as he fell. It seemed to take a long time before the sound of his body thudding into the gravel came from far below. Then they heard police sirens. Tom pointed. There were two police cars tearing across Putney Bridge. They screeched round the corner and began to follow the road down towards the building site. Alex guessed that Miss Maxwell must have finally noticed that they were missing. She must have called for backup.

Tom was soaking wet. His hair was plastered over his forehead. It took him a few moments to recover from what had just happened. "So what was all that about?" he asked.

"I have no idea," Alex said. He had decided at once that he would have to lie. Nobody at Brookland, not even Tom, could know the truth.

"He didn't seem to like you," Tom said.

"He certainly wasn't very friendly," Alex agreed.

The police cars had arrived at the foot of the crane, their lights flashing blue across the yard. A few of the policemen were already searching for Tom and Alex. The others were examining the broken doll that had once been Skoda.

The two boys began the climb down.

TEA WITH SMITHERS

I'd often wondered where Smithers lived. The truth is, I knew almost nothing about him except that he was massively fat, he was bald with a small, almost comical moustache and he liked to wear old-fashioned suits. He manufactured gadgets – secret weapons and so on – for MI6. And that was what he provided for me. He wasn't allowed to give me anything lethal. I never got a gun or anything like that. But he seemed to take a great deal of pleasure in thinking up things that a teenager might have in his pockets (apart from his hands) and his inventions saved my life on more than one occasion.

Anyway, the two of us bumped into each other in Liverpool Street and he seemed very happy to see me. He was the only person in MI6 who I actually trusted. He wasn't like Mr Blunt or Mrs Jones or any of the others who only ever wanted to use me.

"Alex, my dear fellow!" We were standing face to face in the doorway of the building that pretended

Marino Branch
Brainse Marino
Tel: 8336207

to be an international bank, but he was talking so loudly I could have heard him halfway down the road. He had a funny way of speaking, a bit like everyone's favourite uncle or perhaps a head teacher in a small, private school. "What a delightful surprise. I hope we're not using you again. Nobody mentioned anything to me..."

In fact I'd just been in for a debrief. MI6 were closing their files on Dr Grief and everything that had happened at the Point Blanc Academy, and they'd called me in to give them my version of events. Jack always hated it when I went into their offices. She was sure I wouldn't come back. But it had been an uneventful hour and I'd been on the way to the tube station when Smithers had suddenly appeared. I was quite surprised he used the front door. He was more likely to step into a phone box that would turn out to be a lift.

"I'm not going anywhere, Mr Smithers," I said.

"Not another mission?"

"No ... they were just asking me about the last one."

"Ah yes. Dr Grief. I always thought he was a nasty piece of work." He beamed. "In that case, why not come for tea with me? It would be nice to sit down and have a proper chinwag." It occurred to me that Smithers had several chins with which to do it but, of course, I didn't say that. "How about next Saturday at three o'clock?"

"All right." I wasn't sure I did want to have tea

with him but I wasn't doing anything over the weekend and there was a part of me that wanted to know more. I'd first met Smithers a few months ago. I'd been involved in two missions. But as I said, I didn't know anything much about him. Where did he live? Did he have a house or a flat? Did he live alone? Everyone who worked at MI6 was the same. They spent so much time living in the shadows that in the end they became shadows themselves. I had learned that Mrs Jones had two children (although somehow she'd lost them). Mr Blunt was married. Mr Smithers's first name was Derek. And that was it. That was the full extent of my knowledge.

He gave me an address in Hampstead and said it was a ten-minute walk from the tube station. The following Saturday I arrived on time, walking down through the village and taking one of the narrow lanes that twist their way towards Hampstead Heath. It turned out that Smithers lived in a mews. He had a small, pink house with ivy growing up the front. There were three floors and, from the look of it, maybe six rooms. It was the sort of house that might appear in *Mary Poppins* if you've ever seen that old film. I got the feeling there was something not quite real about it. A gnome was standing on the tiny patch of lawn that made up the front garden. I wondered if it was watching me; connected to some sort of surveillance system and the front door bell. Would it blow up if I pressed it the wrong way? You never knew, where Smithers was concerned.

Nothing happened for about five seconds after I'd pressed the bell. I could imagine him heaving himself out of a chair and waddling over to the door. In fact, he didn't appear. There was an intercom set in the brickwork and I heard his voice. "Do come in, old chap! Straight ahead ... the room at the end." The door opened automatically and I stepped into a home that was as old-fashioned as the outside. There was a hallway with black and white tiles, a ticking grandfather clock, antique paintings, a short corridor, a chandelier overhead. I have to say, I was a little disappointed. It was all so ordinary. I closed the door behind me and kept walking. A second door led into a kitchen and living room which ran the full width of the house. Windows looked out onto a small garden behind.

Smithers was sitting in an armchair, tucked away in an alcove. Even on his day off he liked to wear a suit. It seemed that he hadn't waited for me to arrive. He had a plate with three sandwiches balanced on his knee and he was sipping tea out of a porcelain cup.

"How very good to see you, Alex! Take a seat. Please help yourself. I hope you'll find something that you like."

Egg sandwiches, smoked salmon sandwiches, cheese sandwiches, a chocolate cake, scones and cream, fruit, nuts, freshly made lemonade and tea ... there was actually enough for half a dozen people piled up on a table in front of me. I sat down in the seat opposite Smithers and poured myself some tea. Part of me was wishing that I hadn't come. The house was like a theatre set. It wasn't like anywhere I imagined Smithers would live. I got the sense that something was wrong, but I couldn't work out quite what it was.

"So how are you?" Smithers asked. "I heard you nearly got killed in France."

"I was lucky," I said. I didn't want to talk about the chase down the mountain and my near collision with a speeding train.

"Did my exploding ear stud come in useful?"

"I wasn't crazy about the look," I said. "But it got me out of a lot of trouble."

"I'm glad to hear it." Suddenly Smithers was serious. "You know, I do have grave misgivings about MI6 using you," he said. "It's probably illegal and it's certainly immoral. The trouble is, you're too damned useful. You ought to try being less successful."

"If I was less successful, I'd be dead," I said.

"Yes. You have a point. But even so it was very wrong of your uncle to drag you into our world." He glanced at me disapprovingly. "Do please help yourself," he said. "Have an egg sandwich. I used to love egg sandwiches when I was a boy, especially when they were cut into triangles. I'm not quite sure why, but they taste better that shape."

"How did you get into MI6?" I asked. I did as I was told and took a couple of sandwiches.

"You shouldn't ask questions like that, Alex. You know we're not allowed to talk about ourselves." Smithers raised his cup and sipped his tea noisily. His fingers were so plump they wouldn't fit through the handle. He had to pinch it to keep it in place. "I once asked Alan Blunt what he'd got up to at the weekend and he almost had me arrested as a double agent." Smithers laughed to himself, then set the cup down. "But I can trust you, I suppose. I got into MI6 because of my grandfather, Major Arthur Smithers."

"Was he a spy too?"

"Not exactly. He was in the SOE during the war. I don't suppose you've learned about that in school..."

"The SOE." In fact we had read about it in history lessons. "The Special Operations Executive."

"That's right. You've got it in one!" Smithers was clearly pleased. "Formed in July nineteen-forty. It was just after Dunkirk. The French were finished. The Nazis were everywhere. It looked as if we'd pretty much lost the war. So Churchill formed a special unit and famously told them to 'set Europe ablaze'. That was the SOE. A lot of people didn't like them, you know, Alex – because they got up to all sorts of dirty tricks. But Churchill understood. It was a time of crisis. If we were going to win the war, we had to stop behaving like gentlemen.

"Anyway, my grandfather went to work for Station Nine which specialized in gadgets and secret weapons. One of his earliest ideas was the exploding rat."

I couldn't help smiling. I wasn't sure if Smithers was joking or not.

"I'm absolutely serious! It was a dead rat with a bomb in it. One of our agents would leave it on the floor in a German factory and someone would come along, pick it up and throw it in the furnace. And ... *boom*!" Smithers gestured with his teacup sending tea flying onto the arm of his chair. "They also hid bombs in camel droppings. The Germans would drive over them in their armoured vehicles with the same result. The SOE had lots and lots of superb ideas. There was a fountain pen that shot out tear gas. A dagger hidden inside a pencil. A one-man submarine which they tested in the reservoir in Staines. Exploding bicycle pumps, radio transmitters disguised as sewing machines ... they never stopped!

"After the war, old Arthur used to tell me all these stories and I was absolutely fascinated. Apparently he worked on super-strength itching powder, which he planned to put into the Germans' underpants. I know it sounds mad but I swear to you, it's absolutely true. You can check the history books! I was quite a small boy but I began to experiment myself. I had a cousin who used to bully me all the time and the first gadget I ever created was especially for him. It was on his ninth birthday cake. It was rather naughty of me but I'm afraid I mixed potassium chlorate with the candles. It's a highly efficient oxidizing agent and it reacted with the sugar in the icing. The result was a disaster. Instead of the birthday boy blowing out the candles, the candles blew out the birthday boy. His parents weren't at all amused.

"I also got quite a name for myself at school. I was sent to an absolutely horrible place down on the south coast and I'd only been there one week when I was caught trying to post myself back home. When that didn't work, I started making gadgets just to keep myself amused. I managed to speed up all the clocks so we got shorter lessons and I was very pleased when I smuggled a mobile telephone into the end-of-term exams."

"I'd have thought anyone could do that," I said.

"Well, yes," Smithers agreed. "But this was ten years before mobile phones were invented. After school I studied physics and chemistry at Cambridge University and I got a hundred per cent in my final exams. Unfortunately, the authorities found out that I'd X-rayed the questions a week before."

"What did they do?"

"They recommended me to MI6. That was how I got the job. I've been there ever since and I have to say I was getting quite bored until you came along. It's all very well making guns, knives, poison pills and that sort of thing but I find it much more fun making gadgets for you. The bulletproof ski suit, infrared goggles, the motorized yo-yo ... you must admit, we've had some jolly times together."

Jolly times? Smithers was always smiling when he handed out his latest gadgets but I wasn't often smiling when I used them. I was too busy trying to stay alive.

"As a matter of fact, there's a brand-new gadget in front of you right now." Smithers leaned forward, challenging me. I could see the reflection of the light, dancing in his eyes.

"What do you mean?" I asked.

"Exactly what I say. You've got to remember, Alex, at the end of the day my job is to disguise things. For example, take the Nintendo DS I gave you when you went off to deal with Herod Sayle. It was a smoke bomb. It was a bug finder. It had all sorts of uses but the main thing was ... it was invisible. Sayle saw it and he didn't look twice. And that's the point. Not every gadget I make is a weapon but it's always designed to deceive. Right now you're looking at my latest invention but you're not seeing it – which is the proof, I suppose, that it works."

What was he talking about? I was looking at something. I thought it was ordinary. But it wasn't. It was a gadget. What could it be?

Very carefully, I examined everything.

The tea. Sandwiches cut into triangles, the scones, the cake. They could all have been drugged or poisoned, although why would Smithers want to do me harm? The cake could have all the ingredients of a bomb. For all I knew, the icing could be plastic explosive.

"It's not the food," Smithers said. He placed his cup on the table beside him. It made no sound. He was watching me closely.

What else? There was a small, yellow teapot on the table. I lifted the lid. It contained only tea. I widened my search. What about the table itself? It was round, wooden. It looked antique. I reached out and ran a finger along the edge, looking for the telltale hole that might fire a bullet or an anaesthetic dart.

"You're not even close," Smithers said.

He was sitting in a high-backed chair with two arms that curved round like scrolls. Press a button and the whole thing might blast off into the air – but he had nowhere to go. He had his back to the wall and the ceiling curved over his head. A single spotlight illuminated him and now I thought about it, there was something quite theatrical about the way he presented himself. But as far as I could see, the light was ordinary. There was a picture on one wall. It looked like an oil painting, a cornfield, but I remembered visiting Smithers's office on the eleventh floor of MI6. There had been a painting that had started moving even as I examined it ... it was actually a plasma screen connected to a live satellite somewhere above the Atlantic Ocean. And for that matter, there had been a communications system hidden in the potted plant. I got up and went over to the picture. I ran a finger over the surface.

"It's not the picture."

I was beginning to get annoyed. Smithers was still sitting there. In fact he hadn't left the chair since I had come in. He was looking very smug, one leg crossed over the other. I noticed he was wearing bright red socks. "All right, Mr Smithers," I said. "You win. Whatever your latest invention is, I can't see it."

Smithers laughed. "I owe you an apology, Alex. I really wanted to have tea with you but in the end it wasn't possible."

"What are you talking about?"

"Mrs Jones sent me to Singapore. A last-minute assignment. I'm there now."

"Wait..."

"Let yourself out, old chap. I'll make it up to you when I get back." Smithers reached out and pressed something I couldn't see. A second later, he flickered and disappeared. So did the chair he'd been sitting in.

That was when I realized he'd never been there. I'd been having tea with a hologram. I wasn't sure whether to be angry or amused. But at least the cake was real. I took it home for Jack.

CHRISTMAS AT GUNPOINT

My uncle, Ian Rider, always told me that he worked in international banking. Why did I believe him? Bankers don't usually spend weeks or even months away from home, returning with strange scars and bruises they are reluctant to explain. They don't receive phone calls in the middle of the night from people who refuse to give their name and then disappear at the drop of a hat. And how many of them are proficient in kick-boxing and karate, speak three languages and spend hours at the gym, keeping themselves in perfect physical shape?

Ian Rider was a secret agent; a spy. From the day he left Cambridge University with a first in maths and Arabic, he had worked for the Special Operations division of MI6. Just about everything he ever told me was a lie, but I believed him because I had no parents and had lived with him all my life. And, I suppose, because when you're thirteen years old you believe what adults say.

But there was one occasion when I came very close to discovering the truth. It happened one Christmas, at the ski resort of Gunpoint, Colorado.

Although I didn't know it at the time, this was going to be the last holiday we would have together. By the following spring, Ian would have been killed on a mission, investigating the Stormbreaker computers being manufactured in Cornwall. That was just a couple of months after my fourteenth birthday. That was when my entire life spun out of control and I became a spy myself.

Gunpoint had been named after the man who first settled there, a gold-digger called Jeremiah Gun. He'd had a shack up in the mountains and had cheerfully drunk himself to death, leaving behind a handful of gold nuggets and his name. Gunpoint was about fifty miles north of Aspen, and if you've ever skied in America you'll know the set-up. There was a central village with gas fires burning late into the night, mulled wine and toasted marshmallows, and shops with prices as high as the mountains surrounding them.

We'd booked into a hotel, the Granary, which was on the very edge of the village, about a five-minute walk to the main ski lift. The two of us shared a suite of rooms on the second floor. We each had our own bedroom, opening onto a shared living space with a balcony that ran round the side of the building. The Granary was one of those brand-new places designed to look a hundred years old, with big stone fireplaces, woven rugs and moose heads on the walls. I hoped the heads were fake, but they probably weren't.

For the first couple of days we were on our own. The snow was excellent. There had been a heavy fall just before we arrived, but at the same time the sun was shining and the weather was unusually warm, so we were talking the sweetest powder snow and lifts with no queues. We warmed up with a few gentle runs – greens and blues – but we were soon racing each other down the dizzyingly steep runs high up over Gunpoint itself.

It was on the third day that things changed. It began with two new arrivals who moved into the room next door; a father and a daughter. She was just a couple of years older than me. We met outside the lift – the elevator she would say – and by the time we reached the ground floor I already knew quite a bit about her.

Her name was Sahara. Her dad lived and worked in Washington DC – she told me that he was "something in government" and I guessed she was being deliberately vague. Her mother was a lawyer in New York. The two of them were divorced and Sahara had to share Christmases between them. She was very pretty, with long black hair and blue eyes, only an inch taller than me despite the age gap. She'd been skiing all her life – and she was completely fearless. And, unlike me, she had her own boots and skis. At the time my feet were growing too fast and, as usual, I'd had to rent.

Sahara Sands. Her father was Robert Sands, with silver hair, silver glasses and a laptop that never seemed to leave his side. He spent every afternoon in his room, working. Sahara didn't seem to mind. She was used to it, and anyway, now she had Ian and me.

Two more people came to the Granary on the same day as Sahara and her dad. They were sharing a smaller, twin-bed room across the corridor and somehow I knew they weren't here for fun. Maybe it would have helped if they'd tried to smile. That was how I noticed them in the first place, sitting in the bar with two glasses of water, neither of them drinking, not even talking. In fact the two of them never seemed to be far away, although not once did they come over and speak to us. They were both in their late twenties, smartly dressed and very fit. They could have graduated from the same college. The third time I saw them, they were having breakfast. I asked Ian if he thought they were lawyers. He laughed.

"I don't think so, Alex." Suddenly he was serious. He nodded at them, sitting together on the other side of the restaurant. "Try again."

I looked at them more carefully. They were wearing identical ski jackets. They were two tables away from Sahara and her father, not exactly watching them but keeping them in sight. I remembered seeing them on the slopes, about the same distance away. Suddenly I got it. "Are they bodyguards?"

"Better. At a guess, I'd say they're American secret service."

I blinked. "How do you know?"

"Well, their clothes are American. I haven't seen them touch a drop of alcohol and they're watching everyone who comes into the room. But more to the point, they're both carrying guns."

"Under their jackets?"

Ian shook his head. "You could never draw a gun out of a ski jacket in time. They've got ankle holsters. Take a look the next time they're in the locker room." He glanced at me over his coffee. "You have to notice these things, Alex. Whenever you meet someone, you have to check them out ... all the details. People tell a story the moment they walk into a room. You can read them."

He was always saying stuff like that to me. I used to think he was just talking, passing the time. It was only much later that I realized he was preparing me, quietly following a plan that had begun almost the day I was born.

"Are they here with Robert Sands?" I asked.

"What do you think?"

I nodded. "They're always hanging around. And Sahara says her dad works in government."

"Then maybe he needs protection." Ian smiled. "I'm going to set you a task, Alex. Just for fun. I want you to find out their names by the end of the week." He paused. "And the make of their guns."

But the next day I had forgotten the conversation. It had snowed again. There must have been twenty centimetres on the ground, and it was bulging out over the roofs of the hotel like over-stuffed duvets. Sahara and I switched to snowboards and spent about five hours on the chutes, bomb drops and powder stashes at the bowl area high up over Bear Creek.

We had lunch together at a barn-like place high up in the mountains. I had a stew. She ate a salad. She was only sixteen but the waiter didn't seem to notice when she produced a credit card and insisted on paying for both our meals. "It's Dad's," she explained. "He hates to think of me going hungry."

"So what exactly does your dad do?" I asked her.

"I told you. He works for the government. You shouldn't ask questions about him. He never talks about his work." She changed the subject. "Where are your mum and dad?"

"I never knew them," I told her. "They died when I was small."

"That's terrible. I'm sorry." She looked genuinely upset. "I miss my mother a lot when she's not around but at least I get to see her. I wish my parents had stayed together. Divorce is such a stupid idea." She'd bought herself a can of Diet Coke and flicked it open. "You ski really well," she went on. "There's a double black diamond we could try after lunch, if you like. It's called Breakneck Pass and it's meant to be wild. My dad told me to keep away but he doesn't need to know."

"No thanks." I shook my head. "I don't want a

broken leg. Let's take it easy."

"Whatever you say, Alex." She winked at me, but I could tell she was disappointed.

We skied together for the rest of the afternoon and at half past three, with the sun already dipping behind the mountains, we decided to call it a day. We were both bruised and exhausted, soaked with sweat and melted snow. Sahara hurried off to meet her dad for a hot chocolate. I went back to the Granary on my own. I got changed in the locker room and dropped off my board. Then I had a swim in the hotel pool – twenty lengths without stopping. Even at that age, I tried to keep myself fit. After that I went up to the reception area, thinking that I'd wait for my uncle in front of the fire but when the lift door opened, I saw he was already there. He was sitting on the corner of a sofa wearing jeans and a jumper. I was about to call out to him – but then I stopped. I knew at once that something was wrong.

It's not easy to explain, but he had never looked like this before. He was usually laid-back and relaxed but now he was completely silent and tense in a way that was almost animal. Ian had dark brown eyes – people say I inherited them – but it was as if a shutter had come down. They were cold and colourless. He hadn't noticed me. His attention was focused on the reception desk and the man who was checking into the hotel.

People tell a story, Ian had said. *You can read*

them. Looking at the man at the reception desk, I tried to do just that.

He was wearing a black roll-neck jumper with dark trousers and a gold Rolex watch, heavy on his wrist. He had blond hair – an intense yellow, cut short. It almost looked painted on. He was around thirty years old, with a pockmarked face and a lazy smile. I could hear him talking to the receptionist. He had a Bronx accent. So much for chapter one. What else could I read in him? His skin was unusually pale. In fact it was almost white, as if he had spent most of his life indoors. He worked out; I could see the muscles bulging under his sleeves. And he had very bad teeth. That was strange. Americans wealthy enough to stay in a hotel like this would have invested more in dental work.

"You're on the fourth floor, Mr da Silva," the receptionist said. "Enjoy your stay."

The man had brought a cheap suitcase with him. That was also unusual in the land of Gucci and Louis Vuitton. He picked it up and disappeared into the lift.

I walked further into the reception area and Ian saw me. At once, he relaxed. But he knew I had been watching him.

"Is everything OK?" I asked.

"Yes."

"Who was that?"

"The man who just checked in? I don't know."

Ian shook his head as if trying to dismiss the whole thing. "I thought I knew him from somewhere. How was Bear Creek?"

He obviously didn't want to talk about it, so I went up to the room and watched a film before dinner. I'd brought schoolwork with me but so far I hadn't even looked at it. I was always putting it off until the next day. At half past seven, I made my way back downstairs. As I left my room, I noticed one of the secret service men coming out of a doorway across the corridor. He walked towards the lifts without saying anything to me. Sahara and her father weren't around.

Ian and I ate dinner together and everything seemed normal. We talked about school, about skiing, about the news. Ian always wanted me to know about current affairs, which I suppose was also part of my training. He ordered half a carafe of wine for himself and a Coke for me. I must have been more tired than I thought because at around ten o'clock I found myself yawning. He suggested I go up and get an early night.

"What about you?" I asked.

"Oh ... I might get a breath of air. I'll follow you up later."

I left him and went back to the suite, and that was when I discovered I didn't have the electronic card that would open the door. I must have left it on the table. Annoyed with myself, I went back to the dining room. There was no sign of it and

Ian wasn't there either. Remembering what he had said, I followed him outside.

There was a courtyard round the side of the hotel, covered with snow, a frozen fountain in the middle. It was surrounded by walls on three sides, with the hotel roofs – also snow-covered – slanting steeply down. The whole area was lit by a full moon, which shone down like a prison searchlight.

And there he was.

Ian Rider and the man who called himself da Silva were locked together, standing like some bizarre statue in the courtyard. They were fighting for control of a single gun, which was clasped in their hands, high above their heads. I could see the strain on both their faces. But what made the scene even more surreal was that neither of them were making any sound. In fact they were barely moving. Both were focused on the gun. Whichever brought it down would be able to use it on the other.

I called out. It was a stupid thing to do. I could have got my uncle killed. But both men turned to look at me, and it was Ian who took advantage of the interruption. He let go of the gun and slammed his elbow into da Silva's stomach, then bent his arm up, the side of his hand scything the other man's wrist. I had been learning karate for six years and recognized the perfectly executed sideways block.

The gun flew out of the man's hand, slid across the snow and came to rest just in front of the fountain.

"Get out of here, Alex!" my uncle shouted.

It took him less than two seconds but it was enough to lose him the advantage. Da Silva lashed out, the ball of his fist pounding into Ian's chest, winding him. He followed through with a vicious roundhouse kick. My uncle tried to avoid it, but the snow, the slippery surface, didn't help. He was thrown off his feet and went crashing down. Da Silva stopped and caught his breath. His mouth was twisted in an ugly sneer, his teeth grey in the moonlight. He ran a hand through his blond hair, smoothing it back. He knew the fight was over. He had won.

That was when I acted. I dived forward, throwing myself onto my stomach and sliding across the ice. My own momentum carried me as far as the gun. I snatched it up, noticing for the first time that it was fitted with a silencer. It was much heavier than I had expected. Da Silva stared at me as I brought it round, aiming it at him.

"No!" My uncle uttered the single word quietly. It didn't matter what the circumstances were. He didn't want me to kill a man.

Da Silva stared at me. Even at that moment, I saw the contempt in his eyes. As far as he was concerned, I was just a kid, holding a gun. He didn't think I had the nerve to use it.

I pulled the trigger. I felt the gun jerk in my hand. There was no noise, other than a soft ripping sound as the silencer did its work. Even so, the power of the weapon shocked me. I emptied the chamber, one bullet after another, all seven of them. The recoil hurt my wrist. But I wasn't shooting at da Silva. At the last moment I had lifted the gun and I was firing into the air above him, over his head. At last it was over. The gun was empty. All the bullets had gone.

Da Silva stood where he was, unharmed. Very slowly, he reached behind him and took out a second gun. My uncle was still on the ground; there was nothing he could do. I lay where I was, my breath coming out in white clouds. Da Silva smiled. I could see him trying to make up his mind which one of us he was going to kill first.

There was a gentle rumble and a tonne of snow slid off the roof directly above him. It was exactly what I'd hoped for. I had cut a dotted line with the bullets and the weight of the snow had done the rest for me. Da Silva just had time to look up before the avalanche hit him. I think he opened his mouth – either to swear or to scream – but it was too late. The snow made almost no sound, just a soft *thwump* as it hit. In a second he had gone. Buried under a huge white curtain.

My uncle got to his feet. I did the same. The two of us looked at each other.

"Alex..." he began.

"Do you think we should dig him up?" I asked.

He shook his head. "No. Let's leave him to chill out."

*   *   *

"Who was he? Why did he have a gun? Why were you fighting him?"

There were so many things I wanted to know when we finally got back to our room. Ian had phoned the police. They were already on the way, he told me. He would talk to them when they arrived. The gun that he had taken from da Silva was beside him. I could still feel the weight of it in my hand. My wrist was aching from the recoil.

"Forget about it, Alex," he said. "He had nothing to do with me. Da Silva – that's not his real name, by the way – is a wanted criminal and I just happened to recognize him when I saw him outside the hotel. He's been involved in bank fraud."

"Bank fraud?" I could hardly believe it.

"That's right. I was out for a walk and I met him quite by chance. I challenged him, which was pretty stupid of me now I think about it. He pulled out the gun ... and the rest you saw." Ian smiled. "I expect he'll have frozen solid by now. At least he won't be needing a morgue."

If I'd thought a little more, I'd have realized that none of it added up. When I had come upon the two men, they were fighting for control of a single gun. They had dropped it, and then da Silva had produced a second gun of his own. So logic should have told me that the first gun actually belonged to my uncle. But why would he have brought a gun with him on a skiing holiday? How could he even have got it through airport security? It was such an unlikely thought – Ian carrying a firearm – that it had never occurred to me, and I accepted his story because there was no alternative.

Anyway, I was exhausted. It had been a long day and I was glad to crawl into bed. There were all sorts of questions tugging at my mind but I ignored them and fell asleep almost immediately.

Ian was surprisingly quiet the following morning and it occurred to me that he hadn't even thanked me for what I had done the night before. Over breakfast he told me he wouldn't be coming skiing. Apparently he'd spoken to the police when they'd finally arrived, and they wanted him to come to their offices in Cale and tell them as much as he could about da Silva and the fight outside the hotel. There was further bad news too. Somehow da Silva had dug his way out of the great mound of snow. He had got away.

"I would have thought he'd been flattened," Ian said over boiled eggs and grilled bacon. He never ate anything fried. "But he managed to tunnel his way out like a mole. I'm annoyed with myself, if you want the truth. I should have checked."

"Do you think he'll come back?" I asked. The thought made me a little nervous.

Ian shook his head. "I doubt it. He knows I recognized him and he's probably out of Colorado by now. Maybe he's even left the States. He won't want to hang around."

"How long do you think you'll be?"

"A few hours. Don't let this spoil the holiday, Alex. Just put it out of your mind. You can ski with Sahara today. From the way you two are getting on, I'd say she'll be glad to have you on your own."

I didn't know what he meant by that but I didn't argue. In fact, when I knocked on her door an hour later, Sahara wasn't there. It was opened by her father, Robert Sands.

"I'm sorry, Alex," he said. "You're just too late. She left a few minutes ago; she's got a lesson this morning. But she'll probably call in later – I can ask her to meet you."

"Thanks," I said. "I'll be up at Bear Creek."

He nodded and closed the door, and as he did so I looked over his shoulder and saw that he wasn't alone. The two young men were with him; one sitting on the sofa, the other standing by the window. The secret service men. I could see his desk too. The laptop that I'd noticed before was there, surrounded by a pile of papers. Robert Sands was meant to be on holiday but from the look of it, the work never stopped. I wouldn't have been surprised if he'd taken the laptop on the slopes with him.

I went downstairs to the locker room and a few minutes later was clumping out to the ski lift with my skis over my shoulder and my poles dragging behind me. I didn't much like the idea of skiing on my own and wondered if Sahara would even be able to find me ... if she came looking. There were a lot of people around, and the thing about skiers is that they all look more or less the same. On the other hand, I was wearing a bright green jacket – a North Face Free Thinker. She'd already joked about the colour and I was sure she'd recognize it a mile away.

But as it turned out, I saw her before she saw me. The nearest lift to the hotel was a gondola, taking twenty people at a time up to an area called Black Ridge, about a thousand metres higher up. Sahara was right at the front of the queue, standing between two men, and I could see at once that something was wrong. She wasn't smiling. There was something like panic in her eyes. I examined the two men. I had never seen them before but, whoever they were, they certainly weren't ski instructors. They were standing very close to her, sandwiching her between them like they didn't want to let her slip away. One of them was round-faced, fat and white. The other looked Korean. They were both big men – even with the ski suits I got a sense of over-worked muscle. Sahara was scared, I saw that too. And a moment later I saw why.

A third man had gone ahead of them and was waiting inside the gondola. I only glimpsed his face behind the glass but I recognized it instantly. It was da Silva. His hood was up and he was wearing sunglasses, but his pale skin and bad teeth were unmistakable. He was waiting while the other men joined him with the girl.

I started towards them, but I was already too late. Sahara was inside the gondola. The doors slid shut and the whole thing jerked forward, rising up over the snow. I think Sahara caught sight of me just as she was swept away. Her eyes widened and she jerked her head in the direction of the hotel. The message was obvious. *Get help!*

I didn't need telling twice. Sahara was being kidnapped in broad daylight. It was crazy but there could be no doubt about it.

I turned round and began to run.

I was running to get help.

If this had happened six months later, if I'd been older and more experienced, I might have tried to do something myself. After all, the three men didn't know I was there. They weren't expecting trouble. I might have been able to follow them, taking the next gondola and somehow tracking them down. It might even have been possible to stop the gondola, leaving them dangling in mid-air. But this was before I'd been recruited by MI6 and given training with the SAS. I was thirteen years old and on my own in an American ski resort. I wasn't even certain about what I'd just seen. Was Sahara really being kidnapped? And if so, why? According to what my uncle had told me, the man called da Silva was involved in some sort of bank fraud. What possible interest could he have in her?

But then I remembered. Robert Sands was her

253

father. He worked for the government and travelled with his own entourage of secret service men. This wasn't about Sahara. It was about him – and he was the one I had to find.

I stabbed my skis and poles into a mound of snow and ran back into the hotel as fast as I could – not easy in ski boots. Fortunately, it was only a short distance away. You were meant to take your boots off in the locker room downstairs but I just clomped right in, through the reception area, into the lift and up to the second floor. I went to my own room first. It occurred to me that my uncle might not have left yet for the police station and if he was there he would know what to do.

I was out of luck. The room was empty. I turned round and was about to go next door, which was where Sahara and her father were staying, when I heard someone talking. I recognized the voice. It was Robert Sands. He was standing outside on the terrace, talking into a phone. Our window was open and I went over and looked out. Robert had his back to me but I could tell at once that something was wrong. He was completely still and his whole body was rigid, as if he'd been electrocuted. I heard him speak.

"Where is she? What have you done with her?"

Da Silva. It had to be him. He'd taken the girl and now he was talking to the dad, making his demands. What did he want? Money? Somehow, I didn't think so. The Granary was comfortable but it wasn't the most expensive hotel in the resort by a long way and if you were into the money-with-menaces business, there were plenty of billionaires to choose from: movie stars, Russian oligarchs and so on.

Being careful not to make any sound, I leaned forward so that I could see more.

"All right." Sands spoke slowly and his voice was ice cold. I could see his breath frosting in the air. "I'll bring it and I'll come alone. But I'm warning you—"

That was as far as he got. Whoever he was talking to must have cut him off. He lowered the phone, staring at it as if it were somehow responsible.

As far as I was concerned, that should have been it. Robert Sands had two secret service men somewhere in the hotel and this was none of my business. But I couldn't just leave it there. I liked Sahara and in a funny way I felt as if this was all my fault. It struck me now that I could have done something more when I saw her being loaded into the gondola. At the very least I could have shouted and raised the alarm. I told myself that I wasn't going to get involved, that I was being stupid. But I still couldn't stop myself. When Robert Sands came out of his room a few minutes later, I was waiting round the corner, watching him go.

I followed him downstairs. He had changed into his ski suit with his goggles around his neck and – here was the weird thing – he was carrying the laptop I had seen on the desk. It was sticking out of a black nylon bag. As he went downstairs he pushed it inside and fastened the zip. There was no sign of the secret service men – but I'd heard what he said on the phone: he wasn't going to involve them. Wherever he was heading, he was going there alone.

I waited outside the boot room, then followed him across the front of the hotel to the gondola, picking up my skis and poles on the way. He had his skis too. The nylon bag with the laptop was hanging across his chest, slightly hidden under one arm. There weren't many people at the gondola now. Afternoon ski school had begun and the various classes were already practising their snow ploughs on the lower slopes. I watched Sahara's dad hold his lift pass out to be scanned, waited a few moments then did the same. By now I'd pulled up my hood and drawn my goggles down over my face. We got into the same gondola and stood only a few inches apart. Even if he looked in my direction, I knew he wouldn't recognize me but of course he wasn't taking any notice of anyone around him. He looked sick with worry. His eyes were fixed on the mountain peaks high above.

Five minutes later we got out at Black Ridge, a sort of wide shelf in the mountains, with another three lifts climbing in different directions. He put on his skis and I did the same. I knew that Robert Sands was a strong skier but I reckoned I could keep up with him no matter where he went.

I didn't need to worry. He only skied as far as the nearest lift – a double chair – and took it up to Gun Hill. There was just one more lift that went up from here. It led to an area called the Needle. It was as high as you could get, so high that even on a bright day like today the clouds still rubbed against the surface of the snow. Once again I went with him, just a few chairs behind.

Da Silva was waiting for him at the Needle.

I saw Robert get off his chair and look around him. By the time I arrived, a few seconds later, he had already moved away. I slid over to one side, keeping close to the cabin where the lift attendant sat all day, watching people get on and off. From here I saw Robert Sands ski down about thirty metres to a flat area with a sign marked by two black diamonds. I knew exactly where we were. This was Breakneck Pass, the run that Sahara had mentioned only the day before. The name tells you everything you need to know. From this point, it was the only way down, a vicious, incredibly steep run of ice and moguls that started with a stomach-churning, zigzagging chute, continued along the edge of a precipice and then plunged into a wood, with no obvious way between the trees. Not many people took it on and I'd had no hesitation in saying no when Sahara suggested it. My uncle said you'd need nerves of steel to take on Breakneck. Or a death wish.

And there they all were, waiting with da Silva,

the fat man and the Korean man I had seen at the gondola. Sahara was still trapped between them. She was still scared. Nobody could see me. I was thirty metres higher up, and the clouds and snow flurries chasing along the mountain ridge formed a screen between me and them. I wiped the ice off my goggles and watched as the scene played out. Robert Sands said something. Sahara started forward, but the two men held her back. Now it was da Silva's turn. He was smiling. I saw him point at the nylon bag with the laptop. Sands hesitated, but not for very long. He lifted it off his shoulder and held it in front of him as if weighing it, then handed it over. Da Silva nodded to his companions. They let Sahara go and she slithered – I wouldn't even call it skiing – across to her dad. He put an arm around her. The business was finished.

Except that it wasn't. I hadn't decided what I was going to do – until I did it. Suddenly I found myself racing down the slope, my legs bent and my shoulders low, my poles tucked under my arms, picking up as much speed as I could. Nobody was looking my way. They had no idea I was there until it was too late. The next moment I was right in the middle of them, moving so fast that I must have been no more than a blur. Da Silva was still holding the laptop. I snatched it out of his hand and kept going, over the lip and down the first stretch of Breakneck Pass.

The next few seconds were a nightmare as I

found myself falling off the edge of the mountain, poling like crazy to avoid the first moguls and only just managing to get the strap over my head so that the computer was out of my way, dangling behind my back. I nearly fell three or four times. If I'd had even half a second to think what I was doing, I'd probably have lost control and broken both my legs. But instinct had taken over. I was twenty metres down the chute and heading for the next segment before da Silva even knew what had happened.

He didn't hang around. I heard a shout and somehow I knew, without looking back, that the three men were after me. Well, that was sort of what I'd expected. Da Silva wanted the computer. Sands had given it to him. So he and his daughter weren't needed any more. I was the target now. All I had to do was get down to the bottom, which couldn't be more than a couple of thousand metres from here. It was just a pity there was no one else around. If I could get back into a crowd, I'd be safe.

I heard a crack. A bullet slammed into the snow inches from my left ski. Who had fired? The answer was obvious, but even so I found it hard to believe. Was it really possible to ski in these conditions and bring out guns at the same time? The snow was horrible, wind-packed and hard as metal. My skis were grinding as they carried me over the surface. I was grateful that my uncle had insisted on choosing my equipment for me; I was using Nordica twin tips, wide under the foot and seriously stiff. It had taken me a while to get used to them, but the whole point was that they were built for speed. Right now they seemed to be flying, and as I carved and pivoted around the moguls I almost wanted to laugh. I didn't think anyone in the world would be able to catch up with me.

I was wrong. Either da Silva and his men had spent a long time training for this or they'd been experts to begin with. I came to a gully and risked a glance back. There were about thirty metres between us and they were gaining fast. Worse still, they didn't even seem to be exerting themselves. They had that slow, fluid quality you may have seen at the Winter Olympics, when the best skiers in the world take to the slopes, and yet the distance between us was closing all the time. Suddenly I knew that there was nothing to laugh about. I cursed myself for getting involved in the first place. Why had I done it? This had nothing to do with me.

I made it to the woodland and heaved a sigh of relief, my breath frosting in front of my goggles. At least the trunks and branches would make it harder for anyone to take another shot at me. I was lucky I'd done plenty of tree skiing with Ian. I knew that I had to keep the speed up – otherwise I'd lose control. Go too fast, though, and I'd risk impaling myself on a branch. The secret is balance. Or luck. Or something.

I didn't really know where I was going. Everything was just streaks of green and brown and white. I was getting tired. Branches were slashing at my face. My legs were already aching with all the twists and turns. And the laptop was half strangling me, threatening to pull me over backwards. One of my skis almost snagged on a root. I shifted my body weight and cried out as my left shoulder slammed into a trunk – it felt like I'd broken a bone. I almost lost control there and then. One of the men shouted something. I couldn't see any of them but it sounded as if they were right behind me, inches away. That gave me new strength. I shot forward onto a miniature ramp and before I knew it, I'd left the ground, propelled up into the air through a tangle of branches that scratched my face and tore at my goggles.

I was in the clear. The wood disappeared behind me and I fell into a wide, empty area. But I knew before I landed that I'd lost my balance and that this was going to end badly. Sure enough, my legs were pulled in different directions, my skis slipped away and there was a sickening crash as I found myself diving headlong into the snow. My entire body shuddered. I couldn't see. I was sliding helplessly in a blinding white explosion. My skis released themselves and were torn off my feet. I was aware that the surface underneath me had changed. It was smoother and more slippery. I was moving faster. I stretched out a hand and tried to stop myself, but there was no purchase at all. Where was I? At last I slowed down and stopped.

I was breathless and confused. I was sure I must have broken several of my bones. The laptop was round my throat and it almost felt as if the ground was cracking up where I lay. No, it really was cracking up! As I struggled to my knees, I realized what had happened. I had gone spectacularly off-piste. There was a lake on the west side of the mountain – they called it Coldwater Creek. I had landed right next to it and managed to slide in. I was on the surface of the ice. And if that wasn't bad enough, the ice was breaking under my weight.

Da Silva and the two men had stopped on the edge of the lake. All three were facing me. The Korean man and the fat man both had guns. My goggles had come off in the fall and da Silva recognized me.

"You!" He spat out the single word. He didn't sound friendly.

There were about ten metres between us. Nobody moved.

"Give me the laptop," he demanded.

I said nothing. If I gave him the laptop, he would kill me. That much I knew.

"Give me it or I will take it," he continued.

There was the sound of something cracking. A black line appeared, snaking its way towards my foot. I steadied myself, trying not to breathe. I wondered how much longer the ice would hold. If it broke I would disappear for ever. There was no question of swimming for safety. Five minutes in the freezing water and I would die.

"Why don't you come and get it?" I said.

Da Silva nodded. The Korean man stepped forward. He was trying to reach me and I could see he wasn't too happy about the idea. He might have been chosen because he was the lightest of the three but he was an adult, twice as big as me, and he wasn't light enough. On the third step, the ice broke. One minute he was there, the next he was gone, his arms floundering and his face filling with panic as he tried to grip the sides of the hole. His breath came out as great mushrooms of white steam. He tried to scream but no sound came out. His lungs must already have frozen.

He had taken a gun with him. They only had one other. Da Silva snatched it from the fat man – he had already decided he was going to risk his weight on the ice – and pointed it at me.

"Give me the laptop," he said, "or I will shoot you where you stand."

"What will you do then?" I shouted back. I took another step, moving away from the edge of the lake. The ice creaked. I could feel it straining underneath my feet. "You can't reach me. You're too heavy."

"Maybe. But the ice will harden in the night. I'll return for the laptop tomorrow."

"You think it'll still be working? A whole day and a night out here?"

"I'll take that risk!" Da Silva didn't want to argue any more. I could almost see his finger tightening on the trigger. I had absolutely no doubt that he was about to kill me. "I'm telling you, you little swine ... this is your last chance."

"Alex ... get down. Now!"

My uncle's voice came out of the wood. As da Silva spun round, I dropped low, hoping the sudden movement wouldn't crack the ice. At the same time there were two shots. Da Silva had fired first. He'd missed. My uncle hadn't. Da Silva seemed to throw his own gun away. He had been hit in the shoulder. He sank to his knees, gripping the wound. Blood, bright red in the morning sun, seeped through his fingers.

Ian Rider appeared. I had no idea how he'd managed to follow us down from the Needle. I'd never so much as glimpsed him. But that must have been what he'd done. He skied to the very edge of the lake and spoke to me, his eyes never leaving da Silva or the other man.

"Are you all right, Alex?" he asked.

"Yes."

"Come back onto dry land. Don't say anything else. Just give me the laptop, then get your skis back on."

I did as he told me. I'd begun to tremble. I'd like to say it was just the cold, but I'm not sure that would be true.

"Who are you?" da Silva demanded. I'd never heard a voice so full of hate.

"You two can take off your skis. Both of you..." My uncle raised the gun. The two men took off their skis while I was putting on mine. He gestured. They knew what to do. Da Silva and the fat man threw their skis into the lake. Meanwhile, the Korean man had managed to pull himself out. He was lying there shivering, blue with cold.

Both my skis were snapped into place. I was ready to leave.

"Enjoy the rest of the day, gentlemen," my uncle said. He gestured at me and we set off together. Da Silva and the others would have to walk down. It would take them hours – and I had no doubt that the police would be waiting for them when they arrived.

And that was it really. What you might call my first mission.

Sahara and her dad left that day. I thought I'd never see them again, but in fact I met Sahara a couple of years later, and that was when she told me that her father worked in the office of the Secretary of State for Defence. His hard drive had contained classified information about an American agent working in the Middle East. If it had leaked, it would have put countless lives in danger – as well as being a huge embarrassment for the US government. Someone must have paid da Silva to steal it, but when that failed he had engineered the kidnap and the attempted ransom. Something like that, anyway.

I never did find out how my uncle had arrived just in time to rescue me. He said it was just luck, that he'd seen da Silva on the gondola and followed him up the mountain while I was racing back to the hotel. Maybe that was true. He also said the gun he'd used was the same gun he'd snatched in the fight the night before. That certainly wasn't true. The funny thing was we hardly talked about it again while we were in Colorado. It was as if there was an unspoken agreement between us. *Ask me no questions and I'll tell you no lies.*

When I look back on it, I wonder how stupid I could have been not to see what Ian Rider really was. A spy. But then again, I didn't know what I was either – what he'd made me. I remember he pretended to be very angry that I'd put myself in danger. But at the same time I could see that secretly he was pleased. He'd been training me all my life to follow in his footsteps and what happened at Gunpoint had shown him I was ready.

And that was just as well. In a very short while, I'd need to be.

SPY TRAP

NIGHT NURSE

Alex Rider opened his eyes.

He was lying in bed in a room that he didn't recognize. White ceiling. White walls. A single door opposite him. Two windows. A polished, wooden floor. No carpet.

How had he got here? And where, exactly, was he? He lay completely still for a moment, fighting back the first stirrings of fear, trying to work out what had happened to him. He thought back to the evening before. It must surely have been evening or night when he went to bed, but he couldn't remember anything about it. Had Jack been there? Had he been in his room, doing his homework? Looking back into his memory, he saw nothing. It was as if he were standing against a blank screen that was concealing his entire world behind it. His heart was beating faster now. Something was very, very wrong. He didn't even know what day of the week it was. He could have been here for an hour. He could have been here for a year.

He tried to push back the covers and stand up but that was when he made his next, unpleasant discovery. He was too weak to move. He looked down and saw that a needle had been inserted into his arm, kept in place with a neat strip of surgical tape. It was connected to a transparent pipe. There was a plastic bag dangling over his head, feeding him with some sort of colourless liquid, drip by drip.

He was in a hospital or a clinic of some kind – but with no knowledge of what had brought him here.

A car accident?

A bullet wound?

This was bad. Very bad.

Forcing himself to keep calm, Alex flexed his fingers and then his toes. He could feel them moving. That was something. Carefully, he shifted himself in the bed, trying to sense if he had any injuries. As far as he could tell, he was in one piece with no broken bones.

He turned his head and examined his surroundings more carefully – but there was little to add to what he had already seen. The room was perfectly square and very ordinary with no pictures on the wall, nothing to make it more welcoming. There were two wooden chairs and a cupboard but no other furniture. He could make out treetops on the other side of the windows and to one side, a stretch of water that was a greenish blue. It didn't look like the sea. It must be a lake or reservoir. The sun was shining. There was no sound of any traffic, which suggested that he wasn't in London. But he was in England. He was sure of it. There was something about the quality of the light and the shapes of the leaves that suggested he hadn't left the country. This was August, the end of the summer. At least, it had been the last time he had looked.

He became aware of something pressing against his head. He managed to lift a hand – the one that wasn't connected to the tube – and felt with his fingertips. There was a bandage running all the way round, across his hairline and over his ears. So he was injured, after all. He wished now that there was a mirror in the room. He badly wanted to look at himself. If he had been in an accident, how seriously had he been hurt?

He lay back, his head sinking into the pillows. Part of him wanted to call out for help and he might have done, except that his mouth was so dry and his heart was beating so fast that he doubted he would be able to find his voice. Instead, he looked around him for a bell or anything he might use to summon help. There was nothing. A glass and a jug of water stood on a white bedside table. What had happened to his clothes? He was wearing striped pyjamas that he had never seen before. Alex never wore pyjamas in bed – he preferred shorts and a T-shirt. The material felt heavy against his skin. He was half tied down by the sheets and the blankets. There was an emptiness in his stomach and he wondered how long it had been since he'd had something to eat. That was another thing. His watch was no longer on his wrist and there was no clock in the room.

Then, quite suddenly, the door opened and a woman came in, dressed in the white uniform and cap of a hospital nurse. She was small and quite elderly with grey hair, tightly packed around her head, and a thin, curved nose. The way she walked and the glint in her eyes reminded Alex somehow of a bird. Glancing at her fingers, he saw that they were long and thin too. Like talons or claws.

She beamed, seeing that Alex was awake. "Oh! So you're back with us again!" she exclaimed. She spoke with a heavy Scottish accent and a high-pitched sing-song voice. She had a habit of emphasizing some of her words as if they were the ones she most wanted Alex to hear. "The doctor *will* be pleased. How are you feeling, my dear?"

"Where am I?" Alex demanded.

"Don't you *worry* now. You're among friends. I know this must all feel a bit strange to you, but the *main* thing is you've woken up."

"You haven't answered my question." Alex knew he was being rude but for some reason, the more pleasant the nurse sounded, the angrier he became.

She didn't seem at all put out. She was carrying a tray with a thermometer, a flannel and two little plastic cups: one with water and the other with two pills. She set them all down on a table and reached for Alex's pulse. "You're in Wiltshire," she explained. "On the edge of Salisbury Plain. The building we're in is called *Bellhanger Abbey*. It really was an abbey once, until we took it over. By 'we', I mean MI6. We turned it into a *hospital* and clinic. My name is Wendy McDarling but you can call me Nurse Wendy." She had been checking his pulse rate. Now she released him. "You're very fit," she said. "I can see you look after yourself, my dear. You're in *excellent* shape." She paused. "But you don't remember what happened?"

"No." Alex's voice fell. He hated having to admit it. He felt completely helpless.

"You were in an accident," the nurse explained. She reached for the thermometer, gave it a quick shake, then slipped it into Alex's mouth before he could protest. "You were on your way to London, on the motorway. We're not quite *sure* what happened. There's an investigation going on even as we speak. But we think a truck went out of control and crashed into you. Anyway, the car you were in was forced off the road and you got a *nasty* bang on your head. That's probably what's affected your memory. You were brought here to Bellhanger Abbey to be looked after. This is a private hospital ... *very* private. When MI6 operatives come back from their missions, they often have to spend time here. We look after them and

273

we don't let them leave until they're as good as new!" She drew the thermometer out and checked it. "That's excellent!" she announced. "Your temperature is normal."

"I want my phone," Alex said. "I want to call Jack."

"Is Jack a school friend of yours?"

"No. She looks after me."

The nurse sighed. "I'm afraid your mobile was destroyed in the car."

"Then can I use another phone?"

"You'll need to see the doctor first. Meanwhile, I'm going to ask you to take *these*." She held out the pills.

Alex looked at them suspiciously. They were like white maggots lying in the bottom of the cup. "What are they?"

"They'll help you sleep."

"I don't want to sleep. I've only just woken up."

"I'm sure that's what you think, but your body needs all the rest it can get. You've had a terrible shock." Alex still didn't take them, so she added, "If you don't want to take them, I can give you an *injection* instead."

She was smiling sympathetically but Alex was sure there was something threatening in her voice, and if she still resembled a bird, it was suddenly a vulture. Her hand was stretched out. He looked at her wrist with the veins showing dark blue beneath her skin as they wormed their way up her arm. Her dark eyes were fixed on him, daring him to challenge her.

Alex was too weak to argue with her, too confused.

He took the pills.

DARK GLASSES

The next time Alex woke up, it was late afternoon. He could tell from the light. How long had it been since Wendy McDarling had first introduced herself? It felt like that same morning but Alex no longer trusted himself. He had been drifting in and out of consciousness with the result that he had no idea how much time had passed.

Once again he examined himself. He was still wearing the striped pyjamas. That was his first, sour observation. But there was some good news. Turning his arm, he saw that the plastic pipe had been removed. A small plaster covered the area where the needle had entered his arm. And somebody had left a plate of sandwiches and a glass of apple juice on the table beside his bed. The sight of them reminded him how hungry he was. Before he knew what he had done, he had wolfed down two of the sandwiches and drunk the juice, which was cold but too sweet. He felt better after that. More in control.

He wanted to get out of bed and stand up but he was still too weak. He pushed back the covers and examined his legs. The striped pyjamas really were horrible ... the last thing he would have chosen to wear. As far as he could see, apart from the bandage around his head, he was unhurt. The nurse had said he had been in a car accident on the way to London. Where had he been coming from? Why had he been out of London in the first place? Alex shivered. However much he tried, he couldn't remember anything. It was strange and scary ... living inside this empty bubble.

He was quite glad when the door opened and the woman came back in, this time accompanied by a young man pushing a wheelchair. He was dressed in shabby jeans with a tightly fitting T-shirt and Alex could see that his arms were covered in tattoos: butterflies, hearts, flowers ... but also guns and hand grenades. His hair was cut short and he had piercings in one of his ears and the side of his nose. He hadn't shaved, allowing the stubble to spread over his cheeks and upper lip. All in all, he was the last person Alex would have expected to see working in a hospital.

"How are you feeling, my dear?" the nurse asked, using exactly the same words as last time.

"I want to phone Jack," Alex said.

"I know! I know! You told me that this *morning*." So it was the same day. "Jack knows where you are. We've given her a very *full* account of what's happened to you. She's very relieved that you're all right." The nurse moved to the side of the bed. "The doctor will see you now."

"So where is he?"

"He's in his office. This is Ivan. He's here to help you but don't try talking to him as he doesn't speak a word of English. We're to bring you to the doctor's office."

That was good. Alex wanted to get out of the room, if only to see what was on the other side of the door. Even so, he didn't like the idea of being taken in a wheelchair. "I can walk," he said.

"Oh no!" Nurse Wendy frowned and shook her head. "I don't think so, Alex. If you tried to stand up, you'd just fall over!" She gave a signal and Ivan, the man with the tattoos, wheeled the chair forward, then leaned over Alex and scooped him out of the bed. He was surprisingly strong and Alex could do nothing to prevent what was happening. Inside, he was seething that he was so weak, unable to fight back. "You'll be able to walk in a day or so," the nurse assured him.

"As soon as I can walk, I'm out of here," Alex growled.

That made her frown a second time. "I'm sure the *doctor* will tell you when you're fit enough to leave," she said.

"What's the doctor called?" Alex asked.

Nurse Wendy smiled. "Dr Feng."

They wheeled him along a corridor that was both

ancient and modern at the same time. The walls were made of stone and looked like the inside of a church, which, Alex reminded himself, they were. But the polished wooden floor and the lighting were brand new. They passed a lift with gleaming stainless-steel doors followed by a grand staircase with wrought-iron bannisters, sweeping down to what appeared to be a drawing room below. The downstairs windows were barred. Perhaps it was the effects of the drugs he had been given but Alex couldn't piece it all together. Abbey, hospital, hotel, prison ... the building had something of all of them. He took a deep breath and tried to focus on his surroundings. Any detail, no matter how small, might help him later on.

Alex's room was number one. He had seen it written on the door. He was taken past five more rooms, all of them identical to his and empty, but the door of the last one – Room Six – was closed.

"Who's in there?" he asked.

"Nobody," Nurse Wendy replied, a little too quickly. Alex made a mental note. There was something in her voice that suggested she might not be telling the truth.

"Am I alone here?"

"I'm not permitted to talk about the other patient." Nurse Wendy scowled, realizing what she had just said. "I mean, if there *was* another patient, I wouldn't be allowed to talk about him." She was looking angry now, as if Alex had deliberately tricked her. "The doctor will tell you everything you need to know."

They came to the end of the corridor and a plain-looking door with no number or name. The nurse knocked and in response to a single word – "Come!" – she opened it and they went in.

Dr Feng was sitting behind his desk. As Alex might have expected from his name, he was Chinese. He was very round and fat with black hair going grey at the sides and a small beard that began under his lower lip and reached about an inch below his chin. He was dressed in an old-fashioned, three-piece suit complete with a striped tie and a watch chain that stretched across his stomach. There was a stethoscope hanging around his neck. Although it wasn't particularly bright in the room, he was wearing sunglasses. Alex thought he might remove them as Ivan wheeled him in, but they stayed where they were, completely masking his eyes.

Alex quickly examined the office. It looked somehow fake, like a stage set with its shelves full of books, the rugs on the floor, the oversized fireplace. A human skeleton hung in a frame in a corner, with another door just behind it. A large window looked out onto a series of well-kept lawns and hedges that had been cut into precise mathematical shapes: spheres, cubes and pyramids. Three Roman gods were fighting amongst themselves as the centrepiece of a huge marble fountain, the water spraying around them. The garden was enclosed by a tall, wire fence and there was a locked gate at the far end with two men standing guard. A gravel driveway led out, disappearing into thick woodland that obscured any further view. They could have been anywhere.

"Good afternoon, Alex," the doctor said. When he spoke, he revealed slab-like teeth that looked false. His voice was soft, slithering over his lips. "I'm Dr Raymond Feng and it's a great pleasure to meet you." He pointed at his dark glasses. "You'll forgive me for not taking these off. I don't mean to be rude but the truth is I have a slight problem. I suffer from photophobia. It means that my eyes do not like the light. My father had the same trouble with his right eye. My mother, as it happened, suffered with her left eye." He spread his hands. "When I was born, it was soon discovered that I was afflicted in both."

Nurse McDarling and Ivan both left the room. Alex heard the door close behind him. He and the doctor were alone.

"I'm sure you have a lot of questions, Alex," the doctor went on. "The trouble is, you've taken a nasty blow to the head. Your car hit a traffic light and you were thrown forward in your seat. It's lucky you had your seat belt fastened."

"Wait a minute!" There was something the doctor had just said that didn't add up. Alex's brain still wasn't working properly and he had to struggle to work out what it was but at last it came. "How could we have hit a traffic light?" he asked. "The nurse said we were on a motorway and there are no traffic lights on motorways!"

"Did I say traffic light?" The doctor stroked his beard. There was a solid gold signet ring on his fourth finger. "Maybe it was a road sign or another car. To be honest with you, I haven't been given all the details. All I know is that you have concussion and that's confused you. You may be having issues with your memory. Please don't worry. Everything's going to be fine. You just need a little time..."

"Where's my phone?" Alex asked. "Why won't you let me call Jack?"

"Surely Nurse Wendy told you? Your phone was damaged in the accident. In fact it was completely smashed."

Alex tried to work out how that might have happened. Surely, if it had been in his pocket, he would have been badly bruised too. He could only assume that it had somehow fallen out at the moment of impact.

"You have to trust us," the doctor went on. "Jack will come and visit you as soon as I think you're well enough. Right now, you need to rest. We must also work out how badly you've been hurt."

"I don't feel as if I've been hurt at all."

"That's often the way with head injuries. The brain, of course, feels no pain. You can damage it without knowing you've done so and it's actually very difficult to know how badly damaged it is. Do you remember what happened yesterday?"

"No." Alex hated having to admit it.

"You don't remember coming in the car from the airport?"

An airport! As soon as Feng spoke the word, Alex had a flash of memory. For a brief moment he heard the sound of a plane touching down, the roar as the engines were put into reverse thrust. He had been abroad. He had just arrived home. And there was somebody waiting for him, standing beside a car on the runway. Alex thought he recognized him. But then the image was gone, snatched away before he had time to work out who it was.

"There were three of you in the car," Dr Feng added. "The driver and the other passenger were both quite badly hurt ... worse than you, as a matter of fact."

"Where were we going? Who was I with?"

"It's important that you remember these things for yourself, Alex. It's part of the healing process." The doctor picked a bit of fluff off his sleeve. "Over the next few days, you and I are going to have several sessions together. You see, I'm not just a doctor of medicine. I also specialize in the mind. I've been asked by MI6 to help you piece your memory back together again. You're going to tell me everything you can remember about yourself and the missions you've been sent on. I want you to talk to me about your friends at MI6, the people

you work for. It's important you tell me everything
you know."

"Why?"

"Because it will help me make you better. As
soon as I feel that you're on the road to recovery,
I'll arrange for Jack to visit you. You'd like that,
wouldn't you?"

"Yes." The word fell heavily from his lips, as if
he had been hypnotized. Alex wasn't sure if he was
awake or asleep. He felt trapped between the two.
Everything he was seeing and hearing could have
been real or could have been some sort of dream.
"I'm not meant to talk about my work," he added.

"I know. But you can talk to me. You and I are
on the same side!"

Dr Feng pressed a button on his desk. "I'll ask
Ivan to take you back to your room. I'm also putting you on a course of vitamins, to help you
regain your strength. They will be given to you in
your apple juice so there won't be an unpleasant
taste. Just make sure you drink it with every meal."

An apple a day keeps the doctor away. Alex didn't
know why the old saying suddenly popped into his
head. He said nothing.

"You and I will have our first session tomorrow,"
Dr Feng went on. He was clearly going nowhere.
"We'll start with how you joined MI6 – when you
were just fourteen years old! I have to say, Alex,
I've heard a lot about you and I'm delighted finally
to meet you."

The door opened and Nurse Wendy came back in with Ivan, who took hold of the wheelchair. The doctor smiled, flashing his heavy, white teeth.

"You can take him back to his room, thank you, Ivan," the doctor said. He turned to Nurse Wendy. "I'll see him tomorrow at nine o'clock, Miss McDarling. Straight after breakfast. We have a lot of work to do!"

"Yes, Dr Feng."

As Alex was wheeled out, two thoughts went through his head. The first was that it was odd that the doctor had referred to Nurse Wendy as "Miss McDarling". Shouldn't he have called her "Sister"? The second thing concerned Ivan. The nurse had said that he didn't speak a word of English but the doctor had just addressed him in exactly that language and Ivan had seemed to understand.

Whichever way he looked at it, nothing made any sense to Alex. What exactly was going on at Bellhanger Abbey and why was he here?

He intended to find out.

THE CLOWN

Later, sometime in the middle of the night, Alex woke up. He knew at once that something was wrong. The room was pitch-black. There was no light at all. And yet he could see. There was something strange about the silence too. When he called out for help, he couldn't hear his own voice.

There was a figure standing in the room at the foot of the bed. Alex hadn't heard him come in. He could have been there all the time.

A clown.

He had a bald head, tufts of green hair, a grotesque, white-painted grin and a red ping-pong ball for a nose. He was wearing ballooning, black and white trousers, a multi-coloured jacket with handkerchiefs trailing out of the pockets and a spinning bow tie. There was an umbrella hooked over his arm. Alex couldn't see his feet but guessed he would have elongated shoes.

286

Alex had always hated clowns. Jack had taken him to the circus once, shortly after she had arrived. He could only have been seven years old. He still remembered the big tent, the trapeze artists, the jugglers, the contortionists, the fire-eaters. But even then he had found the clowns creepy and almost painfully unfunny. They threw cakes at each other. They squirted soda syphons. They slipped on banana skins. And they drove crazy cars. But they never made him laugh.

This clown wasn't even trying to do that. He was just standing there in the weird darkness that wasn't dark, gazing at Alex with eyes that behind the gaudy make-up, blazed with hatred.

Somehow, without moving, he came closer. Alex felt himself being drawn towards him. The clown was growing larger and larger in his vision. Now Alex could see nothing else.

"Who are you? Who are you working for?" The clown had asked the two questions without moving its lips and, stranger still, Alex was certain he recognized the voice. He heard a roaring sound. Something flashed past – but so fast that he couldn't see it.

He just had time to realize that none of this was happening. That it was all a bad dream.

Then he woke up.

It was the morning of the next day.

* * *

287

DR FENG'S OFFICE: 9.05 A.M. (SESSION ONE)

DR FENG: Good morning, Alex. Did you sleep well?
ALEX: I slept OK.
DR FENG: And you've had breakfast?
ALEX: Yes.
DR FENG: I hope you drank your apple juice.

Subject fails to reply.

DR FENG: Well, let's get started, shall we? What do you remember about your uncle, Ian Rider?

Silence. Subject appears uncomfortable.

ALEX: I don't like talking about this.
DR FENG: It's completely confidential, Alex. You have to let me into your mind. Trust me...
ALEX: No.
DR FENG: You have to let me help you, Alex. You have no choice.

A long silence. Finally, subject begins.

ALEX: It's strange, really. I was so close to him. I mean, he was my closest relative. But I never really knew him. My mum and dad died when I was very small and Ian brought me up. That's what I always called him, by the way. He hated being called "Uncle Ian". He said it made him sound Victorian.

He was always there for me when I was young. He took me on holidays with him but they weren't really holidays ... like when you go to a hotel or sit on a beach. We went camping in the Sahara Desert, canoeing down the Mekong River in Vietnam. He took me skiing, scuba diving, climbing ... and he was always making me learn new things. When I was eight years old it was survival techniques in the Amazon Jungle! He showed me how to collect water by making a still. It was a hole in the ground with a bowl in it and a sheet over the top. I knew what to do if I got bitten by a snake. Stuff like that. When we went climbing, he taught me how to survive an avalanche. What to do if I got lost. How to make a fire without matches. He always made it sound like a game but he was deadly serious. I mean, this was the man who took me to Everest Base Camp when I was eleven. He wasn't just having a laugh...

DR FENG: Go on...

ALEX: ...He was the same when we were together in London. He always wanted me to push myself. I never felt he was bullying me or forcing me to do things I didn't want to do. I wanted to please him. And in many ways I was like every other kid. I watched TV. I played computer games. I hung out with my friends. It's just that I was also going down to the gym twice a week. I was learning different sorts of martial arts. Ian encouraged me to speak foreign languages. I spent one entire summer in Paris and another in Madrid and in that whole time I wasn't allowed to speak or read a word of English. I wasn't much looking forward to it but I was staying with great families. I loved the cities. And in the end I could speak French and Spanish ... as simple as that.

DR FENG: You were too afraid to argue?

ALEX: I told you. I was never afraid of Ian. I respected him. And I did argue with him. The only trouble was, he made me do it in Japanese.

DR FENG: Why do you say you didn't know him?

ALEX: Because it's true. I didn't see him a lot of the time. He was always away on business. I thought he worked in a bank ... that was what he told me and why shouldn't I have believed him? I was looked after by a sort of housekeeper he found. I suppose you could say she was like a nanny, except she wasn't. Actually, she was an American student. She'd come to London to study law but she moved in with us. She got free rent and a bit of money in return for looking after me.

DR FENG: Her name was Jack.

ALEX: Yes. I don't want to talk about her. Not with you. Not with anyone. The point is that Ian was lying to her. He was lying to both of us. He didn't work in a bank.

DR FENG: He was a spy. He worked for the Special Operations division of MI6.

ALEX: Yes.

DR FENG: And he wanted you to be a spy too.

ALEX: I only realized that later. All the time we'd spent together, all the trips abroad, all the stuff he'd made me learn ... he was preparing me. He wanted me to be like him.

DR FENG: How do you feel about that?

ALEX: I wish he'd talked to me. I know he couldn't tell me about his work but after he'd died, after I found out the truth ... it made me sad. We'd had all these great times together. Sometimes, when he took me away with him, I thought I was the luckiest boy in the world. But, in fact, he was manipulating me. What gave him the right to decide what I was going to be? I suppose all adults – mums and dads – have dreams for their kids. But that doesn't mean they have to trick them and lie to them and hide things from them. I don't even know what Ian really felt about me. Did he like me or did he just want to use me?

Subject breaks off. He seems upset by what he has just said.

DR FENG: Are you all right, Alex? Do you want to continue?

Subject nods.

DR FENG: Tell me about the night he died.
ALEX: Do I have to?
DR FENG: It's important for your therapy.
ALEX: I got a phone call ... early in the morning.

Subject pauses.

DR FENG: Keep going, Alex.
ALEX: No. I'm not going to talk about that now. Why do I have to stay here? Why won't you let me call Jack?

DR FENG: You're tired, Alex. You're upset. I'm going to ask Miss McDarling to take you back to your room. We'll talk more later on.

Session terminated: 9.21 a.m.

THE CROW

Alex was still confused. He had told Dr Feng much more than he'd intended to but for some reason he had been unable to stop himself talking. The words had fallen out of his mouth as if they were trying to escape on their own.

He was also sleeping far too much – more than was healthy – but at least he had managed to recover his strength. He was able to get out of bed and he was allowed to get dressed, though not in his own clothes. Nurse Wendy brought him a grey tracksuit and a pair of trainers. It was the sort of kit he might have worn in a football training camp, Alex thought. Or a prison.

But slowly he was getting better – he was certain of it – and sure enough, later on that day, he was told that he could leave his room, not in a wheelchair but on his own two feet. The nurse had changed the bandage for him, assuring him that his wound seemed to be healing nicely. Now she gave him a tour of the abbey, at the same time explaining the rules in her strange, Scottish teacher's voice.

"Bellhanger Abbey is a *top*-secret establishment," she said. "It was a real abbey once. It was founded in the twelfth century and it was inhabited by Cistercian monks until the time of Henry VIII and the Dissolution of the Monasteries. I'm *sure* you learned about that at school, Alex."

"Yes."

Brookland School in Chelsea. His best friend, Tom Harris. Playing football for the first team. One by one, the images flashed through Alex's mind, but somehow they seemed far away. It was as if they were memories that belonged to someone else.

"Centuries later, MI6 turned it into a rest home for agents who had been injured in action," Nurse Wendy continued. She was walking briskly in her white, over-starched uniform, her arms folded across her chest as if she wanted to get this over with as soon as possible. "As a matter of fact, your *uncle* stayed here once – although that was before my time. I'm sure you'll be comfortable here. And the important thing is to get well as soon as possible."

On the way back to Alex's room they once again went past Room Six. As before, the door was closed.

"Who else is here?" Alex asked.

"I told you. I'm not allowed to say."

"You said you couldn't talk about 'him'. Who is he?"

Her little black eyes blinked rapidly. "I'm sure the two of you will meet in time."

They reached the staircase that Alex had seen earlier. He could see now that the area at the bottom was an entrance hall with a heavy oak door leading out. The floor was made out of flagstones with a couple of thick sheepskin rugs on top. Two huge candlesticks stood on an antique wooden table to one side. As they walked down together, Alex almost felt that he was entering the world of *Harry Potter*. Add some talking portraits in frames and a few messenger owls and the picture would be complete.

"I don't suppose you'd like to go outside?" Nurse Wendy asked.

"Yes." Alex was pleased. If they let him out of the building, he might get a better idea of where he was. It might also help him find a way to escape.

The door was unlocked. It led out to the front of the abbey with the neatly trimmed hedges and the fountain that Alex had already seen from Dr Feng's office. A bell tower loomed overhead. Alex was glad to be outside, breathing in the fresh air with the sun on his face, but he still felt like a prisoner. He was standing in front of a fence that was five metres high with searchlights mounted on several of the posts, facing both towards and away from the abbey. The woodland on the other side of the fence looked dark and uninviting – even if he somehow could reach it.

There were two guards standing beside the main gate, both of them dressed in army fatigues with rifles slung over their shoulders. One of them had an enormous dog, an Alsatian, on a lead. Seeing Alex, it pricked up its ears and growled.

"We take security here *very* seriously," Nurse Wendy said. She could see what was in Alex's mind.

"There's no way out," Alex muttered.

"There's no way *in*. We're only thinking of your safety."

"Why should I be in any danger?"

"You're a *spy*, Alex, my dear. You have enemies. We still don't know if the road accident really was as innocent as it seemed. We're still investigating. And until we find out for sure, we have to look after you."

As if on cue, one of the two guards walked over to them, leaving the other man and the dog behind. As he drew closer, Alex saw that he was very muscular, black, in his thirties, with a snub nose that seemed to have been pushed into his face and hair cut so short that his scalp showed through. There was a wire running behind his ear, connected to a radio receiver and a throat microphone.

"This is Karl, our head of security," the nurse said.

The man nodded. "Good to meet you, kid." He had a rough, London accent and the sort of voice that sounded permanently angry, on the edge of violence. "I'm sure you want to explore," he went on, "but there are a few things you need to remember. Never come out here at night. Brutus will be loose in the grounds and he can be vicious."

"Is Brutus your friend?" Alex asked, gesturing at the other man.

"No. His name's Vaudrey. Brutus is the dog. You upset him, he'll rip your legs off. And he's easily upset."

"Right."

"Another thing. You don't want to touch the fence. You hear that buzzing sound? I'm sure I don't need to tell you it's electrified, kid. There are ten thousand volts running through it. You even put a finger on it, you can say goodbye to your arm. You try and climb it, there won't be enough of you left to bury."

"I'll remember that," Alex said. He disliked everything about the security man, particularly the way he kept on calling him "kid".

"We have half a dozen guards working here, including me and Vaudrey and we're all armed." Karl smiled unpleasantly. "As I said, don't come out at night. I'd be very upset if there was an accident."

"I'd be upset too," Alex agreed.

"Let's walk round the back," Nurse Wendy suggested. "I'll show you the tennis court and the lake."

Alex was about to follow her when a strange, whirring sound made him look up. At first, he thought he'd imagined it but then he saw something small and black, hovering above him, silhouetted against the sky. It still took him a moment to work out what it was. A drone!

"Don't worry about that, kid," Karl grunted. "That's also part of our security. We call it 'the Crow'. It's a radar detection system and real-time spectrum analyser. It's equipped with a high-resolution, thermographic camera and gives us three-sixty-degree views of the surrounding area, day and night. It's controlled from the security centre up in the tower."

"Also for my safety?" Alex asked.

"Why else?"

Guard dogs. Guns. Drones. Searchlights. An electrified fence. So why didn't Alex feel safe?

Over the next thirty minutes, Alex explored the layout of his new home, looking for any weaknesses, anything that might offer him a way of escape. Bellhanger Abbey looked huge from the outside, mainly because of the grounds that surrounded it and the single tower that rose up high above it. That was where the bells that gave the place its name would once have been located. Partly ruined, it had been rebuilt with modern plate glass and new bricks, which showed where Karl's security centre had been constructed. They passed a tennis court and a croquet lawn but as they continued round the back of the building, Alex's eye was drawn to the lake that he had glimpsed when he first woke up. It was just beyond the perimeter fence and had to be at least one hundred metres wide. There was a jetty stretching into the water with a wooden dinghy bobbing beside it. An old hoist, a sort of miniature crane used for loading and unloading supplies, stood at the end.

"What's the dinghy for?" Alex asked.

"Dr Feng likes to go fishing." The nurse sighed. "Unfortunately, the lake is full of catfish and they're horrible things. They're all poisonous or inedible."

Somehow, Alex wasn't surprised.

There was a door at the back of the building which led into a common room. Sure enough, there were several fishing rods leaning against the wall, as well as ancient fish, stuffed and mounted in glass cabinets. The sofas and chairs were well worn and comfortable. There were newspapers scattered about and some miniature palm trees growing in pots; the sort of thing you might get in an old people's home. From here, they passed into a library with just a few paperbacks resting on otherwise empty shelves, a dining room with more miniature plants, a snooker room and a TV room. There were fireplaces everywhere but they were empty and unused, as if no one had ever thought to make a fire.

As they made their way into the hall, Alex spotted a notebook and a pencil lying on a table, perhaps left there by one of the guards. He waited until Nurse Wendy was looking the other way, then picked them up and slipped them into his pocket.

It was a small rebellion but it made him feel good. He was beginning to fight back.

Later that afternoon, after he had finished his lunch and been taken back to his room, he took out the notebook and opened it. The pages were blank but that didn't matter. He needed it to help him set out his thoughts. He sat down and made a list of the people he had encountered so far.

DR FENG

WENDY McDARLING

IVAN

KARL – HEAD OF SECURITY

VAUDREY (+ BRUTUS)

Karl had said there were four other guards but the abbey still seemed deserted. Maybe that was why it felt so creepy. From the moment he had woken up, Alex had felt completely alone. And that reminded him of something. Nurse Wendy had admitted that there was one other patient at Bellhanger Abbey. And yet, Dr Feng had said quite clearly that there had been three people in the car when the supposed accident had taken place: Alex, a driver and another passenger. The other two had been hurt worse than him – so why was only one of them here? That was something else that didn't add up.

Something was screaming at Alex, inside his head. They were lying to him. He shouldn't be here. Normally, he would have already started working on an escape plan. It didn't matter that he was surrounded by armed guards and an electric fence and that he still had no real idea where he was. He would have found a way out. But his thoughts were scrambled. His head wasn't working properly. It was as if he were seeing the world through a thick fog.

He spent the rest of the afternoon drawing a detailed map of Bellhanger Abbey – the tower, the fence, the lake, the dinghy – putting in all the features he could remember. Sometime later, he fell asleep. He hadn't even got undressed.

THE CLOWN (2)

Alex opened his eyes.

It was still light outside. How much time had passed? This was the second day since his arrival at Bellhanger Abbey, although it felt as if he had been here for weeks. He was lying on the bed, not in it, still fully clothed. There was a crumpled piece of paper in his hand and once again he read the names, at the same time hearing voices.

"I hope you drank your apple juice." Dr Feng.

"We're only thinking of your safety." Nurse Wendy.

"There won't be enough of you left to bury." Karl.

Had he been drugged? How else could he explain the way he was feeling, the fact that his brain refused to function properly? Alex hated having chemicals in his system. He avoided food with too many additives and E-numbers. He would never have been tempted to smoke. Now it occurred to him that he hadn't been feeling himself ever since the accident – and it wasn't because of what had happened on the motorway. It was because of the treatment he had been receiving, supposedly to make him better.

He looked up and, with a jolt of fear, he saw that the clown was standing in front of him once again, clearly visible in the shadows. The make-up was as hideous as before, the brilliantly coloured hair and clothes clashing, like paint tins thrown at a wall. Alex tried to tell himself that he was asleep, that this was just a nightmare ... but at the same time he knew that it was more than that. Something was fighting inside him. His brain was working overtime, desperately trying to make him remember what had really happened.

Once again, he felt himself being carried forward. He heard the blast of something that might have been a car horn and a man's voice, echoing around him. "Don't worry, Alex!" The clown opened its mouth. Alex saw yellow teeth and a dark hole at the back of its throat. As he lay there, staring into the shadows, the mouth grew wider and wider. Now it was bigger than the head that contained it. The mouth had become the size of the room. Alex was staring into an impossible cave, hurtling towards it.

Alex cried out. He wanted to close his eyes but he couldn't.

The clown swallowed him whole.

* * *

DR FENG'S OFFICE: 5.00 P.M. (SESSION TWO)

Subject appears tired and distracted. Eyes not fully focused. Hair untidy. Clearly has no wish to be here.

DR FENG: Alex, the last time we spoke, you told me how your uncle, Ian Rider, prepared you to be a spy. How were you actually recruited into MI6?

ALEX: I don't want to tell you.

DR FENG: Why not?

ALEX: It's classified.

DR FENG: You remember, then?

ALEX: Yes.

DR FENG: It's important to go over these details. I need to know that your memory is functioning properly ... that there hasn't been any damage as a result of the injury to your head. And as I've explained to you, I work for MI6 too. Have you forgotten that?

ALEX: Why are you keeping me here? I want to leave.

DR FENG: Then the sooner we get through this, the sooner we can make that happen.

A long pause. Subject trying to remain silent.

ALEX: All right ... I was recruited after Ian died. At first, they told me he had been killed in a car accident. It seems to me that MI6 tell quite a lot of lies about car accidents.

DR FENG: You think I'm lying to you?

ALEX: I didn't say that.

DR FENG: Please, go on, Alex.

ALEX: I tried to find out how Ian had been killed and that led me to MI6. I nearly got killed myself ... twice. The first time, I hid in a car crusher and they started it up. And then I climbed out of a window to get into Ian's office.

DR FENG: And what did you find?

ALEX: Nothing. The whole thing was a waste of time. It was a test. Alan Blunt had already decided he wanted to use me.

DR FENG: Who is Alan Blunt?

ALEX: If you work for MI6, how come you don't know that?

DR FENG: I do know that, Alex. I'm just testing your memory.

ALEX: Alan Blunt needed someone to investigate a company called Sayle Enterprises which had a manufacturing plant down in Cornwall. That was where they were making a brand-new computer – the Stormbreaker – and the owner, Herod Sayle, had offered to give one, free, to every school in the UK. Blunt knew there was something dodgy about him and he asked me to check him out. I went into the plant under a false name. There was a boy who had won some competition to visit the factory and I took his place.

DR FENG: What happened to Herod Sayle?

ALEX: Somebody shot him. It wasn't me. I never wanted to kill anyone. And when I was sent on my missions, I wasn't given any weapons, nothing that could seriously hurt someone. Mr Blunt never let me have a gun and I was glad about that. I'm fourteen. It's bad enough that I have to lie to all my friends about what I do. I didn't want to be a spy and I still don't. If they asked me to kill people, I'd refuse. I'm not sure I'd be able to live with myself if I did that.

To be honest with you, if I had a choice, I'd walk away. A lot of the kids at my school would think it's cool to be a spy and to have adventures and miss class and all the rest of it. But I was never given any choice. So far, I've been lucky, but one day I'm not going to be able to walk away. I'm going to end up in a real hospital ... or dead.

And what's really sick is that if I get killed, Blunt won't even care. He'll be annoyed. It'll be inconvenient. But in a way he and Mrs Jones are as bad as the rest of them. They're using me the same way they'd use a gun or a hand grenade or whatever. I'm just a weapon. A secret weapon. And when the day comes that they can't use me any more, they'll simply find someone else. They'll forget about me.

DR FENG: I'm sure that's not true, Alex.

ALEX: I'm tired. I don't want to talk any more. I want to go back to my room.

DR FENG: Of course. I'll call the nurse...

Session terminated: 5.24 p.m.

Lying on his bed, Alex thought about what had taken place.

During the interview with Dr Feng, Alex had been aware of two quite different thoughts, at war with each other in his head. On the one hand, he felt a need to answer every question that was thrown at him and it was difficult to stop himself talking. He actually wanted to tell the truth. But at the same time, he didn't like the doctor and he didn't trust him. And so, even as he was speaking, he was struggling not to give too much away. He hadn't talked about the SAS training he'd received in the Brecon Beacons before he was sent to Cornwall. He hadn't mentioned the fact that MI6 Special Operations were based in a building in Liverpool Street that pretended to be a bank.

He hadn't even intended to mention Alan Blunt's name – and it was interesting that when he had come out with it, Dr Feng hadn't even known who he was.

Alex was talking too much. He knew it. But at least he could control some of what he said.

So far, he'd had two sessions in the doctor's office. Were they really part of some sort of cure, helping Alex to sort out his memories? Or was something else going on? Sitting on his own in his room, Alex tried desperately to focus on his predicament but his brain was still refusing to work. Being at the abbey was like watching a television programme where the picture is distorted and the sound is out of sync.

Just before dinner, Alex had demanded his watch back and he had been surprised when Nurse Wendy brought it to the room. He was still wearing the grey tracksuit he had been given and it was as if the watch was the only part of his old identity that remained. He wondered why it hadn't been damaged or broken. After all, the accident had supposedly destroyed his mobile phone. But he decided not to ask. He was afraid they might take it away again.

He made his way downstairs to the dining room where Ivan would be waiting to bring him his dinner. It felt strange, sitting alone at a table big enough to house a banquet but he had to admit that the food at Bellhanger Abbey was excellent

Marino Branch
Brainse Marino
Tel: 8336297

and there was plenty of it. He certainly hadn't lost his appetite. As he sat down, Ivan brought in steak and chips and poured him a glass of the over-sweet apple juice that accompanied every meal.

The apple juice.

Alex had automatically picked up the glass and had been about to drink. It was a little too warm in the abbey and he was always thirsty. But now he had second thoughts. Dr Feng had told him that he was going to be given a course of vitamins and that it would be mixed with the juice so that there wouldn't be any unpleasant taste. And when they had met, it had been one of the first things he had said. *"I hope you drank your apple juice."* It was always there. Breakfast, lunch and dinner. Exactly the same amount. Alex found himself staring at the dark, yellow liquid. Why did you need to add vitamins to apple juice? Wasn't the drink full of vitamins anyway?

He glanced up at Ivan. The tattooed orderly was standing at the door, watching him intently – exactly the same way that Nurse Wendy had watched him when she had given him his pills. She had almost forced him to take them the first time they met but since then she hadn't ever tried again. Suddenly, Alex was certain. There was something in the apple juice and whatever it was, it wasn't there to improve his health. There had to be a reason why he wasn't himself, why he couldn't think straight. He was holding it in his hand.

He pretended to take a sip, then set the glass down.

"Can I have some ketchup?" he asked.

"Ketchup?" Ivan repeated the word as if he had no idea what it meant.

Alex mimed squeezing a bottle with his hand. He was still convinced that Ivan understood what he was saying but he didn't mind playing along. "Ketchup! To go on the chips."

Ivan looked annoyed. He obviously didn't enjoy having to act as a waiter. But he didn't argue. He spun round on his heel and left the room, heading for the kitchen which was somewhere on the other side of the corridor. The moment he had gone, Alex got up with the glass and looked around him. His eye fell on one of the miniature palm trees, standing in a pot in the corner. He hurried over to it and emptied the liquid into the soil.

He just had time to return to his chair before Ivan returned, carrying a plastic bottle of tomato sauce. Alex was holding his glass to his lips. As Ivan came over to the table, he pretended to swallow and put the glass down contentedly. Was he imagining it or did Ivan look relieved?

"Thanks, Ivan," he said.

Ivan did not reply.

Alex had already decided not to eat the ketchup. From now on, he wouldn't put anything in his mouth if he thought it could be tampered with. It might be that he was imagining all of it. Maybe

Dr Feng, Nurse Wendy and the rest of them really were trying to help him after a bad car accident on the motorway.

But already Alex felt better. He was making his own decisions. He was taking back control.

THE TOWER/ROOM SIX

DR FENG'S OFFICE: 9.30 A.M. (SESSION THREE)

DR FENG: Well, Alex, you've been here for a few days now. How are you feeling?

ALEX: I'm sort of all right, doctor. But I'm not sleeping very well. And I'm tired all the time.

DR FENG: I could ask the nurse to give you some more sleeping pills.

ALEX: Yes. That would be great. I can't think straight at the moment. Do you think it's because of the accident?

DR FENG: Of course. What other reason could there be?

ALEX: Have you found out what happened yet?

DR FENG: I'm sorry?

ALEX: The accident. You said it was being investigated.

DR FENG: I'm still waiting for the report.

ALEX: But it's been days...

DR FENG: Alex, let's talk about you. You were in

> Murmansk very recently. I'd like to know
> what you were doing there.

ALEX: You're talking about General Sarov.

DR FENG: That's right.

ALEX: I can't talk about it. He had this plan.
He was going to start a nuclear war. But
everything went wrong and in the end...

DR FENG: What happened to General Sarov, Alex?

> *Subject becomes visibly distressed. Unable to
> continue. On the edge of tears.*

ALEX: Do we have to talk about this now? I'm
not feeling well. I want to go to my
room.

DR FENG: Of course. Don't upset yourself, Alex. I'll
call for the nurse...

> *Session terminated: 9.37 a.m.*

The session had gone exactly as Alex had planned.

Another day had nearly passed and in that time,
he hadn't had so much as a sip of the apple juice.
It was surprising that the miniature palm tree in
the dining room hadn't wilted and died. Every time
Ivan left the room, Alex had emptied his glass
into it. But he could already feel the difference in
his thought processes. Suddenly he was aware of
everything around him. He was beginning to put
the pieces together: the guards, the Alsatian dog,

SPY TRAP

the drone, the electric fence, the lake, the jetty. It was still possible that Bellhanger Abbey was exactly what it claimed to be: an MI6 clinic for agents hurt in action. That didn't matter any more. Alex was going to find a way out of here.

From the moment he had entered Dr Feng's office, Alex had pretended to be ill and upset – but actually he was neither and he had steered the conversation the way he wanted. He wasn't going to be coaxed into another session, giving further information about himself or anything else. It had been interesting, challenging Feng once more about the accident. Could days have passed without MI6 finding out anything? For that matter, why had neither Blunt nor Mrs Jones been to the abbey to visit him? They weren't the most friendly of people. It was unlikely that either of them would bring grapes or flowers. But they needed him. If they knew he had been hurt, they would want to make sure that he was all right.

There was something else.

It was the mention of Sarov that had done it. At last Alex knew why he had been on the motorway. He had just returned to England at the end of a mission that had taken him from the Wimbledon tennis championship to the Caribbean island of Skeleton Key. He had been recruited by the American intelligence service, posing as the son of two special agents. The adventure had ended on the very edge of Russia, in an extraordinary ship's graveyard in

315

Murmansk, and from there he had been flown home in an RAF jet, the Sentinel R1, normally used for intelligence gathering. Very quickly now, piece by piece, his memory was coming back to him. The plane had landed at an RAF base near Newbury. There had been a car waiting for Alex and also a man, someone he knew. But who was it? Alex still couldn't see his face.

It didn't matter. He was getting stronger with every minute that passed. The memory would come back soon enough.

Half past six was always a quiet time in the abbey, with dinner being prepared and Dr Feng about to head home ... or wherever it was he went when he finished work. That was when Alex left his room, determined to make a proper examination of his surroundings. He headed first for the tower that he had seen from the gardens and which was where the main security office was located. He had already noticed a low, arched doorway with a spiral staircase leading upwards. Moving quickly and silently, he passed through the arch and made his way up. If anyone stopped him, he would say he had got lost. After all, he was fairly certain he was meant to be drugged. And he had a good excuse: the abbey was a warren of archways and corridors.

The staircase was narrow, lit by a series of narrow windows that had been cut into the thick stone walls. The tower was about the same height as a six-storey building but there was just a single room right at the top. Alex stopped beside the door and stood, catching his breath. Then, carefully, he poked his head round and looked into a square chamber with windows on three sides, surrounded by a parapet. The abbey might be centuries old but this room, the security centre, was brand new.

Two men were sitting at a console, with computers, television screens and security apparatus. They were younger than anyone Alex had met so far, maybe in their early thirties. One of them was smoking a cigarette, the other sipping a can of Coke with his legs stretched out and his heels resting on the surface in front of him. They didn't look at all like MI6 agents. In fact, they reminded Alex of the sort of hired hands he had seen both at Sayle Enterprises and at Sarov's villa on Skeleton Key. He took in the rest of the room: a couple of filing cabinets, a solid-looking metal cupboard, a dartboard with six darts scattered across its face. The whole place stank of sweat and cigarette smoke.

Suddenly, one of the men turned and before Alex could duck out of sight he had been seen.

"What do you want?" the man demanded. He had a scar that zigzagged across his upper and lower lip. It had the effect of twisting his mouth into two pieces, as if he were being reflected in a broken mirror.

"I'm sorry." Alex stepped into view, trying to

look lost and innocent. "Dr Feng said I could come up here. I want to look at the view."

The two men exchanged a glance. Then the man with the scar shrugged. As far as he was concerned, Alex was just a kid with nothing better to do. "Sure. If that's what the doctor said..."

There was a glass door leading out onto the balcony. Alex stepped outside and found himself standing behind a barrier that consisted of a stone wall with a series of columns rising up to his waist. If he leant too far forward, he would topple over. The sky was getting darker and Alex was sure there was going to be a storm. He could feel the closeness in the air.

He stood there, examining the lawns far below with the marble fountain and the gate on one side and the tennis court on the other. The electric fence curved round in an almost perfect circle, separating the abbey from the lake with its jetty and crane. From this height, Alex got a sense of the woodland which continued, uninterrupted, all the way to the horizon. He had been told that he was in Wiltshire but the truth was that this was a world of its own, utterly enclosed and with no obvious way out.

A car – a bright orange Lada – pulled out from the side of the building and drove towards the gate. Alex could see Dr Feng in the front seat, sitting behind the wheel like an overstuffed cushion. The two guards, Karl and Vaudrey, examined him briefly before they allowed him to pass. The Alsatian dog sniffed around the wheels and Alex realized that even if he managed to hide in the back of the car, the animal would know he was there. Anyway, he had tried exactly the same thing when he was a prisoner of General Sarov and that hadn't ended at all well. He would have to find another way.

He had the beginnings of an idea. Standing there, with the first, angry gusts of wind tugging at his hair, he began to measure the distances: the height of the fence, the position of the gate, the distance to the first trees and the edge of the lake.

Could it work?

No.

It would be suicide. There had to be another way.

He went back into the security room and this time he noticed the drone – "the Crow" – that he had seen hovering over him when he was outside. It was lying on a work surface with the joystick control beside it. Alex looked at it more closely. It was an ugly-looking thing with four arms stretching out more like a spider than a crow, each one mounted with a black propeller. There was a sophisticated camera attached to its belly, staring across the room with its single eye. That was something else to consider. If Alex did manage to break out of the abbey, he would be tracked every inch of the way. What was the range of the device? He had heard of drones that could fly for up to three miles. The trees would provide him with cover but Karl had told him that the camera was thermographic, meaning that it didn't even need to see him. His own body heat would give him away.

The two security men were becoming uneasy. "That's enough!" one of them said. "You should get back to your room."

"Sure!" Alex smiled as if he didn't care either way. "Thanks!"

He went back the way he had come. He hated having to sound so meek but it was important not to raise their suspicions. Alex had no intention of going back to his room. Dr Feng had left. The entire building seemed to be quiet. He was feeling strong and clear-headed. This was too good an opportunity to miss. He reached the bottom of the staircase and followed the corridor back the way he had come.

Alex was quite certain that he wasn't the only "patient" being treated at Bellhanger Abbey. Nurse Wendy had more or less admitted that someone else was here, and later on, Dr Feng had said that there had been two other people in the car when it had crashed. They had to be in Room Six. It was the only door on Alex's corridor that was permanently closed and he remembered how uneasy the nurse had been when they walked past. That was where he was heading now. If there was someone else in the room, they might be able to tell him what was really going on.

There was nobody around. Alex stopped outside

the room and rested his hand against the handle. He pressed down. The door wasn't locked but that wasn't so surprising. There was no need to keep anyone a prisoner in their own room when the entire abbey was little more than a giant prison itself. Very gently, he opened the door, checking that there was no sound coming from the room. There was nothing. He slipped inside, closing the door behind him.

Room Six was identical to his own except that it looked out onto the other side of the abbey with a view of the main gate. Alex saw the same furniture, the same lack of pictures or mirrors, the same white ceiling and wooden floor, the same bed. There was a man lying on the bed. He was partly concealed by shadow but as Alex drew closer, he was certain that he knew who it was. An older man dressed in the same striped pyjamas as Alex had been given. Hair that was thinning out and a lined, weathered face. His features were slack because he was so soundly asleep, but suddenly, Alex recognized him.

John Crawley. The man who described himself as the office manager at MI6 but who was actually much more. It was he who had first introduced himself to Alex at Ian Rider's funeral, at the same time opening the door into the dark world of espionage. More recently, he had invited Alex to become a ballboy at Wimbledon, pitching him into a confrontation with the Chinese triads which had nearly cost him his life. Crawley had once been an effective field agent himself. Alex had always thought of him as one of Blunt's toughest and most capable operatives. And now he was here, lying helplessly in bed.

The sight of the MI6 Chief of Staff smashed the final barriers in Alex's memory. It was like a falling deck of cards. One after the other, images flashed through Alex's mind and he remembered what had happened.

John Crawley had met him at the air base near Newbury. He had been standing on the tarmac as Alex climbed down from the RAF Sentinel R1. Alex had been exhausted, still drained by what had happened at Murmansk.

"Alex! Good morning. I thought I should come and collect you. How are you?"

"I want to go home."

"I have a car waiting. Mrs Jones wants to see you."

"I don't want to see her. Just take me home, Mr Crawley."

"Of course, Alex. Straight away..."

The car was a silver Jaguar XJ. It was exactly the sort of car that Crawley would drive, only this time he was going to be a passenger, along with Alex. There was a uniformed chauffeur waiting and as the two of them approached, he opened the back door and stood back respectfully. At the time, Alex had barely registered him. He was too tired. But now, with everything starting to make more sense, he saw him more clearly.

Karl! The security man from the gate. How was that possible?

Standing in the bedroom, Alex wanted to shout at himself not to get into the car. But he and Crawley had got in. He heard the clunk of the closing door and a moment later they were on their way, swinging out of the airfield and following a series of country lanes to the motorway. There was a blue sign. He saw it now as he had seen it then. LONDON 64 MILES.

"Would you like some air conditioning, sir?" That was Karl's voice, coming from the front.

"Are you all right, Alex?" Crawley.

Alex hadn't replied, his head resting against the window, staring out.

The motorway was tedious, the cars whipping past. The driver seemed to be in no hurry to get them home.

There was a lorry in the road ahead of them. It was moving quite slowly, hogging the middle lane but, for some reason, the driver made no attempt to overtake. Slowly, Alex became aware of it. The whole thing was covered in pictures and there were words in bright red letters.

DR FENG'S
TOURING CIRCUS.
FUN FOR ALL THE FAMILY.

A clown stared at him, plastered across the two doors at the back. Green hair. White painted face. Red lips. Now the driver was getting closer and closer to the lorry. It was almost as if he wanted to cause a deliberate crash.

"Driver, what are you doing...?" That was Crawley again, snapping out the words.

The driver ignored him. The distance between the car and the lorry was narrowing with every second that passed.

Alex saw Crawley's hand disappear into his jacket. He wasn't reaching for a wallet or a pen. He knew they were in danger. He brought out a gun.

He was too late.

It all happened very quickly. The doors of the lorry flew open, revealing two men standing in an interior that was otherwise completely empty. A metal ramp shot out, slanting down towards the road. Both vehicles were travelling at about forty miles per hour but now the chauffeur stamped down on the accelerator and the Jaguar leapt forward onto the ramp and then up into the lorry. The clown doors slammed shut behind them, swallowing them up.

Crawley had his gun trained on the driver's neck. *"Who are you? Who are you working for?"*

The two men had positioned themselves, one on each side of the car. The car must have missed them by inches as it rocketed in. They were both armed, two guns to Crawley's one, but then Karl turned and Alex saw that the total had gone up to three. He and Crawley were trapped in a doubly enclosed space. Inside a car inside a truck. They were outnumbered. He knew he had no chance.

Crawley had come to the same conclusion. He lowered his gun, turned and spoke quietly to Alex. *"It's me they want, not you. Don't worry, Alex. I'm sure they'll let you go."*

Karl was leaning over the front seat, still holding the gun. There was something that looked like a grenade in his other hand. He dropped it onto the floor, between Alex and Crawley. There was a hiss and a cloud of grey smoke was released, billowing upwards. Karl climbed out of the car, closing the door behind him. It was the last thing Alex remembered. The fumes were choking him. He felt his head spinning. Then he passed out.

Crawley had been wrong. Whoever was behind this wanted both of them. But why? What was the point?

That didn't matter now. The two of them had to get out of here. Alex hurried over to the bed, grabbed Crawley by the shoulder and shook him. "Mr Crawley!" he whispered as loud as he could. He didn't want to bring in anyone from outside the room. "Wake up! This is Alex..."

Nothing. Alex shook him harder.

"Mr Crawley! Wake up!"

It still wasn't working and Alex was afraid someone might come in at any moment. He looked around and saw a glass of water on a bedside table. Without a second thought, he picked it up and threw the contents into the agent's face.

Crawley's eyes blinked open. "Alex...?"

"Wake up, Mr Crawley. You've got to wake up *now*."

"Where are we?" Crawley was still struggling, trying to fight his way back to consciousness.

"We're prisoners. We were grabbed on the motorway. You have to help me. We need to get out of here..."

"What?" Water was dripping out of Crawley's hair. The pillow behind him was damp.

"You have to get out of bed," Alex insisted. "I need your help!"

"Help...?"

But it was no good. Crawley was too heavily drugged. His head fell back and he said nothing more.

Alex was on his own.

JACK

It was dark outside. The clouds were heavy and close. Alex knew that Karl would be waiting for him in the dining room but he was determined to keep moving, to use the silence and the fact that Dr Feng was away from his office. That was where he was heading now. He'd had four meetings in the doctor's office and although he hadn't seen a computer or a phone, surely there must be both. He'd also noticed a second door, behind the skeleton. That might lead somewhere interesting. The most important thing was to get a message out to MI6 or to Jack. He'd been told that his iPhone had been smashed in the accident but, since he now knew there had been no accident, it was always possible he might find it and Feng's office was the obvious place to begin.

The office – like Room Six – was unlocked. Alex went in quickly, flicked the light on and closed the door behind him. The first thing he saw was the human skeleton, dangling on its wire frame in the corner. A warning? Alex briefly examined the different bones. A thought occurred to him. He was alone and he was unarmed. The skeleton might just come in useful...

It took him less than a minute to do what he had in mind. After that, he went over to the second door and opened it. To his annoyance it only led into a small bathroom and although there was a cabinet above the sink, it didn't contain anything apart from a toothbrush, a bar of soap and a small pair of nail scissors. He took the scissors anyway.

He was about to leave when he caught sight of himself in a mirror above the sink – it had been the first time he had seen himself since he had arrived at the abbey. He looked drawn and thin, probably a result of the drugs he had been given. The bandage was still wrapped around his head. He had forgotten all about it. On an impulse, he tore it off. There was no wound, no mark of any sort under his hairline or anywhere else. Alex wasn't even surprised. The bandage had only been placed there as part of the charade.

He went back into the office and examined the desk. Dr Feng liked to keep the place neat. There was almost nothing on the surface. Just two pencils and a notepad. No computer and no phone. Quickly, he rummaged through the drawers. He found more papers, including a typed-up transcript of his own sessions in the room. Alex was wasting time and he was about to leave when, quite suddenly, a phone began to vibrate. It had been turned to silent but it was still making enough of a sound for him to know that it was somewhere near.

Quickly, he threw open the drawers, trying to find it. He couldn't see it. He pulled out a whole stack of letters. Photographs. Then a clinical report "ON THE USE OF SODIUM THIOPENTAL IN ADVANCED INTERROGATION". He took it out and saw an iPhone, concealed underneath. It was his own. He recognized it instantly, sitting in its protective silicone case with his own initials written in blue biro. There was a large slab of chocolate next to it and Alex remembered that Crawley had brought the chocolate with him to the air base. At the time, he had been amazed at the way the MI6 man thought. *You've just saved the world ... I've brought you some sweeties.* But that didn't matter now. He snatched the phone.

"Hello?" he said, hardly daring to believe that he might finally have made contact with the outside world.

"Alex? Is that you?"

He knew the voice at once. "Jack!"

"My God, Alex! I've been trying to reach you for days. I've been so worried about you. Mrs Jones told me that you were back safely from Russia or somewhere and that she'd sent someone to collect you. When you didn't show up, I called her but she wouldn't tell me anything. I knew something was wrong but ... honestly! Those people!"

"I'm safe, Jack. But I need help."

"Where are you?"

"Don't say another word. Put the phone down. If you speak one more word, I will shoot you."

Alex turned round. Karl, the security man who had also driven the car into the circus lorry, was standing a short distance away, holding an ugly semi-automatic pistol which was trained on him. Alex hadn't heard him come into the room. He was still holding his phone. It was inches away from his mouth. He desperately wanted to say the two words – Bellhanger Abbey – that would lead Jack to him, but he knew he didn't dare. Karl meant business. There was a mean glimmer in his eyes and he was holding the gun very still, prepared to shoot. Alex cursed himself. He shouldn't have let Jack speak for so long. Of course she had been surprised to hear from him. And he'd been over-joyed to hear her voice. But he should have told her where he was straight away.

Now it was too late. He clicked the phone off and placed it on the desk. Karl took two steps for-ward, closer to Alex. He was smiling unpleasantly. "That was sensible, kid. Now step away from the desk."

Alex did as he was told.

Karl took a step forward and brought his gun slamming down onto Alex's phone, smashing it. "They should have done that from the start," he said. He examined Alex. "It looks to me like someone hasn't been taking their medicine," he sneered. "What happened to your bandage? Dr Feng's not going to be very happy with you. My guess is that very soon you're going to be trans- ferred to intensive care."

"Who are you?" Alex demanded. "I know this place isn't a hospital. It's got nothing to do with MI6. And you owe me a new iPhone."

"You can take that up with the doctor!" Karl was mocking him. "We've just called him. He'll be here any minute. Right now I'm going to take you back to your room." He gestured with the gun. "After you, kid."

Alex walked towards the door, at the same time reaching behind him with his right hand. Karl didn't see the movement. Nor had he noticed that before he'd come in, Alex had removed one of the bones from the skeleton – the tibia, which ran from the knee to the foot. It was solid and heavy and had been tucked into the waistband of his tracksuit. As he passed the security man, he withdrew it, then turned and, in a single movement, smashed it into the side of his head. Karl cried out. Alex hit him a second time, harder. He felt the bone shudder in his hand. It was enough. Karl slumped to the floor and stayed there.

Alex snatched up the gun. He didn't like fire- arms but there was no way he was going to leave it behind. Dr Feng was on his way back. Karl wouldn't stay unconscious long. He had to get out of Bellhanger Abbey fast and although he'd figured out a plan, he was still fairly certain he was committing suicide.

There was only one way to find out. Alex ran out of the room, making for the stairs.

The first thing he needed was a fishing rod.

Five minutes later, Dr Feng arrived back in his orange Lada. It had begun to rain, lightly at first, but now the clouds had opened and it was pouring down. Karl had recovered and had made his way out to meet him. The two of them stood outside the entrance, getting wetter and wetter, shouting above the noise of the falling water.

"What happened? Feng demanded.

"I found him in your office. He'd found his phone and was speaking to someone. Then he hit me and got away." There was a huge bruise on Karl's forehead. Blood was trickling down over one eye.

"Where is he now?"

"We're searching the building. He has to be inside. The gate has been locked and the electric fence is in operation. The dog is out here. There's no way he can get away."

There was a flash of lightning and Dr Feng howled, bringing up his fists to cover his eyes. He wasn't wearing his dark glasses and the brilliant light had caught him unawares. "This entire operation is a catastrophe!" he screamed. Rain dripped down the sides of his face and off his beard. There was something frog-like about him, standing there, drenched. "The boy must have guessed – and stopped taking the drugs! Somehow he's managed to escape. This is your fault, Karl. You'll pay for this."

A third figure joined them, fighting her way through the downpour under an umbrella. It was the woman who called herself Nurse Wendy. "There's no sign of him anywhere," she screeched, shouting over the clamour of the storm.

"What about the agent – Crawley?"

"Still asleep. I told you the dose was too high! He can't even talk."

"This is a disaster." Dr Feng might have been crying. It was hard to tell with so much water streaming down his face. He collected himself. "Did he say anything to the person on the phone?"

"No."

"There's still a chance that MI6 will manage to trace the call. We're moving out of here. We'll take Crawley with us and begin his interrogation in one of our other locations. But we can't do anything until the boy has been neutralized. Find the boy. Tell the guards to shoot on sight. That's all that matters now. Tell me when it's done!"

There was an explosion of thunder and another brilliant flash of lightning. Dr Feng screamed and, covering his eyes, staggered blindly into the building, leaving the others to continue the search.

OVER AND OUT

Alex had found what he wanted in the common room.

When Nurse Wendy had shown him round the abbey, she had told him that Dr Feng liked to go fishing and Alex had noticed three rods ready for use, each one of them brand new and state of the art with graphite bodies and titanium oxide guides. These were specialist bass and catfish rods, for use in the lake ... but fishing was the last thing Alex had in mind. It had only taken him a moment to loosen and then to remove the aluminium spools. Each one of them came complete with at least one hundred metres of line. He had taken all of them, racing back up to the first floor and along to the spiral staircase.

He knew that the guards were looking for him. He could hear them shouting at each other somewhere in the distance. As he continued forward, he caught sight of someone coming towards him and ducked into a doorway just as Ivan, the orderly who had always brought his food, came rushing past. Alex was lucky that the corridor was dark. The two of them missed each other by inches.

Alex pressed on, out to the tower, through the archway and up the stairs. The security office would be manned, of course. The two men that he had met earlier would be on full alert. But he had a gun ... even if he was reluctant to use it. Hopefully, showing it to them would be enough.

In fact, only one of the men – the one with the twisted lips – was in the security office. He looked up as Alex came bursting in, the three fishing reels grasped in one hand, the gun in the other.

"Get out of your chair," Alex said. "Keep both your hands in sight. If you try anything, I'll shoot you. I mean it."

The man got up slowly. "You're wasting your time," he said. "You should give yourself up before you get hurt."

Alex looked around him. His eyes settled on the metal cupboard. He opened it. There were a couple of jackets hanging there and about a dozen wire hangers but nothing else. It was perfect. "Get in there," he said.

"You might have to shoot me first."

Very casually, Alex brought the gun round and fired, knowing that the thick walls and the height of the tower would muffle most of the sound. He had intended merely to hit the floor, but quite by accident, the bullet actually found its target barely an inch from the man's foot, sending a splinter of wood stabbing into his ankle. The guard leapt up, all the colour draining from his face. "All right! All right!" he exclaimed. "No need to get nasty!"

He hurried into the cupboard.

Alex slammed the door. He had taken out several of the wire coat hangers and he used one to secure the handles, twisting it round. The guard might be able to force his way out but by then, Alex would be long gone. Fortunately, he had seen what he was looking for, the second part of his plan. It was sitting on the console, with the joystick beside it.

The Crow.

Alex's best friend, Tom Harris, had a drone and the two of them had often played with it in Battersea Park, flying it over the Peace Pagoda and the River Thames. They'd always been nervous of getting into trouble as drones were increasingly prohibited all over London, particularly near airports, and the London Heliport was only a short distance away. The moment Alex had seen the Crow, he'd had a vision of using it to fly himself out of here. He couldn't cling on to it, of course. The maximum weight that a drone could carry (he had read about Amazon using drones to deliver packages) was about two kilograms. But if he was careful, if he took his time, he could use it nonetheless.

He tucked the gun into his trouser pocket and, with both hands free, pulled the ends of the fishing lines from all three aluminium spools and tied them to the camera underneath the Crow. Then he took everything outside to the parapet where he had stood only a short time before. He saw that the searchlights had been turned on. The entire area between the abbey and the perimeter fence was now floodlit. It was still raining but for now the thunder and the lightning had stopped. Dressed only in the tracksuit he had been given, Alex was quickly soaked and he wished he had thought to take the guard's jacket before he had locked him up.

Ignoring the muffled thumping and the shouts coming from the cupboard, he went back for the joystick. He guessed it would work exactly the same way as Tom's – weren't all drones more or less identical? – with one switch to go up and down, the other to go left and right. Of course, he would have preferred a bit of time to get used to the machine's sensitivity, to work out how quickly it responded to his commands. Unfortunately, time was something he didn't have. He heard Brutus barking. The searchlights were criss-crossing the grass. Any moment now, Feng's people would notice that the security office had become completely silent and would come running up to find out what was going on. He had to do this now.

He had set the drone down on the edge of the stone bannister. Now he lifted the joystick and activated it. At once, the propellers began to turn. So far so good. Alex did his best to put everything out of his mind: the lights blazing, the men searching for him all over the abbey, the security guard locked in the cupboard, trying to break out, the possibility that more guards might arrive at any time. All that mattered was the black metal and plastic machine in front of him. He pressed on one of the controls, accelerating the propellers, and the Crow lurched into the air, more like a drunken animal than a bird. Alex gritted his teeth as it toppled to one side, seemingly about to crash into the wall of the tower, but at the last moment, desperately manipulating the controls with his thumbs, he was able to hold it steady. The Crow continued upwards, carrying the three nylon fishing lines with it. When it was a couple of metres above his head, he paused, examining the lines which glinted in the light and the rain. Taking a deep breath, he guided the drone away from the tower. The three lines stretched out, high above the ground.

Now came the difficult bit. The drone had crossed the electric fence, still trailing the triple fishing line. It hovered over the jetty. Alex pressed down, lowering it, then cursed as it dipped too far, briefly out of control. Forcing himself not to panic, not to try and rush things, he steadied it, then guided it round the hoist that stood at the water's edge, effectively looping the line around it. Behind him, he could hear the guard pounding at the cupboard but the twisted metal coat hanger seemed to be holding up. Far below and out of sight, the dog was barking frantically as if it alone knew what was going on. The lights were fanning out left and right, searching for any movement but not looking in the one direction that would have revealed all. Alex had steered the drone over the L-shape formed by the top of the hoist and its outstretched arm. It was hard to be certain, with the rain driving into his face. With one sodden sleeve, he wiped water away from his eyes. Had he done it? He was about to find out.

He stabbed sideways with his thumb, pressing the control on the joystick and bringing the drone back to him, the three reels still emptying their load. Effortlessly, the drone soared up and across towards the tower, a good Crow returning to its master. Drops of rain splattered off the black plastic. Now there were no fewer than six lines trailing behind it: three going out, three coming back. He would need that extra strength. The drone hovered in front of him. Alex brought it gently down. All three spools were empty. Alex saw that he had used almost all the line: there couldn't have been more than a few inches left. But he had achieved what he wanted. He had connected the tower and the jetty, using what must have been the thinnest bridge in the world.

Would it hold his weight? Again, Alex remembered his uncle. Ian Rider had often gone fishing and had done his best to persuade Alex to come with him, although Alex had never seen the point of killing any animals in the name of sport. Even so, Ian had talked about his equipment. Alex knew that fishing lines were given test ratings that could be as low as one or as much as one hundred and eighty kilograms. He didn't know if these lines were monofilament or braided and they probably had a diameter of no more than two millimetres. But he was fairly sure they'd been designed for big fish ... Nurse Wendy had mentioned catfish, which might weigh up to nine kilograms.

At the end of the day it was all guesswork, but the last time Alex had stood on a set of scales, he had weighed in at around fifty kilograms. There were six lines stretching out from the tower to the lake. Suppose each one was capable of holding nine kilograms. Six times nine equals fifty-four. It wasn't a huge margin but surely, together, the lines would be strong enough to take his weight.

He was about to find out. He was going to slide out of here, over the electric fence. If he didn't actually clear it, if his foot touched the wire, he would die. If the fishing lines broke, he would die. If the guards looked up and saw him, he would die. But if he simply waited for them to find him, the result would be exactly the same. He had no choice. He couldn't think of any other way.

He cut the lines off the drone, using the scissors he had taken from Feng's bathroom, then tied them round one of the stone columns of the bannister, ensuring that they were as tight as possible. Finally, he grabbed hold of two of the wire hangers he had taken from the cupboard and bent them into an upside-down U-shape, curving over the line. He held one end in each hand. Taking a deep breath, he looked down.

He still couldn't bring himself to go. It was raining harder again and he was half-blinded. It was a very long way to the ground. It suddenly struck him that this whole scheme was madness and he was about to give up and find another way when he heard the door of the security office burst open and somebody shouted.

Alex heaved himself over the edge of the tower and jumped.

He fell, incredibly fast, as if he had simply leapt to his death. He was certain that the lines – all six of them – would break. But then he lurched back upwards and felt a jolt in his arms that told him the fishing lines were holding and that he was dangling in the air like an oversized puppet. Or a fish. His hands were hooked into the bent wire, barely able to keep their grip as he shot down the line. He couldn't feel his fingers. The rain whipped into his face. The electric fence rushed towards him in a blur.

He was too low! His feet were going to plough straight into it. Crying out, Alex curled his legs upwards, putting more strain on his stomach and arms. He folded his knees into his stomach, desperately aware that his feet were still too low. The wire was suddenly very close. He saw the rain hitting it and imagined the current running through it. He closed his eyes, waiting for the shock.

But then, somehow, he had passed over it, missing it by less than an inch. He wasn't going to be electrocuted. But there were other ways to die. He was travelling too fast. In about one second's time he would hit the wooden hoist and that would smash every bone in his body. Alex felt the wind and the rain slamming against him. He could hardly see at all. At the last moment, hoping he had judged it right, he swung himself sideways and let go.

He hurtled through the air. He must have been travelling at forty or fifty miles per hour, as fast as a car. For a horrible fraction of a second, he felt himself twisting, falling into nothing. Then his feet hit water. He had missed the jetty and plunged into the lake. Was it deep enough? The thought hadn't even reached Alex's mind before he was sinking into utter darkness, bubbles erupting from his nose and mouth, drowning. He floundered with his arms, kicked out with his legs. Everything was confused.

Then he broke the surface. He was on the other side of the fence, outside the abbey but, reaching down, he realized that he had lost the gun when he hit the water. He was unarmed. Worse still, the guards had seen him. They knew what he had done and they were already shouting for the gate to be opened. Alex was soaked, he was terrified, he was half-frozen. And he still hadn't got away.

THE FOREST

They were coming after him.

Dr Feng, Karl, Vaudrey, Ivan, Brutus ... Alex didn't know how many of them there were. Perhaps Nurse Wendy had even joined them too. He could hear the dog yapping, not far behind, and only hoped that the rainfall would deaden his scent and, for that matter, the noise he was making as he fought his way through the wood.

There was a flash of lightning, a vast wall of it, blocking the way forward and briefly illuminating ancient trees snarled together in knots, thick leaves shaking in the wind, endless raindrops hanging in spiders' webs all around, paths that led nowhere, moss, toadstools, grass ... everything frozen in black and white. He had absolutely no idea where he was going. The forest might continue for miles. He couldn't even be sure that he was still running away from the abbey. He had lost all sense of direction and it was only the sounds of his pursuers, always behind him but getting closer that told him which way to run.

His foot caught in a root and he was sent flying forward, crashing into the ground. Fortunately, soft mud broke his fall but when he stood up again he was even more disoriented than before and, worse, he found that he had twisted his ankle. Every foot-step brought with it a jolt of pain that travelled up his leg, into his knee and thigh. He was still drenched from the lake but, impossibly, the rain was making him wetter. He could feel the strength draining out of him.

Should he continue, or perhaps climb a tree and hide? He could lose himself in the branches and wait for daylight. Would he survive a night in this storm and did he even have the strength to pull himself up out of sight? He was still trying to make up his mind when he stumbled through a tangle of bushes, thorns tearing at his clothes, and found himself in a large, circular clearing.

There was a little more light here, the moon somehow penetrating the dense, grey clouds. It gave Alex hope. Perhaps, if the trees were thinning out, he might actually have made it to the other side. Could there be a road nearby? He listened out for any traffic but there was nothing. He was in the middle of the countryside at night in a storm. Still he pressed on with new strength, ignoring the pain in his ankle. Bellhanger Abbey must have been built near a community. Surely he would find it.

He was halfway across when Brutus found him.

The Alsatian dog came bounding out from the tree line and stopped for a moment, barking furiously. Alex turned and saw it, a dripping ball of fur, blazing eyes and white teeth. It barely looked like a dog at all; more like a wild beast out of one of those medieval paintings ... a vision of hell. Three men emerged behind it. Alex couldn't make out their faces. It didn't matter. He was fully exposed, in the middle of the clearing. They had seen him. Slowly, knowing the chase was over, they began to move towards him.

There was nothing more Alex could do. The men were armed with rifles. Even if he turned and tried to run, they could shoot him down. Brutus could reach him in seconds. He had done everything he could. But it was over.

The men drew closer. Alex could hear the dog growling.

Alex recognized Karl. Without saying a word, determined to get this over with, the head of security lifted his rifle. He took aim.

There was a shot.

Karl toppled backwards, dropping his own weapon. At the same time, the Alsatian launched itself towards Alex. There was a second shot. The dog yelped, tumbled over, then limped away.

The shots had come from behind Alex.

Alex turned and saw half a dozen figures – men and women all dressed in black – emerging from the forest. One of them shouted, "Get down!"

Alex wasn't sure if the words were meant for him or for the men from the abbey. He didn't care. He fell to his knees anyway, taking himself out of the line of fire. Dr Feng's people had given up the fight. They were standing with their hands raised and Alex knew that somehow MI6 had found him.

Someone he didn't know came over to him. "Are you all right, Alex?" he asked.

Alex got to his feet. He was soaking wet, scratched and exhausted. His ankle was on fire. He drew a breath. "Never felt better," he said, then collapsed, unconscious, to the ground.

"I thought you might like to know about Bellhanger Abbey," Mrs Jones said.

"Actually, I'm doing my best to forget about it," Alex replied.

"I'm sure."

The deputy head of MI6 Special Operations was sitting on the sofa in Alex's front room. Alex was opposite her with Jack Starbright next to him. This conversation was supposed to be classified, top secret, but she would never have left him alone when this woman was in the house. If Jack even blinked, she was afraid Alex would be spirited away to Russia or Cuba or anywhere else MI6 needed him. It worried her. They never left him alone.

"How did you find me?" Alex asked.

"That was easy. We'd been looking for you and Crawley ever since the two of you disappeared and we had agents all over the south-west of England. But it was the moment you answered your mobile phone that did it. We were able to lock into the signal and we put together an assault team straight away. They were moving in when they found you.

"Lucky I called," Jack muttered.

"Lucky I answered," Alex agreed.

"But what was it all about?" Jack demanded. "Why had they kidnapped Alex and Mr Crawley in the first place?"

"The whole thing was an information-gathering exercise," Mrs Jones explained. "Dr Feng – if that's his real name – was working for a foreign intelligence service and his job was to find out as much as possible about MI6 Special Operations. He was particularly interested in you, Alex. The idea of a fourteen-year-old boy volunteering to be a spy is a very unusual idea..."

"I never volunteered," Alex reminded her.

"...And they wanted to know who you were and how much you'd achieved." Mrs Jones went on, ignoring him. "Somehow they found out you were on your way back from Murmansk and set up a trap. They snatched you and John Crawley just after you landed. Both of you were drugged. You were given a cocktail of Rohypnol, which made you sleep and confused you, and Sodium Thiopental, which is also known as the truth drug. I'd be interested to know how much you told them, incidentally."

"I didn't tell them anything," Alex growled. That

wasn't quite true but he hadn't told them anything that was important. Anyway, the question had annoyed him. Mrs Jones always put her own interests first. "So which foreign intelligence service were they working for?" he asked.

"We still don't know," Mrs Jones replied. The man called Karl was killed in the crossfire. McDarling, Vaudrey and the rest were ordinary criminals who had been hired by Feng. As for Feng himself, we're interrogating him. He's not talking but he may have been paid by the Chinese or the Russians. They're both extremely aggressive when it comes to intelligence. It might even be the Americans. Under their new president, I wouldn't put anything past them."

"Well, it was nice of you to call in," Jack said. "But if you don't mind, we have to be moving on. Alex is heading off on holiday for a couple of weeks and we need to leave for the airport."

"Oh." Mrs Jones got to her feet. "Anywhere nice?"

"Just somewhere in the sun." Jack was determined not to tell her – although she knew that MI6 could find out in seconds.

"You certainly deserve a break, Alex. Enjoy yourself!"

In fact, Alex was heading for the South of France. He had been invited on holiday by his friend, Sabina Pleasure. He was going to be spending a couple of weeks with her parents in an area known as the Camargue. Upstairs, his bags were already packed.

What Alex didn't know was that a Russian assassin was also making his way to the same location and that, very soon, the holiday would become the start of yet another mission, this time pitting him against a pop star with plans to change the world.

Alex Rider needed a holiday. But it was the last thing he was going to get.

THE ALEX RIDER SERIES

ALEX RIDER
ACTION
ADRENALINE
ADVENTURE

THE MISSION CONTINUES AT
alexrider.com

Alex Rider – you're
never too young
to die…

Alex Rider has 90
minutes to save
the world.

High in the Alps,
death waits for
Alex Rider…

Once stung, twice as
deadly. Alex Rider
wants revenge.

Sharks. Assassins.
Nuclear bombs.
Alex Rider's in
deep water.

THE ALEX RIDER SERIES

ACTION. ADRENALINE. ADVENTURE.

alexrider.com **/alexrideruk**

He's back –
and this time
there are no limits.

One bullet.
One life.
The end starts here.

Alex Rider
bites back…

Get your hands on
the deadly prequel.

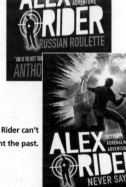

Alex Rider –
in the jaws
of death…

Even Alex Rider can't
fight the past.

Photograph © Jon Cartwright

Anthony Horowitz is the author of the number one bestselling Alex Rider books and the Power of Five series. He enjoys huge international acclaim as a writer for both children and adults. After the success of his first James Bond novel, *Trigger Mortis*, he was invited back by the Ian Fleming Estate to write a second, *Forever and a Day*. His latest crime novel, *The Word is Murder*, introducing Detective Daniel Hawthorne, was a bestseller. Anthony has won numerous awards, including the Bookseller Association/Nielsen Author of the Year Award, the Children's Book of the Year Award at the British Book Awards, and the Red House Children's Book Award. He has also created and written many major television series, including *Collision*, *New Blood* and the BAFTA-winning *Foyle's War*. He lives in London with his wife, two sons and his dog, Boss.

You can find out more about Anthony and his work at:
www.alexrider.com
@AnthonyHorowitz